A STORYTELLING OF RAVENS

R. H. DIXON

D0104795

CORVUS CORONE PRESS

Front cover by Carrion Crow Design.

A CIP catalogue record for this title is available from the British Library.

ISBN: 978-1-9997180-2-2

Corvus Corone Press.

For my readers

Other books by R. H. Dixon:

EMERGENCE

A STORYTELLING OF RAVENS

'Without obsession, life is nothing.'
John Waters

1

Twenty minutes after Sarah Jane Miller's dad had left the house, her mother took two pre-packed holdalls from the downstairs cupboard.

'What're those for?' Sarah Jane asked. She was halfway through a bowl of sugar-topped Cornflakes but lowered her spoon back to the bowl so she could pay closer attention to her mother's curious behaviour.

'Just hurry the hell up, will you?' Roxanne Miller unhooked a car key from the peg on the kitchen wall then checked her wristwatch. 'We're going away for the weekend.'

'No we're not.'

'Yes we are. If your dad can go gallivanting all over the place, so can bloody well I.'

'Where're we going?' Sarah Jane's face twisted at the unexpectedness and inconvenience of this new development; she'd anticipated a weekend at home, reading and writing and hanging out with her cousin Pollyanna, not spending unnecessary time with her mother.

'It's a secret.'

'You mean surprise.'

'No.' Her mother's eyes flashed with a certain amount of impatience. 'It's not for your benefit, smart arse, it's a secret because you're not to go blabbing to your dad.'

'Why not? Why's it a secret?'

'Because.'

'Because *why?*'

Her mother struggled to the back door with the holdalls; the task made difficult because of the five-inch wedges on the shoes she wore, which were almost always kept for special occasions. 'Because we're going to stay with Dean. *Uncle* Dean.'

'Who's Uncle Dean?' Sarah Jane watched, unwilling to help. 'And why would Dad care that we're going to stay with him?'

'Because your dad doesn't like him.' Roxanne Miller dropped the bags and opened the back door. 'But I do. And life's too short.'

'Dad doesn't like Aunty Sonia but you always tell him when we're going to visit her.'

Roxanne breathed in deep and fast, creating a sharp nasal hiss. 'Hardly the same thing, Sarah Jane. *No one* likes Aunty Sonia.'

Sensing and enjoying the fact she was calling her mother out on a big fat lie, Sarah Jane asked, 'Have I met him before? Uncle Dean.' As well as being more short-tempered than usual, Roxanne Miller was acting altogether too strangely and had that cagey, can't-lie-for-shit look, the one she got when she told Sarah Jane's dad that the expensive dress she'd just bought had been hanging at the back of the wardrobe for the past five years. It was a look that fooled no one, however well-planned and credible the untruth was. 'It's just, I don't remember having met him. And I didn't realise you have a brother."

'I don't.'

'So he's Dad's? I thought there was just Uncle Trev on Dad's side.'

'No, he's not your frigging dad's brother either.'

'So how's he my uncle?'

Roxanne Miller huffed, her glossed pink lips becoming unpleasantly thin. 'Does it even matter?'

'Well, yes, how can you say he's my uncle when clearly he isn't?'

'For God's sake, Sarah Jane, can't you just leave it

alone? You're always asking bloody questions. He's my cousin's wife's brother, *okay?*'

'Liar.' Sarah Jane lifted her spoon and slopped soggy cereal back into the bowl. Grinning openly about her dilemma, she hadn't yet decided if she'd oblige her mother's request not to tell Dad. 'What's my silence worth?'

'Me not smacking you in the mouth?'

'You wouldn't dare.'

'Wanna bet?'

Sarah Jane shrugged, she didn't doubt it. 'Pollyanna will have to come too.'

'Suppose I don't have a choice. Just don't tell your dad about any of this. I mean it!'

Sarah Jane said nothing.

'Promise you won't or I'll drop the pair of you off at Uncle Trev's and you can spend all weekend watching him get shit-faced on Special Brew while Tyson craps all over the front room and Aunty Kelly has that weird friend of hers round, the one with the frizzy hair who spits when she talks.'

Sarah Jane's own lips tightened at the threat. 'Alright. But you'll have to make it worth my while.'

'Just hurry the frig up and get ready, will you? And tell Pollyanna to keep her bloody mouth shut as well.'

Sarah Jane sloped off to get dressed and complain to her cousin that they'd be going away for the weekend with some uncle of dubious family connection. As it was, Pollyanna didn't mind. In fact, she said it sounded fun.

Twenty minutes later the three of them left. They travelled north on the A1 till they were somewhere beyond the River Tyne. Roxanne Miller explained to the girls that Uncle Dean was recuperating after being seriously injured in Afghanistan. He'd served as a sergeant there for two years and, although the information she had was sketchy at best, she said after leading his men into a compound, somewhere in the Helmand Province (and, no, she didn't know where exactly), disaster had struck when one of them had stepped on an explosive device (and, no, she didn't know the ins and outs of this either and Sarah Jane was under NO circumstances allowed to badger Uncle Dean for further details). Three soldiers had been killed outright and Uncle Dean, who was standing close enough to the blast to be blown off his feet, was hospitalised for months. He lost the sight in one eye and was lucky not to have lost his left leg. But now, almost two years on, following numerous operations that involved metal plates and pins, and lots of physiotherapy sessions, he was up and about, walking again. Very recently he'd been diagnosed with PTSD, though, and his wife (some heartless bint called Claire) had filed for a divorce. Which was why, according to Roxanne, they were paying him a visit, to help cheer him up. As it was Sarah Jane didn't care about the divorce stuff and had no idea what PTSD stood for (and doubted her mother did either, else surely she'd have said). But the fact that Uncle Dean had been in the army was hugely impressive. She'd never met a sergeant before. Or anyone with one eye and a metal leg. So the trip was now massively more favourable than staying at home.

Once at Uncle Dean's house they switched from Roxanne Miller's car to his before heading further north. Roxanne sat in the front passenger seat, closest to Uncle Dean, with her hair all perfect and face too pretty, while Sarah Jane was stuck in the back with Pollyanna. Pollyanna sat unspeaking for the most part, her goon-face enthralled by the passing countryside scenery, whereas Sarah Jane could hardly take her eyes off Uncle Dean. She'd already decided that Dad didn't need to know about him. Her silence had been sealed. Airtight.

Uncle Dean was mesmerising. Her mother blatantly thought so too; she laughed and touched his arm too much in an infuriating display of kitteny playfulness that made Sarah Jane's jaw lock tight.

After a while, perhaps because he was aware of the silent attention he was receiving, Uncle Dean caught Sarah Jane's eye in the rear view mirror and, in a voice almost as baritone as the revs of the car's engine, said, 'So, how's school? Any favourite subjects?'

Instantly Sarah Jane worried that he'd be able to see what she was thinking. His dead eye was white, the colour of a mood stone depicting boredom or frustration – probably because of her mother's incessant prattle, she thought – but his blue eye, the one that was still very much alive, looked vibrant enough to delve right into her thoughts and sift through them one by one. To know that she was besotted with him in a way she never could be with Kieran Stock, the most popular kid at school, because when it came down to it Kieran Stock was just a boy. Moreover, a boy who had never been blown up. She broke eye contact and looked instead at Uncle Dean's large, accomplished hands on the steering wheel. Hands that had handled real guns and weaponry, she thought. Hands that had known physical pain and hardship. Hands that had, perhaps, killed. She felt her cheeks flash hot, but managed to say, 'English and drama,' without sounding completely idiotic to her own ears.

'So, we have an aspiring actress maybe?' He sounded genuinely enthused.

'Not likely,' Roxanne Miller interrupted with a laugh, spoiling the rapport. 'Pollyanna's the actress.'

At the mention of her name Pollyanna turned, eyebrows raised, and Sarah Jane glowered. Pollyanna shrugged, indifferent, and returned her attention to the side window, evidently happy to sit this one out. Sarah

Jane tightened her hands into claws, dug her nails into the leather upholstery by the sides of her legs and imagined smashing her mother's head through the windscreen. 'I'd like to be a scriptwriter actually,' she said, trying to control the fire in her voice in case it burnt what little scrap of mature credibility she imagined she'd been left clinging to.

Roxanne Miller snorted mild amusement, but Uncle Dean cast a disapproving look that silenced her. Sarah Jane fell in love with him a little bit more.

'Hey, sounds cool,' he said. His eye, the one that was still alive, striking blue, winked at Sarah Jane, making a new wave of heat on her face cripple her ability to react or reply with any sense of unabashed dignity. She looked down again to the scars on his hands. The webbing of white on tanned skin. She imagined them bloodied; how they must have looked right after the bomb. Red. Sore. Agony.

Her heart. Right now.

She considered there might be a network of scars all over his body. Beneath his clothes. Ones she couldn't see. Ones his wife no longer wanted to see. Claire, she thought, really must be a bint. When he started talking to her mother again, Sarah Jane felt comfortable enough to study his profile some more. His blonde hair, once kissed by hostile foreign sun, was pulled into a messy, short ponytail and he had the beginnings of a beard that was dirty blonde. Not a 'dad' beard, but a rugged display of confident maleness. An effortless virility because he'd survived what many wouldn't have. The mangled flesh of his hands, and perhaps elsewhere, had healed. Knitted back together. And the whiteness of his dead eye was a badge of honour. It might be blind, but Uncle Dean had seen more than most ever would. Shrapnel had erased blue, but with white came wisdom and courage.

Sarah Jane was sickly dizzy on new emotions which

felt like a bellyful of E numbers fizzing up inside her, the concoction of artificial chemicals going straight to her head. She couldn't make sense of how she could possibly feel, to the extreme extent, the way she felt, or why. Uncle Dean was physically attractive, that was true, but this lazy observation didn't explain her absolute want nor the desire that burned in her core like lava. Rather, he was soul-captivating on some mysterious, primal level that Sarah Jane had never encountered before. So, while berating herself for her uninformed choice that morning to put on a hoody with a purple unicorn printed on the front, she continued to watch him, taking him in, for the remainder of the journey.

It was at least another two hours till he announced, 'Here we are,' before pulling off a winding country lane onto a narrow access road, then parking on a gravelled area to the side of a large wooden cabin.

The place seemed unreal. A pocket of idealism in the middle of nowhere. Not at all what Sarah Jane had expected. Not that she'd known what to expect; she didn't know Uncle Dean well enough to form any real ideas or opinions of the type of man he was beyond the army sergeant she imagined, or of the places he kept. His cabin was weathered and aged to a degree that it fit snugly into its environment and, although massively impressive, it was not a showy piece of architecture that looked primped to scream *Look at me!* with any arrogant sense of boastful pride. Instead it was a comfortable presence that looked as though it had risen from the ground and grown alongside the trees. A tall, quirky tower rose from its westerly corner, making it look like a fairy tale prop; an organic woodland palace that wasn't visible unless you left the beaten track and *really* looked for it. To the front of the cabin lay a huge expanse of water, as smooth as a mirror. It stretched as far as mountains on the horizon that were the colour of chestnut mushrooms. And to the rear, across the one-vehicle access road, was a thickly wooded area.

Uncle Dean pulled on the handbrake and threw Roxanne Miller a wink. 'Welcome to my home in the woods.' Then he turned to the backseat and said, 'Make yourselves at home, girls.'

More than happy to accept his invitation, Sarah Jane hurried from the car. As she did, a raucous chatter of deep-voiced birds broke any tranquillity that might have been. Looking up at a large tree that stood alone by the west wall of the cabin, its full height scratching the bottom section of the tower, she saw its autumnal branches were busy not just with the rich orange of dying leaves but also with black feathery bodies. A murder of crows, she thought, delightedly. She skipped across the gravel, around the back of the car, skimming Uncle Dean's paintwork with light fingers, and helped Pollyanna from the back seat.

'I'm Rapunzel and this is where I'm going to live from now on,' Pollyanna said, looking up at the tower. Its slate roof was a colder shade of grey than the late afternoon sky and its windows were impenetrable-black.

'You'll have to stay here forever in that case, shit for brains, because no prince in his right mind will want to come and rescue you,' Sarah Jane said, trying to determine if the tower's windows were obstructed by blackout blinds or whether the darkness lay within.

Pollyanna narrowed her eyes at her cousin's contempt, but didn't argue.

As the girls crossed the lawn to catch up with Uncle Dean, two birds from the tree swooped down and perched on the guttering above the veranda, their feathers black-velvet under the sunless sky. Sarah Jane decided they were too big to be crows and must therefore be ravens. Neither flew away when she and Pollyanna passed beneath, both just watched; their eyes inquisitive, intelligent.

'Hi,' Sarah Jane said, tilting her head back to maintain eye contact. The birds hopped along the guttering with a cheeky synchronicity which matched the girls' pace, and one of them cawked a deep enthusiastic response.

Sarah Jane left Pollyanna on the veranda and followed Uncle Dean through the cabin's front door. He was a few inches shorter than the doorframe itself and his shoulders almost spanned its width. He walked with a significant limp, his left foot swinging out to the side due to the obvious limited mobility in his knee. Sarah Jane wondered which parts beneath the flesh were metal and whether he could feel the plates and pins grating and grinding, cold, against what was left of his damaged, splintered bones. She watched with great interest as he moved about the cabin, flicking switches down to test lightbulbs and opening blinds to let the last of the day's light in. He cast his car key onto a worn, wooden coffee table in front of the couch and rounded everyone together before declaring a tour of the place. First he talked them around the lounge and kitchen then, while Pollyanna sat by the enormous lounge window watching a paddling of ducks out on the lake, he ushered Roxanne and Sarah Jane upstairs, their feet noisy on the wooden steps, while he trailed awkwardly behind. He opened the first door on the left and Sarah Jane peered inside. The air was musty, unused, and the space dark because the raven-tree outside partially obscured the window. Sarah Jane could hear the birds' boisterous babble and wondered if they were happy or cross to have company again. She had no idea how often Uncle Dean used the holiday cabin, but judging by the layer of dust on a nearby chest of drawers, she didn't think very.

A king-sized bed, positioned centrally on the back wall, was covered by a thick velvet throw, maroon in colour. Like a royal robe laid out. And a large stag's head was affixed to the wall above the bed's headboard. Its glass eyes watched them with a black sadness and the number of tines on its antlers suggested it might have been King of the Woods, once upon a time.

'Is this your room?' Sarah Jane said to Uncle Dean, even though she knew it must be.

'Yeah.' He ran a finger along the top of the drawers, distracted, and frowned at the grey fuzz it collected. 'How on earth can an empty house gather so much dead skin?'

'Dust,' Roxanne Miller corrected. She was standing out on the landing, gripping the doorframe as though the room and her better judgement forbade her from entering but her feet were feeling wayward and so she had to stop them from moving forward.

'What's in there?' Sarah Jane pointed at a heavy-looking oak door to the right of the bed. Its iron lock was sucking on a key and it looked like the sort of door that must surely conceal dusty heirlooms and family secrets.

'Nothing,' Uncle Dean said, side-stepping to block her advance. He took her by the shoulders and spun her round, then pocketed the door's key and guided her back out onto the landing. 'That is, nothing that need concern you, sweetheart.'

'But,' she looked up at the ceiling, 'does it lead to the tower?'

'Never you mind.' He steered her along the landing to the other first floor room. This was a smaller space with a double bed dressed in plain white linen. A virginal display in contrast. An oil-painted swan swum forever on calm blue waters above the bed, its beauty depicted in summery, seemingly effortless, strokes by some unknown artist. Roxanne Miller set her bag down, claiming the room as her own. Sarah Jane ground her teeth together.

Back downstairs Uncle Dean showed all three of them

where the bathroom was. Then, at the end of the corridor, next door to the bathroom, was a spacious twin room, decorated blue, where Sarah Jane and Pollyanna were to sleep. From their window they could see the woods behind the cabin. It looked like an uninviting, monstrous place, Sarah Jane decided almost immediately. A place where thorns and nettles and poisonous plants would be the most pleasant things to be found. The front-most trees were like gnarled, bony sentinels, guarding all that might reside in the mossy, mulchy darkness, held close and tight between boughs and trunks, beneath the golden awning of another year's dead summer.

'Whispering Woods,' Uncle Dean said. He positioned himself by the window, folding his arms over his large chest.

'Why's it called that?' Sarah Jane moved closer to him under the pretence she might see better.

'Because of the trees.' His voice was a low rumble of gritty caution and Sarah Jane could sense that a nervous edginess had taken hold of him because of the way he was standing, all angular and stiff. 'The trees sometimes talk.'

Unsure what to make of this claim, Sarah Jane grinned and said, 'That's silly.' But when she looked up, she saw that his blue eye was serious and succinctly more disturbing than the white one.

'It's true,' he said, with a wink. 'And anyone that can hear them, for sure, will go slowly and irreversibly mad.'

2

Rough fabric prickled Callie Crossley's right cheek, bare arm and consciousness. She was lying on her side, struggling through dark, incoherent thoughts. Then she groaned and opened her eyes – awakening to even darker and more incoherent thoughts. Her head hurt and she couldn't move her arms because her hands were bound behind her back. Perhaps even more worryingly, she couldn't see. At all. Couldn't even move her tongue to speak (or scream) because there was something jammed inside her mouth. Something soft, like a handkerchief. Or a sock. Or…who knew, it could be anything!

Fully awake now, she knew she was in a different kind of nightmare altogether. A very real one. When she tried to stretch her legs her feet met with something that created a hollow-sounding thud. Panic swelled in her chest and she kicked out, harder this time, causing similar reverberant thuds to vibrate beneath her.

Fucking hell, I'm boxed in!

With this newer, starker realisation the darkness sealed itself around her with a more suffocating density and the air seemed suddenly thin. There was no sound except that of her own breathing, which she knew was too rapid. She wondered when she'd run out of oxygen. This thought, in turn, made her breathe even faster, to the point of hyperventilation.

Calm down, just calm the shit down. Think rationally.

But this isn't *rational.*

I don't care. Just think, think, think dammit!

Mentally backtracking, Callie thought about what she'd been doing last: getting drunk and socialising at

Antonio Drake's private party at his UK home in Kensington. The cosy shindig was in celebration of *Ampato Curse*, the sequel to *Juanita Heat* in which Drake's stellar performance as brooding anti-hero Angel Grind had since branded him as some sexy Hispanic Indiana Jones type. The action-adventure, which had topped the charts for weeks on end back in 2014, had seen Drake's character Grind battle against time and countless obstacles to claim back the Inca Ice Maiden that had been stolen by fanatical madman Donovan O' Sheath. O' Sheath, played by classic British television scoundrel Rothbury Clime, had planned to invoke the Incan God by offering up the ancient mummy along with a new sacrifice, his own step-sister, till Grind thwarted his plans and defeated him halfway up twin-peaked mountain Nevado Huascarán in northern Peru. And now *Ampato Curse* was forecasted to be just as much of a blockbuster. Callie Crossley wasn't totally convinced, however. Aside from the fact Drake's rapport with leading lady Elspeth Moore in *Ampato Curse* lacked the chemistry he'd shared with Rowena Murray in *Juanita Heat*, the storyline felt weaker by comparison and rushed in its completion. Just another sequel for sequels' sake. Callie hoped to be proved wrong though. For the longevity of her own career, she *wanted* to be proved wrong.

She'd swigged champagne at Drake's party and chattered enthusiastically about her own part in the movie – bungling historian Rosie Montgomery who wore stereotypical nerd glasses and a tweed jacket with elbow patches - to all that asked, and there had been plenty, until she'd had enough and just wanted her pyjamas and slippers on. She'd made her excuses then left. Bizzle and Franky, her security men, met her at the door and escorted her towards her waiting car. That was the last she could remember.

So where was she now?

Where in the world was so dark and cramped?

The prickly fabric beneath her felt like…what?

Well, *felt.*

The lining of a car boot.

Oh fuck, I've been kidnapped!

Callie had been warned of the risks. Countless times. Had always taken the warnings seriously. Especially recently. Which was why she always had Bizzle and Franky close to hand. But where were they now? She couldn't recall being manhandled or roughed up. Nor could she recall Bizzle or Franky reacting to anyone who shouldn't have been there outside Drake's home. And yet here she was, trussed up in what she suspected was the back of a car.

Had someone drugged her at the party?

She didn't think so. Having downed more than quadruple her recommended daily allowance of alcohol, Callie felt surprisingly clear-headed. But then, adrenalin could do that couldn't it? Maybe she *had* been drugged. She rolled onto her back, knees pointed up. Her bound hands dug painfully into the softness of her buttocks and her arms hurt, so she rolled back onto her side. A piteous sob clawed its way up her throat but was cut short, muffled by the warm, unpleasant gag in her mouth. This was too awful to bear: the knowledge of being in danger offset by the definitely not knowing why. The best she could hope for was a kidnapper who wanted some sort of ransom. She had enough money to guarantee a safe release, if that's what it was about. But, depending to whom her kidnapper made the initial monetary demand might also (depending on the types of movies you'd seen) depend on how many fingers she would lose before serious negotiations got underway.

Gah.

Another idea occurred to her then. What if she was in

the back of her own chauffeur's car? Maybe Landon was in on some dodgy-bastard, money-making scheme with Bizzle and Franky.

No way! Too paranoid.

Is it? How well do you really know those shady fuckers?

Not very, I suppose.

See!

She tried straightening her body lengthways again, even though she knew it didn't fit. Not even close. Again this served to make her feel maddeningly claustrophobic. She jolted upwards, a frustrated bid to make more space, somehow, and hit her head on the underside of what she presumed was the parcel shelf.

Arrrggghhh. Need. To. Get. Out. Have. To. Get. Oh wait!

A news report about a woman who'd been bundled into the boot of a family saloon by a would-be killer sprung to mind. Callie recalled the woman had knocked a back light out of the white Passat; a car nobody would have suspected had such an unusual cargo had she not then stuck her hand out of the hole she'd made. This tactical move meant the woman attracted the attention of several fellow road users, most of whom reported her hand-waving to the police. As a result, she was then saved from whatever horrors her kidnapper had had planned for her. A nice, tidy ending.

Callie's situation was very different, however. She realised that. The car she was in was stationery and there were no sounds – traffic or otherwise – to suggest anyone else was nearby. But still, she had to try. Had to do something. Couldn't just lie there waiting till there was no oxygen left and her lungs shrivelled up or exploded or deflated or did whatever they do when there's no air left to breathe. She nudged her stilettos off and felt about with her bare feet, searching for the nearest rear light. When she found it, she reared her left leg and hoofed the inner side of the fitting with the ball of her foot. She felt it slacken, but it didn't give. She tried another three times, harder each time. On the fourth attempt it fell out and a powdery waft of daylight killed the darkness next to her feet, highlighting the close proximity of her box-like confines even more.

Oh fuckitty fuck, I need to get out.

She jabbed one foot outside into cool air and jiggled it about, making mad grunting noises behind the gag as she did. She could hear birds now. Crows, she thought. And it was the cawing of these birds and the light breeze that danced open-aired freedom about her toes that made her think, most likely, she hadn't been stashed away in a garage or some other secure lock-up where no one would ever find her. She kept rotating her ankle, wriggling her toes.

Please see me. Someone? Anyone! Please. I NEED to get out.

But after ten minutes had passed, Callie's foot became still and she began to sob; an awful sound like a large dog having a seizure, she thought. But she couldn't help it. Couldn't stop. Was too distressed. Couldn't control nor contain the internal terror that made her lungs incapable of filling up anywhere close to capacity – or even half way. She'd been stolen and tied up and locked away. And the arm she was lying on had gone numb and she needed a drink of water. A champagne hangover was beginning to kick in and her mouth was dry, the gag having soaked all of the moisture from it.

What did any of this mean? Was she going to die?

Not like this. Please, not like this.

She pulled her foot back into the boot space and shuffled about, rearranging herself so that she lay on her front. The imminence of pins and needles about to spread up her entire arm tingled; the nerves angry about having been starved of blood for too long. She tried screaming again, a noise that wasn't loud beyond her own head. A noise that did not much more than hurt her throat. She banged her feet against the hollow, sturdy walls of her confinement to make as much racket as she could. To vent her frustration. Surprisingly, she felt anger building. Which was good, she thought. If she could feed this inner rage it would help her not to fall into emotionally-weak pieces. But after only a few minutes had passed she grew tired. Fell still. Felt less angry already. And sobbed.

Then she heard something. Something beyond her tiny cell. A door creaking open. Close by. Her heartbeat became even more erratic and she strained over the sound of her own breathing to detect more sound. A person, perhaps. She felt hopeful, nervous, frightened and elated.

Please let it be the police.

Or Bizzle and Franky.

Or anyone *who doesn't want to do awful things to me.*

She was sure she could hear footsteps now, someone approaching slowly – cautious or deliberate, she couldn't tell. A steady advance. Grass rustling subtly in a way it hadn't before. A certain expectancy charging the air, prickling dormant senses not usually used when danger didn't present itself to this degree.

Then the birds were shouting, excitedly. What could they see that she couldn't?

Callie held her breath; her lungs burning with the effort. She could sense that whoever was out there was standing not two feet away. Her kidnapper having come to relay his intentions, perhaps, or merely toying with her. Or coming to play holy fuck because she'd kicked the rear light of his car out. Or maybe it was a chance passer-by, as she'd hoped.

Her bladder twinged and she thought she might wet

herself. She considered screaming a muffled scream against the gag, in case whoever it was went away without knowing she was even there. But there was a click and the boot opened. Daylight poured in, blinding her. When her eyes adjusted to the new brightness she saw a figure standing over her. It was then that she filled her lungs and screamed.

3

'What do the trees in Whispering Woods talk about?' Sarah Jane asked.

Uncle Dean shrugged. 'Suppose that depends on what it is they have to tell you.' His blue eye sparkled with mischief, but his dead one conveyed a solemn truth.

Sarah Jane's own eyes glittered with excitement. She shifted her weight to her right leg, so her arm was touching his. 'Do you know any stories? About any of the people that have gone mad.'

'A couple.' He smiled; his teeth were white and straight and somehow, falsely or not, substantiated genuineness. 'There used to be a man lived here as it happens. Old Mally Murgatroyd.'

'You mean *here?*' Sarah Jane pointed to the floor. 'In this cabin?'

'Yep. He lived alone. Went doolally. Some say it was cabin fever, but maybe he'd always been a tongue sandwich short of a picnic.'

'Sounds like the picnic was better off that way,' Pollyanna said. She was looking out of the window from across the room. Next to her was Roxanne Miller.

'You think?' Uncle Dean seemed to consider this. He scratched his chin and the whiskers there sounded coarse against his fingertips. He smelled of cologne; a citrus musk. Sarah Jane breathed him in, becoming more and more inebriated on infatuation.

'One evening, late August, quite some years back,' he said, his voice still low, 'something really awful happened here.'

It was then, right at that moment, Sarah Jane felt a

change in the atmosphere, as though Uncle Dean's words had commanded a shift in the fabric of reality. She imagined the room was listening and changing mood to suit, altering to accommodate his story like an emotional chameleon that recognised their morbid interest and need for tragedy. All at once every bit of warmth that the earlier sun had left behind was spat out through the open bedroom door and the air became instantly cold; as cold as the blue of the covers on the two single beds. Sarah Jane shivered. She looked out at the woods, needing and longing to know its darkest secrets so she could ponder them as if they were her own. There was a murderousness about Whispering Woods and she wanted Uncle Dean to go right ahead and weave its stories into the here and now so she might glimpse beyond its frontline, to see what was really in there. To feel what it was like. To know if its insides lay ghastly and stinking beneath countless deciduous summers or if the frostbite of each winter was enough to have cleansed the horror of the trees. She wanted to walk through the undergrowth with Uncle Dean leading the way, the pair of them kicking up dead leaves with the toes of their boots. She tingled with excitement and all the while was aware of a delicious warmth on her arm – the warmth of him radiating through the fabric of his shirt sleeve. 'What happened that was so awful?' she asked.

'Some broken-down motorists on their way home from a camping trip stopped by. A man, a woman and their two kids.'

'Then what?'

'Take a guess.' Again he smiled; it was a smile that didn't denote any sense of favourable outcome for the family in the tale, but a smile that crushed down on Sarah Jane's heart nonetheless, adding more weight, more pressure, till it actually hurt.

'Old Mally Murgatroyd killed them?' she asked.

He drummed his fingers on the sill, a quick-fire sequence of confirmation, then pointed a finger gun at her. 'All except the small boy.'

'But why?'

He shrugged, looked puzzled for a moment as though he'd never considered this, then said, 'Why does anyone do anything?'

Sarah Jane pressed her arm even closer against his. 'How did he do it? Kill them, I mean. Did he butcher them?'

'Sarah Jane!' Roxanne Miller, still standing by the doorway, folded her arms over her chest. 'Why do you always have to be so bloody horrible?'

'Did it with a filleting knife,' Uncle Dean said, seeming not to hear Roxanne Miller's voice, let alone her disapproval. He was staring out of the window now, trancelike, unreachable. The room was breathing all around them. In. Out. In. Out. Big. Small. Big. Small. 'Hacked all three of them up, right there in front of the little boy.' His head jerked round then, and he regarded Sarah Jane with the most intense blue. 'Can you imagine that? His mam. His dad. Then his big sister.'

Sarah Jane could. She half-smiled. 'Then what?'

'Old Mally Murgatroyd, he sautéed their flesh and made himself a stew for dinner. Made the boy eat some of it too.'

'Oh come on, Dean,' Roxanne Miller objected.

'Once he'd had a bellyful,' Uncle Dean went on, 'he left the boy here and went out into the woods and hanged himself.'

'Wow.' Sarah Jane was still trying to determine if he was winding her up, but the white of his dead eye made it impossible for her to tell. 'But *why?* Why would he do that?'

'The trees, they told him to. That's just how it is,

sweetheart. Those touched by the madness of Whispering Woods do all kinds of crazy stuff. It's like the trees…'

'Dean!' This time Roxanne Miller made sure she was heard.

Uncle Dean turned to her, startled, fully aware, his thoughts completely back in the room with them. 'It's okay though,' he said, raising his hands in apology, 'not everyone hears the trees anyway.'

'What happened to the boy?' Pollyanna asked, her voice a ghostly addition to the conversation.

'Stayed here,' Uncle Dean said. He edged away from the window, his eyes not leaving Roxanne Miller's.

'How long for?'

'Hard to say.'

'Where is he now?'

'Look, I think we've all heard enough silly stories for one day,' Roxanne Miller said. She was glaring, but her eyes lacked any *real* reproach. 'I'm sure tales like this aren't good for young imaginations.'

'Yeah, sorry. I, uh, I'm sorry.' Uncle Dean winced and Sarah Jane hated her mother more than ever for having made him look momentarily weak. It wasn't a look befitting an ex-army sergeant. He owed her nothing, least of all an apology just because she was too feeble-minded to deal with the truth and the more unsavoury aspects of life.

Roxanne Miller shook her head and flashed him a different kind of sullen look which, deliberately or not, gave way to a certain sexual tension that brought a touch of uncomfortable warmth back to the room. She then turned and made off towards the lounge and Sarah Jane scrunched her fists tight, her nails burrowing into skin, when she saw how Uncle Dean sighed after her. The memory of the orphaned boy who'd eaten bits of his parents and sister lingered in the uncomfortable silence like a stewing argument and Sarah Jane thought of ways to encourage it. But nobody said anything for a while.

'Maybe I'll tell you the rest some other time,' Uncle Dean said at last.

'Can't you now?' Sarah Jane said, hopefully, her hands relaxing a little. 'She won't hear. And I won't tell.'

Uncle Dean laughed and nodded. His blue eye shone. 'You're funny, kid.' But he turned and left, taking with him the knowledge of Whispering Woods.

The girls stayed in their room to unpack and Pollyanna drew the curtains against the woods, even though day hadn't yet faded to dark. Sarah Jane removed clothes and toiletries from her holdall as loudly as she could, the room absorbing her bad mood. Less than an hour later everyone was eating tuna-topped baked potatoes at the dining table in the kitchen and there was no further talk of death or mutilation. Not even the merest mention of Whispering Woods. Afterwards, once the plates had been washed and cleared away, they all watched television in the lounge: Roxanne Miller on the couch with the two girls and Uncle Dean in a shabby, leather armchair on his own. Every now and then Sarah Jane caught the adults exchanging glances, glances that made her toes curl under and temples pulsate.

Just after ten Uncle Dean brought a bottle of Malbec from the kitchen and Roxanne Miller ordered Sarah Jane and Pollyanna to bed. They went begrudgingly but without argument.

'Do you think Uncle Dean's story was true?' Pollyanna said, once she and Sarah Jane were settled into their individual night-soaked cocoons of duck down, listening to the soft, rhythmic sound of the night's first rain. She'd taken the bed by the door, leaving Sarah Jane with the one by the window – the one closest to Whispering Woods.

'You're such an idiot, Poll.' Sarah Jane was staring at the ceiling above the door. Greyness and shadows decorated the walls and furniture, and the smell of the woods was right there with them: a natural but indefinable smell that made her think of foliage decomposing on top of damp soil, under which scores of earwigs, woodlice and worms crawled, scurried and slithered. 'Course it wasn't true.' And yet Sarah Jane had mindfully turned her back to the window, wary of the ghosts that might be breathing against the glass pane.

Since Uncle Dean had spoken of Whispering Woods earlier she imagined he had roused its victims from any ill-begotten slumber, bringing their torment back to life with his, the storyteller's, second-hand words. And now disturbed, she thought it likely that they would want to get inside the cabin to bring their stories even closer. To whisper in her ear, in their own words, about the madness they'd suffered. They might even want to climb inside and make her...

A burst of exaggerated laughter made its way to the girls' room. Anger immediately took over where fear left off. Sarah Jane scrunched her eyes shut and lay rigid, squeezing her hands closed so her fingernails bit into her palms.

'Something must be funny out there,' Pollyanna thought to say.

Sarah Jane's fists clenched even tighter; she didn't want to think about it. Tried to think of something, anything, else but couldn't help imagining her mother, right now, touching Uncle Dean's arm and smiling that infuriating smile. When she didn't say anything in response to her cousin's observation and a heavy, brooding silence had stretched out too far, Pollyanna said, 'I wish this place was mine.'

Sarah Jane clicked her tongue in disdain. 'Liar, you're too much of a scaredy cat to live here.'

'Am not. You said yourself that Uncle Dean's story was just made up.'

'Even so, you wouldn't *dare* stay here alone.'

'Yes I would. Easy peasy. And I'd never want to leave.'

'Careful what you wish for, *Rapunzel*.'

'Don't be such a mong.'

'Shut up, tit head!'

'Make me, ginger nut.'

'Ha! Says you!'

'Dick-splat!'

Both girls then fell into fits of laughter and soon Sarah Jane was wiping her eyes and groaning because her belly ached. 'I'm pleased you came, Poll.'

'Me too,' Pollyanna said, her words hiccupped with a lingering giggle. 'What do you think we'll do tomorrow?'

'Not sure.'

'Reckon Uncle Dean will show us the sights?'

'Dunno.' Sarah Jane became gravely serious in an instant.

Oblivious to her cousin's sudden mood dip, Pollyanna asked, 'Do you think he has a boat for the lake?'

'Dunno.'

'He *must* do though, mustn't he?'

'I don't know.'

'Cor, you don't know much do you? What's the matter?'

'Nothing.'

'Yes there is.' Pollyanna sat up, her duvet crinkling noisily. 'What is it? Tell me.'

'Nothing,' Sarah Jane said. 'Just leave me alone and go to sleep.'

A few moments passed before Pollyanna guessed, 'It's him, isn't it?'

'Who?'

'Uncle Dean.'

'What about him?'

'You're acting all funny because of Uncle Dean.'

'What's that supposed to mean?'

'You fancy him.'

'No I don't!'

'Yes you do. You've been staring at him *all* day.'

'Haven't.'

'Have.'

'Shut your stupid face.'

Pollyanna laughed. 'Ha! I can't believe you fancy Aunt Roxanne's *boyfriend*.'

'I said shut it!' Sarah Jane's head was suddenly pounding and she could feel hot blood swelling behind her eyes.

'Else what?'

'I'll kill you.' Sarah Jane rolled over so that her back was turned to her cousin. So that she now faced the window-wall that stood between her and the ghosts of Whispering Woods. 'And he's *not* her boyfriend.'

Pollyanna laughed again. 'What would you call him then? Her *special friend?*'

When Sarah Jane failed to reply Pollyanna eventually lay down again, but Sarah Jane could tell she was grinning; her cousin's smugness was as thick as the darkness that seeped from the woods and encapsulated the cabin. She felt ill with anger. It wasn't long before the ensuing silence between the two girls was disturbed by another peal of over-the-top laughter from elsewhere in the cabin. Sarah Jane ground her teeth together so hard her face ached and she made a low grunting sound; a sound that escaped before she could stop it.

Pollyanna sniggered and whispered, 'Sarah Jane and Dean, sitting in a tree, K-I-S-S-I-N-G.'

'Fuck off, Poll,' Sarah Jane said, no longer caring how loudly she spoke.

'Eee, I'm telling.'

'I don't *fucking* care!'

'You will when Aunt Roxanne belts you one.'

'You're *so* dead.'

'Not.'

'Are.'

'Yeah well, I hope Aunt Roxanne is snogging Uncle Dean's face off right now. It'd serve you right.'

'Well I hope you have horrible dreams about Whispering Woods, ones you never wake up from.'

'Well I hope those two ravens come and peck your eyes out while you're asleep and then when you wake up and can't see I hope Old Mally Murgatroyd sticks you with his knife.'

Sarah Jane held her breath, determined not to respond anymore. If she did she knew she'd lose it. Eventually she fell into an angry sleep and dreamt of dark spaces and black shapes and never-ending shadows in a labyrinth of woods, which tried to entangle her. Trees scraped her skin, puncturing and burrowing, their branches trying to fill her arteries. Night slithered all around her and over her, with reptile sleekness, and she could smell something familiar, something that urged her to continue further on into the woods, thicker and deeper, where the smell, she knew, would be stronger. There was a distant murmuring. Whispering. She could hear her name being called. Over and over. Again and again. And she knew then what it was, that smell. It was him. The clean tang of Uncle Dean blended with the life and death of Whispering Woods.

When she awoke it was still night time. Something had disturbed her, but she didn't know what. She sat up and looked into the crushed-velvet darkness, her heart hammering. 'Poll?'

Gentle snoring suggested her cousin was sleeping, so Sarah Jane eased out of bed. As she did, the room lit up white-blue; an electric blaze through the thin fabric that covered the window. Seconds later deep, resonant thunder rumbled overhead and underfoot. Sarah Jane stood still, allowing her eyes to adjust to the dark, which settled back into place like heavy curtains. When Pollyanna still didn't stir, Sarah Jane snuck from the room and crept down the corridor towards the lounge, listening all the while for signs that her mother and Uncle Dean were still up or the trees of Whispering Woods were uprooting and repositioning themselves so the cabin would be lost in their midst come morning.

In the lounge, rain lashed against the windows that overlooked the lake and another flash of lightning highlighted that the room was unoccupied. The last coals in the wood burner had died to a burgundy ember and two empty wine glasses sat side by side on the coffee table. Sarah Jane stood close to the window and put her hands on the cold pane; a flimsy transparency given all that might be out there, watching. The lake was a combined blackness with all of its surroundings, and only when lightning flashed could Sarah Jane see where it lay. For a fleeting moment she thought she saw a figure at the lip of the shore, to the far right, but when lightning flashed again she saw nothing. Wind screamed through slits in the wooden window surround and she imagined the tree at the side of the house, the raven-laden branches buffeting about and the ravens themselves huddled tight against the trunk. She also thought about the trees to the rear of the cabin. Whispering Woods. The place where the once majestic King of the Woods might have lived before his head was mounted onto Uncle Dean's bedroom wall.

The night here, at this place, was horrific. So dark. Arcane. But it was excitement not fear that coursed through Sarah Jane's veins. She found it impossible to feel overly afraid. Not because she was especially brave, but because Uncle Dean was upstairs. If Whispering Woods was to swallow the cabin whole, the fallen sergeant, her uncle by convenience, was there to protect them. He would know what to do. Probably knew all there was to know about Whispering Woods and much worse besides.

Sarah Jane cast a glance towards the wooden staircase and saw his bedroom door was ajar. She stood there bare-footed, imagining him. Reckoned if she was quiet enough she would be able to sneak upstairs and peak into his room. See him sleeping. Beneath the King of the Woods. Beneath maroon velvet. Before she knew it she was edging up the stairs. Quietly, softly. Her feet clammy on the wooden boards. Halfway up lightning flashed, illuminating everything in the lounge below. Then thunder raged. The sound of her heart. She stopped and leaned her back flat against the wall and breathed in deeply.

Almost there.

Sensing Uncle Dean close by, she responded to the invisible pull with which his strong presence reeled her in. Her heart hot and heavy, filling her veins with a ferociousness that made her feel lightheaded. On the landing now, her fingers touched the doorframe. She buzzed with anticipation. Angled her face to the gap. Looked into the war hero's lair. And, at once, stopped breathing.

Uncle Dean wasn't asleep. Nor was he lying in bed. He was standing in the middle of the room, naked. Light blonde hair hung loose to his broad shoulders and his body was a taut mass of muscle and war story braille. His pubic hair was the same dirty blonde as his beard and the sight of his penis made her face flash hot. Still, she couldn't look away. Not even when lightning flashed and his body was imprinted onto her retinas, for her to take away, to savour. She should have left. Gone back to bed. But Uncle Dean, right now, in this moment, was the most hypnotic thing she'd ever seen. Imperfect perfection. A Norse god in an erotic oil painting. She couldn't move.

Thunder followed; her heartbeat rapturous.

Then just as quickly, it perished.

Roxanne Miller stepped into view, equally as naked as Uncle Dean.

No.

No! No! No!

Her mother touched Uncle Dean's bare chest, caressing scar tissue she had no business caressing, and stepped on some explosive device inside Sarah Jane's head.

BOOM!

White heat filled Sarah Jane's thoughts and she scrunched her fists and closed her eyes against the blast. She wished everyone in the world was dead, including herself, because this was too awful. Too hideous to contemplate. As powerless and defunct as the King of the Woods, she was nothing more than a silent spectator to what was happening in Uncle Dean's room. Haunted eyes to watch and be ignored.

An ugly duckling.

No! Just no!

She felt the pull of Whispering Woods and stopped resisting it. Its menace wrapped around her like black wings in an instant and she allowed herself to be enveloped till she could barely breathe, till all of the darkness she could possibly know came rushing inside of her, filling all of the empty gaps and making her more whole than she thought she ever had been. Whispering Woods' energy was a depraved, ravenous, almost touchable thing, and it channelled through her ferociously. She could hear its voice too. Not the blast of a thousand trees talking all at once, but one voice. Quiet.

Whispering. Filling her head. Urging her to do things. Bad things. Things that would make her feel good. Like necking the beautiful swan and drinking its blood and eating its flesh and decorating Uncle Dean's bed with its white bloodied feathers, sewing them onto the maroon throw. This internal, external rage continued to charge, building to an awful, debilitating crescendo, till eventually Sarah Jane saw nothing but red. So much red. Maroon all over everything.

4

Smiler woke early. No strange thing. The birds in the ash tree were caw-cawing their observation that the sun had come up again. As if one day they expected it might not.

Chance would be a fine thing.

There was a mob of about thirty of them lived there, at the side of the house. Smiler heard them all the time, especially when he was in his room, but mostly on some subconscious level. He went through to the lounge with a mug of black coffee and a packet of cigarettes, as he always did, to watch out the window for interesting weather. Or wildlife. Or anything. Anything at all. The last thing he expected to see was a black Bentley GT parked up on the front lawn.

Fuck me sideways!

Dropping his morning fix, he raced along the hallway to the front door. His breaths came out in excitable gasps and his hands trembled, fingers not doing exactly as he wanted, as he undid the door's security bolts.

Someone's come. Someone's here!

He pulled the door open then ran outside, not caring that his feet were bare or that he was wearing nothing but underpants. Seven-day-worn underpants. Jumping from the top step of the veranda, he landed at the edge of the dewy lawn and breathed in the chill-fresh morning air. He stood still, his bare skin bristling, and saw that it was still there. The Bentley. A monstrous black thing in its surreal state of *being there*. Smiler hardly dared to move again in case it was a mirage and that by making any more quick movements he might provoke it to fade out of existence. Or disappear in a sudden mental blip. From this distance he couldn't see anybody inside. He glanced about the garden for signs of a driver. When he saw none he chanced creeping forward. The car remained where it was and the birds in the ash tree cheered him on. Or laughed. He couldn't quite decide. Either way, suspicion gnawed at his initial hopefulness and his guts began to churn because of another new detail he noticed only now: one of the Bentley's rear lights was lying on the lawn and its misplacement looked wholly inappropriate. Like a pulled nail on a lady's manicured hand. Still, he continued on. Stalking and creeping till he was at the rear end of the car. Peering in through the back windows, he saw that the black leather seats were empty. Something didn't feel right. Something about the whole situation felt staged. Wrong. He was so tense with edginess, the muscles in his arms and neck ached. And there was something else. Even though the Bentley being there and its detached rear light lying on the lawn seemed too intentionally odd, neither of those things worried him nearly as much as the number plate did: L0S 3R.

Was it a personal slant against him? Or an elaborate trap: the car set out to lure him into some other realm of hell?

Seriously, could things get any worse?

Soon find out.

He reached out, breathed in deep and popped the boot.

Inside was a plump blonde. Early thirties. Bound up. Her blue eyes implored him with a genuineness that only true terror could substantiate. Then she screamed. Well, tried to. A gag was bunched in her mouth, strapped in place with a length of red ribbon tied like a gift bow at the back of her head. Smiler almost did a scream of his own. He cast another quick glance around the garden and down by the lakeside, to make sure nobody was lurking behind bushes, watching him. But there was no one. Not that he could see. He reached down and tackled the gag away from the woman's mouth and said, 'Whoa, whoa, calm down. It's okay.'

'*Okay?*' The woman's eyes bulged. She began moving her jaw up and down, then swiped her tongue around her stale-red lips. 'It most certainly is *not* okay.'

Smiler held his hands up and took a step back. 'Alright, alright, chill. So it's not okay. But, I mean, do you know who did this? Like, who brought you here?'

'No. No I bloody don't.' Her eyes were glassy and if not for the anger that seemed to be counterbalancing her upset, Smiler reckoned she'd be a hysterical wreck.

'Who are you?' he asked, tugging on his bottom lip, unsure what else to say or do. He'd never found himself in this kind of situation before.

'Who am *I?*' she said, squirming about and managing to rise up onto her knees while looking him up and down. 'Who the fuck are *you?*'

5

'Holy shit.' Callie Crossley's eyes became wide, stark recognition stealing her ability to blink. *'Joey Chaplin?'*

The man, barely into manhood, who was standing there in poisoned-white underpants, scratched the back of his head and sighed. 'Miles Golden actually.'

'Same bloody difference. What the hell are *you* doing here? And…*what the hell happened?'*

'I'm not sure I know what you're asking.' Miles Golden shrugged. A random strong gust of wind blew front sections of his hair across his eyes. He tucked the strands behind his ears and, in doing so, created a severe centre parting that looked not to have known shampoo in a long while. 'Are you asking me what happened to you? Or what happened to me?'

Callie groaned and closed her eyes. She had a soul-crushing feeling that his being here and the reason he looked like he did would somehow link with the reason why she was here. It seemed to be turning into *that* kind of a day – and getting decidedly grimmer by the minute. Whatever the reason for her winding up in the boot of a car, though, gut instinct told Callie Crossley that Miles Golden was not her kidnapper. She didn't know him personally, but knew of him. And, rightly or wrongly, didn't feel threatened.

Miles Golden had achieved fame in British Sitcom *Only Me*. His onscreen character Joey Chaplin helped turn him into an iconic floppy-haired, baby-oiled poster-boy. At one point his blonde hair, white teeth and golden abs meant his name was as sweet as butterscotch on any teenaged girl's tongue, but now, standing there, he made Callie think of loose hair in scummy plugholes and food floaters in dishwater. Of George Romero extras and inbred yokels. Miles Golden had deteriorated to a degree of, quite possibly, non-rectifiable awfulness. He was almost unrecognisable.

What the hell happened indeed!

His once-waxed chest was now smattered with irregular patches of hair, as if he was stuffed with wire and nylon and it was poking through where the skin had become threadbare. His naturally blonde hair was no longer styled, instead it sat just past his shoulders, straggly and greasy. His skin was pocked with spot scars and pores. It carried all the dullness of someone with a serious vitamin deficiency and was jaundiced rather than tanned. Callie doubted he'd brushed his teeth in months. His trademark white smile was now steel-grey along the gum line and missing a couple of teeth at the sides. She'd also bet he hadn't done a single push-up in all the time he hadn't brushed his teeth, because his neat six-pack was now a rounded, doughy paunch above the waistband of his over-used underpants. Most depressingly, perhaps because of some emotional endurance known only to him – and this proved way more significant than any of these other skin-deep beauty fails – his once bright, azure eyes were now dreary. No longer a source for any right-minded teenage-girl's fantasy. His youthful zeal was gone. Stone dead. Beyond cajoling back to life, she thought, because he looked as though he'd lost the will to exist. Whatever had happened to Miles Golden frightened her.

'Name's Smiler, by the way,' he said, in that ratchetty adolescent voice of his, not seeming to notice Callie's automatic, yet unintentional, repugnance upon recognition of him. Either that or he was indifferent to it.

Wearied by sparring emotions – fear, exhaustion and pity mostly – Callie shuffled about on her knees and showed him her bound wrists. 'Here, undo this will you?'

At first he looked about, as though expecting someone else might appear. Then he began to unpick the knot in the rough manacle of cord, remaining hesitant all the while, as though worrying about whether he should untie her or not.

'Do you have any idea why I'm here?' Callie asked, turning back to face him and rubbing her chafed wrists. She tried to stand and almost fell.

'None at all.' Smiler took hold of her hands, steadying her as she clambered from the back of the car. Her fitted Versace shift dress made the effort more ungraceful than it should have been and she almost fell on top of him. As soon as her feet were on grass and she was standing upright, she pulled her hands away and looked around, to take in her surroundings properly.

An oddly shaped log cabin, shabby and unloved, old but well-crafted, seemed to be the only building around. Its presence loomed like a thundercloud and she thought it could be no random accident that her kidnapper had parked the Bentley up on this particular lawn, in this particular patch of could-be-fucking-anywhere. The cabin seemed to regard her with quiet menace from the black windows of its tower room, like it knew her already. And it terrified her that it might. Above its lower section she could see the treetops of a woodland behind and to its front there was a massive lake. Its vastness and blackness made Callie feel nauseous and unreasonably afraid. She shivered. Unfamiliar mountains bordered the lake's furthermost edges. Forever away. A mere backdrop that was unreachable. Perhaps unreal.

'I take it you don't recognise me?' she said, meeting Smiler's dull gaze again.

The decaying teen pin-up's expression became vague and he continued to stare at her for a few moments. His eyes were like plastic buttons that had been left on a window display too long. Sun-damaged. Faded blue. No emotion. No life. Eventually he shook his head. 'Should I?'

Callie suppressed a sigh. 'Suppose not.'

'Are you meant to be famous or something?'

'I'd begun to think so.' She bent to pick up the offensive piece of material he had removed from her mouth just moments before. It looked like a balled-up, used white cotton handkerchief by her feet. She pulled it taut. Her breath caught. A set of words had been scrawled in crude black ink; each letter had bled, growing numerous spider legs, but was still readable in its abruptness: **DEAD TO ME**. The message inspired a new dread, making the blood in Callie's veins feel freezer-chilled. It was a confirmation of sorts that her kidnapper was a vitriolic psychopath and not some ransom opportunist after all.

'Whoa, what's that mean?' Smiler asked, reading the note.

'That I've pissed someone off.' Not wanting to touch it anymore, Callie let the swatch of fabric fall to the floor. 'That someone hates me.'

But who?

That was the ultimate question, the mystery that had hounded her for weeks. Because this note wasn't anything new or even all that surprising in itself. She'd received her first death threat around three months ago and, thereafter, got a new one every other day. Always similar in context and style, but not method of delivery. On this occasion the note-scribbler had risen to some new level of terrorism. It was impossible to determine from the messages, which were never longer than five words, or the handwriting, just who her tormentor might be. She couldn't recall having done anything so terrible as to warrant the kind of hatred that was being directed at her and, furthermore, she couldn't understand why she'd been dumped at some cabin with some has-been teen star whom she'd never met before and appeared, now, to be some kind of junkie in need of rehab.

Rehab.

Her agent Sam Dent-Worth always said she drank too much. This could hardly be part of some intensive get-dry programme. *Could it?*

As though feeling excluded from her thoughts, Smiler asked, 'Any idea who would do something like this to you?' His pale, blotchy arms were folded over his chest and his eyes showed concern – but for Callie or himself, it was hard to tell.

'You'd think so wouldn't you?' She glanced around the garden, feeling a wave of paranoia as black as the lake wash over her. She felt trapped yet exposed. Imminently threatened. Like whoever had done this, whoever had busied themselves for weeks on end sending malicious notes direct to her home via Royal Mail and leaving others wedged beneath her car's windscreen wipers, tacked to her front door, stuffed in the keyhole of the summer house in her back garden, tucked beneath the doormat on her front porch and folded beneath her cat's collar, was watching. Right now. Enjoying this whole charade. Probably laughing.

'Where is this place?' she asked, wringing her hands together and concentrating on remaining outwardly calm, because whatever was going on she was determined not to be made a fool of any further. Determined not to give her kidnapper the satisfaction of seeing she was blind-drunk on fear.

'Whispering Woods,' Smiler said.

'Where's that?'

'I dunno.'

'Why not?'

Smiler seemed embarrassed by his own answer and shrugged. 'I dunno, I just...don't.'

Callie felt a small seed of anger budding inside of her again and was keen for it to grow into something huge. 'Is this some sort of celebrity reality show?' she asked, her voice raised. 'Are people watching us? Now? Is it live? Are we on TV? Right now?'

'Whoa, whoa, chill.' Smiler held his hands up and shook his head. 'No, we're not on TV. Not that I'm aware. I don't know where Whispering Woods is that's all, I'm just...here.'

'So this isn't your place?' Callie pointed and looked at the cabin. It was looking right back.

'No.'

'Then whose is it?'

'I dunno.'

'So why are you here?'

'Someone brought me.'

'Who?'

'I dunno.'

'How don't you know?'

'I never saw. I don't remember. One day I was just...*here*.'

Callie's anger crashed again, giving way to a deep terror that was anchored on realisation. 'Were you kidnapped too?'

Smiler fidgeted with his fingers, his eyes not maintaining contact with hers for much longer than a blink or two. He lacked any of the arrogance or cockiness she might previously have stereotyped him with. Again he shrugged. 'Maybe. I mean, I guess.'

'You *guess?* What kind of sense is that?'

'None, I suppose.'

She groaned. 'You *definitely* don't know who owns this place?' This time she wanted him to say that he did more than anything else. She wanted to discover that this awful situation was some elaborate, albeit desperately unfunny, joke because that would be a whole lot less scary than the other possibilities and scenarios that were forming and developing in her mind; scenarios involving psychopaths with penchants for butcher's blocks and thumb screws, drill bits and pliers.

'No,' he said. 'I'm just kept here.'

'Kept?' She felt faint and, in that moment, couldn't think of a more horrible word. Champagne-bile felt like it was trying to burn a hole in her gut. 'Like, against your will kind of kept?' She needed clarification. To be sure.

Smiler looked puzzled. 'Well, I don't want to be here if that's what you mean.'

Callie's face went numb. Was she to become what Miles Golden had become? Her lungs felt leaden, her heart even more so. 'But, who keeps you here? And what do they do to you?'

'Nobody does anything to me.' Smiler unfolded his arms and laughed; a humourless sound as flimsy as dead leaves. He gestured all about them with his hands. 'It's Whispering Woods,' he said. *'This place* keeps me here.'

'You're not making any sense.' Callie edged backwards. Was he a victim like her? Or was he insane? It was hard to tell. Which made her even more uneasy. She felt an unpredictable upwelling of emotion rapidly amounting to *something* inside her.

Smiler looked wary, as if sensing it. 'Why don't you come inside with me?' he said. 'I'll get dressed. Then we'll use the car and get out of here.'

'Go inside with you? Oh no. No way. I'm not going in *there!'* Callie was looking at the cabin again. Its tower windows looked empty, but full. It was staring. Mocking. Studying her. 'If the keys are in the car, I'm leaving right now.'

'No. Don't. Please.' Smiler clutched his midriff, as if in pain. 'Please don't leave me here. I won't be long. I just need to grab some clothes.'

Callie massaged her temples. Too much was happening. There was too much nonsensical, not enough solid information being imparted. Her hangover headache was intensifying. She couldn't think straight. Wasn't sure what she should do. 'I don't trust you, Golden,' she said. 'I don't trust any of this.'

'Smiler,' he corrected, appealing to her with eyes that were like fragments of sky trapped beneath old glass. 'It's Smiler, please. And try to trust me. If you can. I'm not so bad. Not really.'

Callie bit her lip. If she tried to leave now he might try to restrain her by wrapping his bare arms around her and clinging on. Or he might turn violent. Could she fight him off? She wasn't sure. But what was she meant to do? Take a sneaky shot while he didn't suspect? Lay him out on the deck before taking a flyer in the Bentley? Actually, that sounded rather appealing. But then, what if he was telling the truth? What if he *was* being held captive? He certainly didn't look in a good way.

'Why don't you come inside?' he urged. 'I'll explain a bit more when I've got some clothes on. It's just, this is kind of awkward. Standing about like this. And I'm cold.' He folded his arms across his chest and Callie saw his skin was like gooseflesh.

She sighed. How could she walk away? It would be heartless of her to leave without him, especially when he seemed so desperate. He looked pitiful. Like a mistreated dog. 'Fuck it, Golden,' she said, 'I'll come inside while you get dressed. But if this is a trick, I swear to God!' She left the threat hanging, unsure what she meant to threaten him with anyway. An arse-kicking? A dunk in the lake? A cut and blow dry?

Smiler smiled – a smile that would have been attractive had he still been – and held up his hands. 'I swear it's not a trick.'

He turned and cut across the lawn towards the cabin. Callie trailed not far behind. Barefooted. Anxious. The birds in the tree started hollering again, as if making excited bets amongst themselves about what the outcome of her decision to go inside would be. 'What's up with them?' she called out to Smiler. 'What are they shouting about?'

'Oh don't worry, that noise is pretty standard,' he said, waving his arm dismissively. 'The ravens, they're always here.' He hopped up the steps onto the veranda and held open the cabin door, motioning for Callie to enter first. 'And Pollyanna,' he added. 'Pollyanna's always here too.'

6

Right from the start Callie Crossley didn't completely trust Miles Golden - or Smiler, as he preferred. His boy-face was a bit too sinister, like the face of an old ventriloquist's doll. Big blue eyes that should be appealing were anything but and his mouth, once crafted by some high-end orthodontist no doubt, was dull and discoloured. It seemed he'd been put in a box, this cabin, and forgotten about. But who was the puppet master, Callie wondered, and who was Pollyanna? He'd refused to say when she'd asked. Said she'd see for herself, soon enough.

Inside, the cabin was dull and dingy. Too much wood, not enough light. Not enough housekeeping. The place smelt damp, a festival ground for asthma and allergies. She felt threatened. Hemmed in. Like coming inside with Smiler was a huge mistake. So why had she?

Because you're Callie 'Too Much Empathy' Crossley, that's why.

But the guy needs help.

Oh he needs help alright! And let's see how much empathy he *has when he's flaying you with a chainsaw!*

The day was panning out terribly, her worst by far, and Callie expected it might get hideously worse. She'd seen low-budget horror films with similar themes: lead protagonist (usually female) makes a bad choice (sometimes based on misguided compassion, sometimes sheer stupidity), ensuring gruesome consequences for herself and often everyone else around her. Total sting in the tail tales. Different kind of role to the ones she was used to playing, of course. Comedy was Callie's forte, recently crossing the line into action-adventure. Not that she was particularly funny in real life. Callie Crossley was simply deemed too curvy by society or the media or whoever it is that decides a sixteen dress size is too big to be much more than the film's stooge.

Well it certainly looks like you stooged this!

Grit ground beneath her bare feet as she followed Smiler along the entrance hallway. The spongy carpet felt like moss in a woodland thicket. Dust-bunnies scarpered, clinging to skirting boards, and Callie wondered if it was too late to turn around and go back outside. Back to the car. To make off without...

'I won't be a sec,' Smiler said, as though he knew what she was thinking. 'Then we'll get going.'

Callie tried to force a smile, but none came. She followed him further into the den, till they were standing in a large, dingy lounge area. The walls were overbearing, clad in dark pine. They didn't look as though they'd seen a duster or polish in years. No pictures hung on them and there was nothing to identify who the owner of the cabin might be. Thick cobwebs draped the ceiling like voile; their creators having been left to build spidery palaces and citadels unhindered for goodness knew how long. Daylight shone through a massive window that overlooked the lake, cutting a blunt wedge out of the gloom and sharing it with the room's thick dust motes. The section of gauzy light hung in the air, unnatural and angular, while the rest of the room dwelt in mid-range to dark shadow. In front of this lakeside viewing area, highlighted by the swatch of dust-diluted sun, was a redheaded girl of around thirteen. She was sitting in a wheelchair, watching them with sly interest.

Something about the girl pulled at dormant memories, making Callie gasp out loud. She immediately felt uneasy. Unsettled. Threatened. There was something recognisable about the girl, but it was an ungraspable familiarity as with old dreams.

Pollyanna?

She looked like a porcelain doll, fragile and creepy, and her skin had a grey-white sheen to it; mushroomy-pallid as though it had never been touched by direct sunlight. Thin wisps of grey swirls rose from her left hand where she cinched a cigarette between her middle finger and forefinger. Smoke added an extra layer of museum age to the room, clinging to the air in light whorls but not doing much to detract from the stink of damp. Through the haze, the girl regarded Callie with what Callie could only interpret as instant dislike.

'Pollyanna,' Smiler said, 'this is Callie Crossley. Callie, this is Pollyanna.'

'Why are you here?' Pollyanna asked. Her voice was a bronchial croak, each of her breaths a wheezy labour on lungs which Callie imagined must be damp with mucous and shrivelled with decay. Her eyes were large and impossibly black, surrounded by papery skin smudged grey with bad health and bitterness. Definitely not enough love. When she brought her hand up to take a draw on the cigarette the movement was slow and stiff, making Callie wonder if she'd got her all wrong. Pollyanna looked adolescent and yet, at the same time, the way she moved seemed ancient. Thirteen going on ninety, her frame osteoporosis-fragile.

'Don't worry,' Callie said, reluctant to be drawn into whatever spat the girl was baiting for. 'I won't be here long.'

Prompted by this admission, Smiler set off running up a flight of creaky stairs to the first floor. His bare feet slapped noisily on bare wooden boards, creating gun-shot echoes in the lounge that suggested an emptiness much emptier than the room actually was. Before disappearing through an open doorway at the top, he called back, 'Gimme a few minutes.' Then slammed the door shut.

'Time remains stagnant in this place.' Pollyanna said, her voice strangely monotone. She was gazing out at the lake and Callie wasn't sure if she was talking to herself.

'Excuse me?'

The girl's eyes remained on the lake. Her hair was long and untamed and Callie thought it looked like it hadn't been trimmed or combed in forever. It shone the colour of autumn leaves, Hallowe'en-orange in brilliant morning sunshine. Only there was no brilliant sunshine in this place. Just waxy, lazy light. Curling a strand of red hair around her forefinger, winding and wrapping, again and again, Pollyanna looked circumspect. A grey – it might have been black at some point – shirt dress sat above her knees and she wore nothing on her feet. Her knee joints were swollen knots of cartilage and gristle on skinny legs and her hands were adorned with skeleton-fingers. She took another slow draw on the cigarette, then breathed smoke from her nose. 'Why are you here Callie Crossley?'

'Not by choice, I can tell you,' Callie said, unsure which was worse to inhale: the girl's second-hand smoke or the cabin's mould spores. Both of them, she imagined, were now coating her airways and clinging to her lungs. She coughed into her hand, an attempt to dislodge them.

'And you think we chose?' Pollyanna flicked ash onto the floor. She did it with such instinctive casualness that Callie was offended. She rose onto the balls of her feet, so the carpet, an unfathomably coloured organism, touched less of her. 'I dunno,' she said, finding it hard to conceal her disgust, 'you tell me.'

But Pollyanna, it seemed, was done talking for now and slow seconds passed where neither of them said anything. At least, not out loud. Everything was quiet except for the muffled noises of Smiler getting dressed upstairs. Eventually it was Callie who broke the silence by asking, 'I take it there's no telephone in here?'

An untrustworthy smirk played about the girl's lips. 'Of course not.'

'Who are you?'

'Pollyanna.'

'I figured that already.' *Smart arsed little shit.* 'But who are you? Where are you from?'

'Why would where I'm from define who I am?'

Callie took a slow, deep breath and counted to three. 'Do you live here?'

'Where else? The garden?'

Keep going. Just keep pushing me. Callie's worn patience was turning to deep agitation and her voice became strained. 'Does anyone else live here with you?'

'You already know the answer to that.'

'There's just the two of you then?'

Pollyanna nodded and cast a sideways glance at Callie, her impossibly old eyes sly and calculating.

Callie pretended not to see. She glanced around the lounge again and ran her hand along the mantelpiece. *Why am I here?* She looked at her fingertips. They were black. 'Does Smiler look after you?'

At the suggestion Pollyanna's eyes seemed to darken, if that was at all possible. 'I look after myself, thank you very much!' she said, betraying her act of grown-up cool with a churlish tone.

Callie smiled, pleased to be a source of such irritation. 'But you must only be what? Thirteen? Fourteen?'

'Your point being?'

'That you're pretty young to be fending for yourself, aren't you?'

'Well really it's none of your business.'

'How long have you been here?' Callie decided to try a different angle.

Pollyanna puffed on her cigarette. She blew smoke in Callie's direction and looked up to the right in thought.

'How long? Let's see. How long does it take to fly to Orion's belt and back?'

Callie blew out her cheeks, exasperated by this new nonsense. 'That's impossible to say.'

'Even more so if you have to unbuckle it.'

'What the hell are you talking about?'

'Just answering your question.'

Callie couldn't comprehend the girl or the situation. Wasn't sure she wanted to. Again she took a deep, aggravated breath. Counted to four. 'Alright, Little Miss Cryptic. Whatever. Now tell me who owns this place.'

Pollyanna laughed; an awful grating sound. 'Nobody owns this place, stupid. *It* owns *you*.'

'That doesn't make sense.'

'It's not supposed to.'

'What's not supposed to?' Smiler was standing at the top of the stairs now, fully clothed. He was wearing a washed-out Guns 'N' Roses t-shirt and worn blue jeans. He'd pulled his hair back into a ponytail, but looked no less dreadful.

Callie scowled. 'Why are you living in the middle of nowhere with a little girl, Golden?'

He rubbed the back of his neck and his face reddened. 'I, er, it's not what you think!'

'You think you're so bloody great don't you?' Pollyanna said, glaring at Callie with an intensity so hateful that it could only express a yearning for sudden death. 'Flouncing in here with your big hair and big tits like you own the place. Well, just so you know, you don't! You don't know a thing either. You have no idea what's going on. You're a nobody in here. Everyone's a nobody, but especially you. Understand? You're *nobody*.'

'Whoa calm down, Poll,' Smiler hurried down the stairs, his hands held out in some effort to placate her. 'Let's just go, shall we?'

'*Go?* Where do you expect to go?' Pollyanna turned on him, no less riled.

Callie sighed. 'To the nearest village to call the police would be a good fucking start.'

Again that awful, humourless laugh. 'This is what I'm talking about,' Pollyanna said. 'You don't know a thing. There is no village.' Then for no sane reason that Callie could think of, she stubbed the cigarette out on her own bare thigh, all the while staring Callie down. She didn't even flinch.

'There *is* a village,' Smiler said, his voice sounding wearied. He kept his attention on Callie and didn't react at all to Pollyanna's display of self-harm. Perhaps it was as normal an occurrence, Callie thought, as the raven-noise outside.

'So we'll go there,' she said, desperate by now to get going.

'There's nothing there though,' Smiler told her. 'Nothing but empty houses and shops. No people.'

'So we go further afield, what's the problem?' Callie was feeling increasingly impatient. 'Wherever the road takes us. It's not like we're on the fucking moon, is it? There's got to be loads more villages. Towns even. Hell, cities if we keep going.'

'Won't work,' Pollyanna said.

'What won't?'

'The car.'

Callie crossed her arms. Counted to five. 'How would you know?'

'Just do.'

'Full of optimism, aren't you?'

'Optimism's for idiots.'

Callie's hands flexed. She imagined them around Pollyanna's neck, squeezing and crushing till the last ragged breath rasped out of the girl's wizened lungs, rendering her as silent as the cabin's dust motes that swirled all about them. The thought was so sudden and vivid it shocked Callie, but she felt no guilt. Only a faint pang of regret that she wouldn't actually do it. 'I'll tell you what *I* think's idiotic, sitting about doing nothing!'

Smiler sighed. 'She's right, Poll. We have to at least try.'

'And preferably before whoever brought me here comes back for his fucking car and finds me not in it!' Callie moved to the window, pulsing her fists, and peered out at the Bentley. It was waiting on the lawn. The lake beyond seemed to imitate its blackness.

'Yeah,' Smiler agreed. 'Whoever it was must be out there somewhere.'

'Probably watching us right now.' Pollyanna turned her head and smiled, her eyes displaying sadistic glee.

Smiler didn't retort, he simply frowned at her in a way that a low-profile father might chastise his vocally errant child in public. To Callie, he said, 'Are you sure you have no idea who might have done this to you?'

Callie huffed and slapped her thighs in a display of extreme aggravation. 'Yes, I'm bloody sure.'

'It's just that note, *Dead to me.* It sounded pretty personal.'

'Of course it sounded pretty personal,' she said, running her fingers through her hair and squeezing her eyes shut. 'This whole fucking thing is personal! A complete bloody nightmare in fact.'

'And for you,' Pollyanna observed, 'it's only just begun.'

Callie counted to six. Balled her hands. Felt like punching a wall. She saw orange, not red, behind her eyelids. And when she opened her eyes again she still saw orange: Pollyanna's hair. 'I can't take anymore of your shit.' She turned and headed towards the hallway, the dirty, dry cat's tongue fibre of the carpet scraping the bottom of her feet. 'You can stay here and be nobodies together if that's what you want. But me? I'm leaving.'

When she got to the door and pulled it open Pollyanna called out to her in a voice that was unruffled; its portentousness somehow substantiated by the creeping dread given off by the cabin itself, 'No you're not. This place won't let you.'

7

'Pollyanna you have to come.' Smiler's words came out broken, thick with lingering adolescence.

'No. No, I don't.' Pollyanna remained by the large window, looking out across the lawn towards the Bentley. Smoke-polluted sunlight captured her in a retro-photo haze like she'd been there since the 60s. She looked like a skeleton vacuum-sealed in white shrink-wrap skin with hair, an exotic orange fungus sprouting from holes that had been pecked in the plastic by demented birds.

'Okay, you don't *have* to,' he said. 'But I'd like you to.'

'Liar.' Still, she turned to see his expression. To see if he meant it.

'No I'm not.' Frown lines fell into place too comfortably on Smiler's face, adding an extra twenty years, easy. 'I *do* want you to come.'

She regarded him for a while longer, unspeaking, her mean, anaemic lips pulled tight.

'*Please,*' he urged.

She huffed to convey some annoyance – at her own doubt or his persistence, he couldn't tell – and there was a deep rattling noise in her chest as she did so, like a cat purring miserably. 'What's the point?' she said, turning back to face the Bentley; the black atrocity that had delivered Callie Crossley straight to their door.

'*Smiler!*' And there was her voice, calling from somewhere outside. '*Are you coming or what?*'

'Yeah!' Smiler raised his eyebrows at Pollyanna in sheepish apology.

Silence then followed; an unbearable indicator of two

resolute decisions having been made and coming between the two teenagers, perhaps marking the end of their forced friendship. A friendship they'd both come to depend on, because misery enjoys company and, aside from a few items of worn clothing, Smiler and Pollyanna had had nothing but each other for quite some time.

Reluctant to look at him now, it was Pollyanna who spoke first. 'Better be quick, mustn't keep the fat cow waiting.'

'Hey, that's not nice.'

'I'm not nice.'

'Yes you are.'

'Liar.'

'Look, if you won't come with me now I'll send someone back to fetch you.' Smiler's right leg was shaking with nervous adrenalin and he was twisting the hem of his t-shirt into a ball in his fist, making it even more creased. 'We'll get out of this, I promise. We will. Haven't I always said that?'

Pollyanna's own fists were in her lap, tightly closed like oyster shells. Tightly closed like her mouth. Words were her pearls now and she decided he could no longer have them.

'Poll? Please. Come on.' He made eyes at her, which in the past might have won her over. 'It's not too late to change your mind.' But she didn't look. Wouldn't. Couldn't be swayed. He slammed his palm down on the bannister and swore, then ran outside in case Callie Crossley left without him.

As it was, Callie was standing in the middle of the lawn, arms folded over her chest, accentuating a cosy cleavage. She was glamorous but bedraggled in a morning-after kind of way and she stood out against a backdrop of stippled grey sky and a dark lake that had been spilled onto harsh greenery. Harsh because it was an unknown wilderness that stood between her and home. Overgrown plants bordered the lawn, their barbed stems, for the most part, prickly and unkind. The only flowers that bloomed belonged to weeds. This was a hopeless place.

'What's her problem?' Callie asked.

'Leave her be.' Smiler shook his head. 'She's been here a long time. It can't have been easy.'

'I didn't say it had.' Callie turned and started towards the Bentley, across the lawn that was strewn with clover patches and unblown dandelion heads. 'I'm in no mood to take shit from teenagers though.' She scowled back at him, her long blonde hair catching in her mouth as she did. 'So you've been warned.'

'Hey, I'm nineteen!'

'Exactly.'

'Whoa, condescending much?' Smiler jumped off the veranda and hurried to catch her up, his loose shoelaces flapping about. 'I'm an adult.'

'Just about.' Callie opened the driver's door of the Bentley and breathed in deeply. The smell of leather upholstery was glorious compared to the cabin's insides, but something didn't feel right. The key in the ignition should have made her sag with relief; instead it felt too easy. Too considered. As though her kidnapper had laid a meticulous trap and she was playing right into his or her hands. But what else could she do? What choice did she have?

None.

'Get in, boy,' she said to Smiler over the car's shiny roof. 'Let's go for a drive.'

Without needing to be told twice, Smiler jumped into the passenger seat and rubbed his hands together. He turned and smiled at her. Subtle dimples in his cheeks turned into crevices, reminding her, oddly, of spoon gouges in freezer-burnt ice-cream. 'I can't believe this is really happening,' he said.

Callie settled into the driver seat, running her hands over the steering wheel, and played out, in her head, the conversation she'd have with the first policeman they came by. She'd list off times, whereabouts and the names of people she'd last seen, and the dark-haired, bearded constable with the kind, brown eyes would be impressed by her calm manner and perhaps even in awe, but quietly so, that she was Callie Crossley. He would probably ask for her autograph and a selfie, if he was playful enough. Maybe he'd even offer to buy her an after-work drink at his local, to help ease the shock of her ordeal. That would be nice. Really nice. But all the deep concern she imagined etched onto his ruggedly handsome face faded to nothing when she stepped on the Bentley's brake pedal and turned the ignition key.

Nothing happened.

She tried again. Not even the faintest of chugs. She checked to make sure the automatic transmission was in neutral. Three times. It definitely was. Still nothing. Slamming her hands against the steering wheel, she screamed through gritted teeth and felt her eyes brimming hot.

No! No! No!

Smiler was watching her with dread. His complexion had taken on a new level of sickliness and the deep spoon-crescents in his cheeks were gone. 'What is it?' he asked, even though he could surely see what the predicament was.

Callie reached down to the foot well and popped the bonnet, too upset to answer, too angry to address sheer idiocy. Her hands were shaking and she wasn't sure what to do next: open the bonnet, look inside, then what?

'Do you know what you're doing?' Smiler echoed her thoughts, adding pressure she didn't need. His voice sounded reedy with desperation. It annoyed her immediately.

She got out of the car and stomped round to the front. 'Does it look like I know what I'm doing?'

'Er…?' He wasn't sure. So he went to stand with her.

It soon became apparent that it wouldn't have mattered if Callie was the most highly skilled mechanic in the world, because when she opened the bonnet there was nothing where an engine should be. Nothing but a gaping hole of fresh air. An engine bay framing lawn. Both of them stood gawping for an indeterminable amount of time before Callie broke the spell of shocked silence with, 'Un-fucking-believable.'

Smiler was hunched over the bonnet, standing so close to Callie that the hairs on his arm tickled the skin on hers. 'Where's it all gone?'

Callie straightened. She squared her shoulders and gave him a hard stare. 'Maybe *you'd* like to tell *me*.'

'What?' He took a cautious step back and started picking at a scab in the corner of his mouth. 'How should I know?'

'Because you two creepy little shits are in on this together.' Callie pointed to the cabin's lounge window where they could see Pollyanna watching. 'Wednesday Addams is fucking loving this.'

'No.' Smiler shook his head. 'We had nothing to do with it. I swear.'

'Then how come she knew the car wouldn't start?'

'She didn't. She's just pessimistic about everything.' Smiler had become flighty. Unpredictable. His nerves like stacked matchsticks that might tumble and fall or ignite and go up in flames.

Pity and mistrust warred within Callie, neither instinct dominating the other. She wasn't sure how to read him, he was so convincing. She looked up to where the sun was hiding beneath an old, bobbly blanket of grey cloud in an attempt to cleanse her eyes of his face, otherwise she thought she might punch it. But looking up made her feel trapped. Beneath this particular stretch of sky, for all she knew, she could be anywhere in the country. Anywhere in the world. Her head spun like she might have drunk ten bottles of champagne at Antonio Drake's party. The sky throbbed, or maybe it was her eyes, and she was aware of the lake's blackness even though she wasn't looking at it. It was silent, but horribly there. And the cabin, she could feel it glaring at her, victorious. She reached out to touch the Bentley's raised bonnet, to steady herself, then looked at Smiler's face again. Everything slowed down. Too abruptly. She felt sick. She filled her lungs with clean air. 'If you're lying,' she said with strong conviction, 'I swear to God I'll kill you.'

Smiler held his hands up in full acceptance and together they went back to the cabin.

Pollyanna was waiting in the hallway for them, like an old doll that had been left too long at the back of a dark, mildewed cupboard, unfed with love. One that talked when you really didn't want it to. When it wasn't supposed to. One that moved when your back was turned. When the lights went out. Always creeping. 'Told you it wouldn't work.'

'Don't fucking start,' Callie said, aware at once of the cabin's damp smell; the insidious, festering stink that would make her lungs rattle and throat itch if she stayed for much longer. She could feel an unhappy kitten unfurling in her chest already.

'You swear too much,' Pollyanna told her. Her black eyes glistened like roaches' backs in the shadows of the boxy passageway and her stick-thin arms stuck out at right angles from the wheels of her chair.

'And you're a little shit, what of it?'

Pollyanna sneered, her tiny teeth like popcorn kernels.

'Will you two stop bickering?' Smiler said, the plea mostly directed at Callie. 'It's just, like, can't you both *try* to get on?'

'We *could*, but what'd be the point?' Callie squeezed past Pollyanna and made her way to the lounge. 'It's not like I'm staying in this shit tip.'

'Oh? Where are you off to?'

'There's got to be somewhere else I can get to by foot.'

Pollyanna did a three point turn and wheeled after her. 'With no shoes?' She was enjoying this way too much.

She also had a point. Beyond driving off in the Bentley, Callie hadn't considered how else she might escape. She scrunched her recently pedicured toes into the horrible carpet and cursed the fact she had no sensible shoes. 'If that's the way it has to be,' she said, 'yes.'

'Look, I've had plenty of time to find somewhere else,' Smiler said, fiddling with the scab on his mouth again and making it bleed. 'And there isn't anywhere. Certainly not that you can reach by foot.'

'There's *got* to be,' Callie insisted, crossing her fleshy arms over her chest and making the crease of her cleavage stretch right up to the base of her throat.

'But there *isn't*. There's no escape.' His expression conveyed scared desperation, which made Callie think he was telling the truth. At least, what he believed to be the truth.

She sighed. Counted to three. Felt like weeping. '*Please* tell me this is a joke,' she said. Her demeanour was suddenly weary, her limbs felt weak. All of the rage in her had depleted and she surrendered to the despair that was pressing down on her, trying to grind her spirits into the terrible depths of the carpet beneath her feet, alongside goodness knew how many years' worth of cigarette ash and dead skin. 'Candid Camera, maybe? Or some brand new show I've not heard of? Did someone set me up? Did they? Tell me. Was it my agent, Sam? Or

Franky? Bizzle? Freya? Emma? Or...*Landon?* Was it him?'

'Hey, I wish it was a joke,' Smiler said, wiping blood from the weeping sore on his mouth with his thumb. 'At least then there'd be a way out for all of us.'

A loud thudding noise from somewhere above in the uppermost realms of the cabin reverberated through wooden panels and floorboards, making all three of them look up to the ceiling and freeze. Callie could almost feel the weight of the building bearing down on her. She felt breathless and woozy and insurmountably scared.

'See,' Pollyanna said, with not even the tiniest amount of smugness. 'I told you this place wouldn't let you go.'

8

'You can't just go nosing about!' Pollyanna moved with great finesse. She skirted round the couch at surprising speed and stopped at the foot of the stairs, glaring up. Her eyes were like cold pieces of basalt.

Smiler was already trailing after Callie. He turned and frowned at Pollyanna. 'Let her look, Poll. Let her see what she wants to see. Let her see there's no one else here.'

'But she has no business…'

'Just leave it, Poll. What does it matter?' He lifted his arms then let them fall to his sides. 'We have nothing to hide.'

Pollyanna didn't argue, but she stewed at the bottom of the stairs; her arms folded and her entire countenance in a funk.

Callie glanced down. She thought about saying something, but decided against it. Antagonising the girl wasn't in the least bit constructive. Her primary goal was to validate Smiler's claim that only he and Pollyanna resided in the cabin, beyond that she wasn't yet sure. Bickering with a teenager didn't score highly on her list of priorities though, so she pushed open a door on the landing and stepped into one of two first floor rooms.

A warm staleness of too much Smiler and not enough ventilation greeted her, as well as the sight of a large unmade bed. The bed had a grubby velvet throw crumpled around its base and an example of taxidermy-grotesque mounted onto the wall above it. Callie supposed the stag's head had been an intentional display of stagnant death by whoever had put it there originally, but now, however many years later, it had degraded from freshly-killed grandeur to decrepit monstrosity. Its fur was thick with dust and age, its eyes comatose-black. She hated it immediately.

Smiler touched her elbow, making her start. 'This one's mine,' he said, indicating the room with a tip of his head. 'Yours will be the next one along. If you decide to stay, that is. But, to be honest, I don't see any other option. Sorry.'

Callie made a belligerent face. She had no desire to claim a room in the cabin as her own. She'd sleep outside in the tree with the ravens before it came to that. 'What's in there?' she asked, pointing to a closed door next to the unmade bed.

Smiler frowned. Again. 'I dunno. I've never been able to get inside to see. It won't open.'

Looking upwards, Callie attempted to work out the layout of the cabin from where they were standing, trying to remember its shape and how it had looked from outside. 'The tower's right above this room, isn't it?' she said at last, shivering as she recalled how its windows had watched her with private black humour as she'd stood with the words DEAD TO ME in her hands, pulled fresh from her mouth, while nothing in the world made sense anymore.

'Er, yeah.'

'In that case, I'm guessing that's not just a storage cupboard,' she said, pointing to the locked door.

'No, I don't think so.'

She gave him a curious look. 'Is there another way to get up there?'

Smiler shook his head.

'So, wait.' She paused, needing to clarify the situation in her head. 'You're telling me there's only *one* door to the tower and you can't open it?'

Lowering his gaze to the floor, he shrugged. 'Er, yeah.'

Incredulous at the thought of having unexplored space above them, Callie laughed. It should have been a nervous sound, if anything, but came out forced and perverse; wholly inappropriate given the situation, yet uncomfortably comfortable in its surroundings. The out-of-control shrillness and suddenness of her own maniacal outburst terrified Callie. Almost as much as the dark possibilities that lurked overhead. Smiler regarded her warily. She covered her mouth with her hand and stopped laughing, feeling awkward and horrified and altogether too edgy. 'Shit, there could be *anything* up there!' she said, wide-eyed. 'Why the fuck haven't you tried forcing it open?'

'Don't think I haven't.'

'Not hard enough, obviously.'

'Obviously.'

'Maybe *I'll* try.'

Smiler's lifeless eyes became sardonic for the briefest of moments. His old self shining through? He stood back and gestured to the door with an open hand. 'Be my guest. Let's see you in action.'

Callie's mouth tightened at the challenge. She hadn't meant right this minute. Still, she tried barging the door with her shoulder a few times and rattled its handle up and down. The handle's mechanism was stiff, but she felt metal grinding against metal, and the wooden door trembled against its wooden jambs. Like Smiler had said though, it was locked. No amount of pulling and shoving would open it. She'd need tools for the job. A hairpin. A chisel. A sledgehammer.

Smiler's eyebrows were raised when she looked at him, like he expected her to do something else. So she bent and looked through the long keyless keyhole, even though she expected there would be nothing to see. There was only blackness. But it was a blackness that seemed to have enough substance to poke her in the eye if it wanted to. A blackness, she thought, that might seep out and touch her. Her scalp tightened and she shivered when some dreadful intuition told her that by looking into this blackness she had alerted something unseen of her presence.

She straightened up and backed away. 'Okay, let's see this other room you were talking about, Golden.'

Inside the next room she hoped to find a film crew camped out. A whole group of faces that would look up from amidst cameras and monitors and other electrical equipment and shout, 'Surprise!' At which point Miles Golden would reveal he'd been wearing theatrical makeup all along and that Pollyanna was his kid sister or something. Instead, when she opened the door, she found an empty room that was filled with too much red and white. Satin bedsheets were a large haemorrhage against stark white walls, and a canvas above the bed, the only decoration in the room, was an abstract splatter of red. An arguable piece of art that looked to have been created with all the speed and frenzy of a severed jugular. Three piles of folded clothes, menswear by the looks of it, were stacked on the floor along the window wall. 'Whose are those?' was the first thing Callie thought to ask.

'I'm not sure.' Smiler stayed on the landing, poking his head inside the room without stepping over its threshold. 'I always presumed they must belong to whoever owns this place.'

That idea chilled Callie. Because if that was the case, then where was he? Might he be behind the door to the tower? A dark entity existing in blackness, in whatever state of life or death? Maybe he was the mastermind behind this situation, spying on them and plotting his next move. Or a third-party removed from the equation, murdered, his body hidden by someone else so that his property could be used for ill intent. Or maybe, ignorantly or not, he was someone who simply let the place out to kidnappers and sociopaths who bore no clearly defined grudges against the people they took. Whatever his circumstances, the absence of the owner of the abandoned clothes bothered Callie. A lot.

She stepped over to the window and looked out. Trees crowded the rear of the cabin, forming a blockade, and went on as far as she could see in a tangle of dark green, orange and brown post-summer foliage. She was trapped; hemmed in by woods on one side and water on the other. The wind threw a handful of dead leaves at her face, but the window caught them. Still, she jumped. She thought she saw movement in the darkness between two thick trunks below, but on closer inspection saw nothing unusual. Just branches waving.

'Whispering Woods,' Smiler said.

'Lovely, I'm sure.' Already Callie wasn't interested. She hated woods. Hated outdoorsy stuff. Hated walking. Hated this place. She turned from the window and picked up a pair of jeans from the nearest pile of clothes and held them up. Levis. Thirty-four inch waist. Probably about right for Smiler these days, but the leg length was too long. Next she picked up a checked shirt. Barbour. Large. Didn't mean anything.

'They were in my room originally,' Smiler explained. 'I put them in here because it felt sort of weird having someone else's stuff around me. Took a while to get to that stage though. At first I slept on the couch, you know, till I knew for certain there was just me and Poll. I mean, Poll always said that was the case, but, like you, I doubted it. I didn't believe her. I mean, there was no reason for me to *be* here. I'd never been here in my life and I didn't know Pollyanna from Adam. After a week or two went by and there was nobody else, that's when I decided I had to get used to living here as comfortably as I could. What else could I do? So I cleared the other room out and tried to make it my own.'

'Why didn't you just use this room?'

'I dunno.' He picked at his chin, making the skin between sparse whisker growth turn red. 'It just never felt right.'

Strangely, Callie could understand. Something about the room didn't feel right and given the choice she reckoned she'd have taken the one with the stag's head too. Even if it meant being closer to the oppressive, breathing blackness that was behind the tower door. She'd have wedged something up against the door's handle and plugged its empty keyhole with damp tissue paper. But whatever dwelled in that blackness no longer seemed as threatening as the red and white room she was standing in now. Something bad had happened in here. Something terrible. She could sense it like sometimes she could sense oncoming rain. Ghost-white walls reflected a malevolent unrest, preventing it from soaking into the cabin so it might settle and lay still. Instead, this bad energy from distant or recent past kept a frenzied momentum between walls and ceiling, all the while being sucked in and blown out by sleazy bedsheets.

'Looks like rain's on the way,' Callie said, wondering whether if she touched the bed the satin would absorb her fingers and pull the rest of her in.

'Yeah,' Smiler said. He was biting the inside of his mouth, his attention outside again. 'I'd hold off exploring Whispering Woods if I was you.'

Callie went back to the window and considered the intent of the clouds. 'I think I'd rather get wet than stay here any longer than I need to.'

'But when it rains it *really* rains. I'm not even kidding. You'll end up in trouble if you go out there.'

'Compared to the trouble I'm caught up in here? I think I'd rather risk the rain.' The whole sky was moving fast; a turbulent inflow of storm-grey. Callie turned round and cast the Barbour shirt onto the bed.

'You aren't in danger here,' Smiler said. 'But you will be if you go out there.'

'Not in danger? Are you kidding me?'

Wind showered grit against the window and the first spots of rain began to fall.

'Look, whoever the Bentley-driving note-scribbling head case is, he's not in the cabin, is he?' Smiler said with a certain amount of hand-talk going on. 'You're safe here with me and Poll.'

'I don't believe you,' Callie said.

'I wish you would.'

'Well I don't.' Callie looked down at her feet. 'Are there any spare shoes in here?'

Smiler groaned. 'You aren't *really* thinking about going out there are you?'

'Yes.'

'What if *he's* out there though? And besides, it'll be dark before you know it. You can't be out there in the dark.'

Callie got down on her knees and looked beneath the bed. He was right, of course. How far would she get in the woods once night fell?

'There aren't any shoes if that's what you're looking for,' Smiler said.

Unable to determine if he was telling the truth or not, Callie supposed it didn't matter. Not at that moment. The first pangs of thunder grumbled in the distance, marking the incoming storm as a sulk above the mountains beyond the lake. Its arrival could be imminent. She would go nowhere just yet.

Back downstairs they found Pollyanna in the kitchen placing foil parcels onto a baking tray. 'I hope you like baked potatoes,' she said, not looking up from the task in hand.

Confused by the display of calm domesticity in the

wake of the tantrum Pollyanna had thrown not yet half an hour since, Callie hesitated for a moment before answering, 'Er, yeah.'

Pollyanna looked up and smiled. *Smiled!* Beneath the kitchen's fluorescent strip lighting she appeared to be a different girl. Not entirely approachable, because there was still an underlying wildness about her, but certainly a lot less hostile. The light had removed shadows from her face and given her skin a marginally healthier tone. Her eyes were less black, more darkest brown. More human. And Callie could see now that she might have been pretty before the cabin had taken her for itself.

'Lucky,' Pollyanna said, still smiling, 'because there's not much else except roasted, boiled, fried or mashed. There's always raw of course, but no one eats raw potatoes. They're slimy. And cold. Like tongues. And slugs. Do you like slugs, Callie Crossley?' An element of trickery crept to her eyes.

Callie's guard was raised again. 'Not particularly.'

'Me neither.'

'We also have tuna,' Smiler said, rounding the kitchen table and stooping to pull the oven door open so Pollyanna could slide the baking tray inside.

'Not today we don't,' Pollyanna said. 'I threw it away.'

'Why?'

'Because I'm sick to death of it. It makes the whole place stink. And it makes my hands stink. It totally stinks. And I hate it.'

'But you kept the chocolate, right?' Suddenly Smiler looked worried. He began picking at the scab at the side of his mouth.

She laughed, her eyes teasing. 'Yes, I kept your stupid chocolate. Though I nearly never. It's not good for you, too much.'

Thunder complained. Louder this time. It had rolled a

tiny bit closer.

'Smiler, you know how you said you've been here a long time?' Callie said.

'Yeah.'

'And that there's nothing in the nearby village. Like no other people or shops or anything.'

'Yeah.'

'Then where the fuck do you get potatoes, tuna and chocolate from?' She put her hands on her hips, feeling massively duped.

Smiler continued to pick at his mouth. She wished he wouldn't.

'That's the thing, you see,' he said. 'This is gonna sound crazy.'

Callie bent over, resting her elbows on the kitchen table. She cradled her head in her hands and closed her eyes. 'Even crazier than the rest of it?'

'Maybe. I dunno. Probably. Yeah.'

'Go on, hit me with it.'

'Well, every day the cupboards get restocked with the same stuff.'

'By who?'

'I dunno, that's the thing. The food's just...*there*.' He looked to Pollyanna for support but she said nothing, so he turned back to Callie. 'It's true, stop looking at me like that.'

'Seriously, how can you not notice someone filling the bloody cupboards?' Callie opened the nearest one and peered inside. It was empty.

'I dunno. It just appears. Every morning there's, like, a new stash of potatoes, tuna, chocolate, coffee and cigarettes.' Nervous energy made his fingers busy. He fiddled with his bottom lip.

'Isn't that a bit random?'

'Well yes, very,' he agreed. 'And pretty damn tedious. But that's the way it is.' As if to further validate what he'd said, he then thought to add, 'I mean, I never used to smoke before I came here.'

Callie shook her head. *Unreal.* 'Haven't you tried to catch out whoever it is who leaves the stuff?'

'Of course. Me and Poll stay up loads, waiting in the kitchen and guarding the cupboards all night. But even when we sit awake for a full twelve hours, sometimes longer, we always find the same things in the cupboards. It's always baffled us.'

Callie covered her face with her hands. 'Right now I actually don't know whether I want to laugh or cry.'

'If you have the luxury of choice,' Smiler said, shrugging, 'definitely laugh.'

9

Throughout dinner Pollyanna remained quiet, inwardly thoughtful, while Callie and Smiler made small talk (mainly about the weather and when it might be safe to venture out). Her lack of conversational input bothered Callie. She wanted the girl to open up and say something, to give further insight as to who she was and what link she had with the cabin, if any. But she just sat there, fiddling with her fork, mashing crumbly white potato around her plate. After a while, unable to bear the girl's silence or her fork's *tick-tick-tick* any longer, Callie laid her own knife and fork down on the worn table top and fixed her with a firm stare. 'When did you first come here, Pollyanna?'

Smiler stopped chewing and froze, as though she'd asked something particularly daring and outrageous. Lightning flashed through the kitchen window at the same time. It was nothing more than a pink subtlety in the artificial brightness, but the fluorescent strip lighting hummed and flickered above, making all three of them look up. The sound of thunder charged closer.

'Feels like years,' Pollyanna said, returning her attention to her plate. Pressing her fork down onto the leftovers again, she made lined patterns. 'But it can't be.' She arranged the flattened potato so it looked like a flower head on the glazed blue ceramic. Or the sun shooting rays. 'Unless I'm dead.' She met Callie's gaze then and held it. 'I do consider *that* a lot.'

Callie's thoughts floundered for a moment. It wasn't the answer she'd expected. She cupped her hand and forced a small cough into it. She wanted to make some kind of remark but couldn't think of anything to say that wouldn't sound patronising. So she didn't say anything. None of them did.

The weather was then overly loud above their shared silence, the wooden husk of the cabin amplifying each sound of the wind and rain, which by now was driving down an eerie fury. Callie didn't think she'd seen so much rain in a single downpour. It was relentless. She could no longer see Whispering Woods from the window; it was nothing but a dark smear on the glass. The clouds were overripe and they raged with thunder, which was never directly overhead but always within the periphery of the lakeside shelter. Each sky-explosion had enough bass to rattle drinking glasses in the cupboard above the sink. They vibrated like a charm of hummingbirds singing of the dangers of nature. Callie wondered whether if the thunder got any closer, the glasses would smash into pieces. Subsequently she found herself hoping so, because they belonged to the cabin and she hated everything associated with it. Its damp smell had already become less noticeable, she realised. Subconsciously accepted, perhaps. This disturbed her, immensely. She promised herself she *would* get out, shoes or no shoes. If not today then definitely tomorrow. Before it was too late. Before the cabin captured her and made her another of its permanent residents. Another trophy. She couldn't bear the thought. Hated the idea of some unseen sadist restocking the kitchen cupboards with the same lousy food, day in, day out, while scrutinising her from some secret place. Watching her fall to pieces; physically as well as emotionally. Playing this game. Whatever game it was.

One I refuse to play!

And all the while the red and white room above them weighed down heavily, bleeding into Callie's thoughts. A festering malignancy that gnawed at her subconscious like the itch of a lump that shouldn't be there.

They cleared the table and nobody spoke. Callie washed the plates and cutlery, Pollyanna dried them with a damp tea towel and Smiler put them away into cupboards and drawers. By the time they were done the sun had given up the ghost and the rain was still coming. Callie accepted, regretfully, that she would have to stay overnight. Her subsequent announcement came as no surprise to Smiler or Pollyanna. Smiler suggested he air the red and white room, but she declined the offer and said the couch would do fine. To which he nodded his understanding and accepted her decision without further comment.

Pollyanna, who radiated a substantial anaemic glow, went to bed just after eight. Smiler said she often did. She slept along the corridor, next door to the bathroom, in a room Callie hadn't yet seen. Which, if she was honest, she wasn't sure she wanted to.

When there was just herself and Smiler, Callie felt less uptight. By no means relaxed, but not as on edge. She took a knife from the kitchen, unsure if she felt safer or not because of it, checked the security bolts on the front door in the hallway, then went through to the lounge to settle down for the rest of the evening. Smiler followed and set to work lighting the log burner.

For the next two hours they occupied either end of the couch in front of the fire, their legs glowing and itchy with orange heat, and held stilted conversations about television and fame, which seemed trivial and ridiculous given all that was happening. It was an undiscussed mutual decision to avoid talking about their captivity and the general awfulness of their plight, however, because until the storm cleared there was nothing they could do. They both recognised and respected this fact.

Callie held onto the knife and Smiler sat with the poker in his hand and a family-sized bar of Dairy Milk in his lap. Every so often he would offer her a square, but she never accepted. Their light-hearted banter was intermixed with regular bouts of awkward silence, and during these silences they listened to the thunder and the rain and waited for something to happen. Something unpleasant. Because it was a day for unpleasant things to happen.

When nothing unpleasant or otherwise had happened by ten-forty and the fire had almost burned out, Smiler declared it his bedtime. He stood up and stretched, his t-shirt lifting to reveal his soft stomach. 'Are you sure you'll be okay down here?' He looked anxious. Perhaps worried in case Callie disappeared, deliberately or not, while he slept.

'I'm sure I will be,' she said, managing a smile; a weary effort that in some way showed she shared part of his anxiety.

'Well, shout if you need me.'

'Thanks.' *I think.* She was unable to imagine a scenario that would prompt her to call his name.

At the foot of the stairs he stopped and fingered the light switch. 'Want me to turn the light off or are you staying up a while longer?'

Callie's heart quickened and she resented him for asking. For highlighting a new problem. The idea of being doused in darkness wasn't at all a happy one, but she knew if Smiler didn't turn the light off now she'd only have to do it herself later. Then she'd have to find her way back to the couch in the dark. With bare feet. And that thought made her feel entirely too uncomfortable. She gripped the knife's handle tighter and pulled a scratchy wool throw from the back of the couch over herself, especially her feet, and nodded.

'Night then.'

Once alone in the moonless black, Callie stretched out on her side and used a saggy cushion as a pillow. She wished she had a bottle of wine. Or vodka. Or anything over twelve percent proof that might help her through the night. Because she had a feeling it would be long and arduous, sleepless and terrible. Shadows leapt up the walls with every irregular flash of lightning, for which thunder didn't always follow, and rain laced the windows. She closed her eyes but couldn't slow her thoughts, so she looked to the lake which she knew was out there somewhere.

Elsewhere in the house she could hear water dripping; a sound that might have been there all along but was detected only now that the darkness had augmented her other senses in the wake of partial blindness. She imagined a bathroom tap not tightened properly, letting water loose to drum against white enamel. Or the toilet cistern dripping. Or a weak joint in a kitchen pipe. Or rain water seeping between wooden joints in the saturated cabin and *drip-dripping* into the hallway. It could be any or all of those things, but it was also highly likely, she thought, that the lake was swallowing them.

Soon the dripping ran red. In Callie's mind, blood trickled down the walls of the red and white room. Oozing. Seeping. Bleeding. She managed to fall asleep to its rhythmic, unhurried endlessness and immediately her dreams were dark and uncertain, transporting her outside into the woods, where she was surrounded by trees that spat leaves and harried her with balding limbs. There was no rain in this place, but the wind ripped through the latticed branches of a million trees till it howled loud enough to rouse the dead. Its wolf breath bit her skin and thrashed her hair. She was standing still, but panted as though she'd been running. With each chest heave, her breath came out like ghostly entrails; white vapour that was whipped upwards and dispersed to the wind. Two large black birds watched her from above. Perched on a bare branch, their backs hunched against the wind, they babbled in bird-speak, repeating a sequence of caws that sounded something like *Hookin'* and *Moonin'*. Over and over.

When Callie tried to move she couldn't. She looked down and saw that her feet were ankle deep in mud and dead leaves. Struggling to free herself, becoming hysterical with panic, she found that the ground, the very foundation of the woods, wouldn't ease its grip. Wouldn't let her go. She pivoted her body and saw the cabin some way off, obscured by a dark jumble of branches and trunks. But closer, much, much closer, was an emaciated figure lying face down on the ground, swathed in a long, old fashioned white nightgown. Callie groaned and tried kicking her feet free, but the earth held firm and made her watch as the figure sat up with movements that were unnatural and jerky. Like a parody of death reanimated.

'Pollyanna!'

The girl was covered in soil, and earwigs nested in her dulled red hair. Her black eyes were vacant but she grinned some awful vindictive grin. 'Listen to the trees, Callie Crossley,' she said. 'Hear them in your head and you'll have the answers. You'll know why you're here. You'll know why I'm here.'

The trees bore down on Callie as though they'd been prompted, their angry faces defined by black whorls in bark. But their mouths were quiet. None of them spoke. Callie cowered on her knees and whimpered. She clawed at the earth around her ankles and felt it collect beneath her nails. The trees poked her with spiky branches, breaking her skin till she bled, and the ground became tighter, threatening to break delicate foot bones.

'But I can't hear them,' Callie said, wiping tears from her cheeks with dirty fingers. Her whimpering voice was drowned out by the surrounding noises of branches and leaves rustling. 'The trees, they aren't saying anything,

Pollyanna!' she screamed. 'How will I know if I can't hear them?'

Pollyanna laughed at this and crumpled to the floor, as though her bones had turned to mush. She lay in the same face-down position in which Callie had first seen her, like a waif sacrificed to the woods by some immoral someone or something.

Callie let out a long frustrated cry. When she was done her throat hurt and her ears rang. She felt the earth loosen and crumble around her ankles. Pressure eased from her feet and there were crawling sensations across her skin where roots slackened and unanchored her. 'You will,' she heard Pollyanna say.

She looked to the girl who was clearly dead and realised she couldn't have spoken. Maybe it was the trees all along, Callie supposed. Maybe they *had* spoken to her.

Then there was another voice, hushed and urgent. A woman. 'Can you see her? Is she there? Are you sure?'

Callie awoke with a start, certain this voice had been real; right here with her now, beyond the safety net of dreams. The words continued to resonate in her head. She sat up, heart crashing, and asked, 'Who's there?'

The question was met by silence.

Lightning flashed and there came a giant clash of thunder. Callie jumped. The storm was directly overhead. Scary, loud. There was a new coldness to the air which permeated the thick, stiff blanket around her, making it even more unpleasant against her skin. She shivered and pulled it tighter about her shoulders.

'Is someone there?' she asked the room.

Again no answer.

She felt for the knife, needing it close, and found it by nicking her fingertips on its blade; it had slipped down the crevice between the couch's arm and cushion while she'd slept. Cautiously, steadily, she rose to her feet, wincing at every creak her bones and the couch made. Some ten feet away the stair spindles rose up to the ceiling like an empty ribcage. Callie scrabbled over to its base and smacked the light switch on the wall with her hand.

Nothing happened.

Shit!

The storm must have knocked the power out, hardly an omen of menace. She stood unmoving, trying to decide if she believed that. Yes. She did. But this logic made her no less scared because what about the voice she'd heard?

A bolt of pink lightning split the sky and zipped down over the lake, illuminating for the briefest of moments not only the landscape outside but the lounge as well. Callie saw no one else in the room with her. Thunder shook the cabin and it sounded like all of the trees in Whispering Woods were sparring.

Creeping to the window, gripping the knife close to her chest, she saw that rain was still lashing the outside world. It was heavier than any rain had a right to be. And the engineless Bentley was, of course, still on the lawn. A black mechanical carcass that served no purpose other than to mock her. *LOS 3R!*

She touched the glass and somewhere behind her a floorboard creaked.

Someone was there in the lounge.

She spun round and saw nothing but darkness and shadows interspersed.

'Smiler?' she whispered, hating that her voice made her sound so weak and afraid. 'Pollyanna?'

There was no reply. But in the shadows something breathed. There *was* someone there. She could sense it.

Can you see her?

She could still hear that voice in her head.

Is she there?

The hairs rose on all the exposed parts of her skin and she found she could no longer move.

Are you sure?'

So she stood listening. And waiting. Knowing that each torturous second was aeons away from dawn. Then something brushed against her arm. Warm. Human. Skin. She fell backwards, her lungs gasping for air. Her elbow smacked against the huge window. *Ow!* She pressed her back against its cold pane and held the knife out in front, ready to strike. But there was no one there. She'd felt someone touch her, yet no one was there.

She sobbed soundlessly and leaned heavily against the window, her legs threatening to give way. Another rupture of lightning lit up the sky and garden. She whipped her head round with a groan; her brain had registered something out on the lawn that hadn't been there before. As blackness reclaimed the garden she screamed.

Instantly there was movement upstairs, then the door to Smiler's bedroom was flung open. Emerging onto the landing, his silhouette was even blacker than the night. 'What is it?'

'Quick!' Callie told him, her back still pinned against the window.

'Why? What's going on?' Smiler was already rushing down the stairs. Once he reached the bottom he ran, surefooted, and leapt over the couch to reach her.

'Look!' She was pointing to the garden, her hands shaking.

'What? What is it?' he said, standing next to her now. 'It's too dark, I can't see.'

'There's a body. Out there. On the lawn.'

10

Wind screamed in Callie's face as she pushed outside. It snatched the door from her hands, slamming the brass handle against the cabin's outer wall and creating a gunshot *crack* above the noise of the storm. The door then ricocheted back. Callie dodged out of its way but it caught Smiler on the shoulder and knocked him backwards into the hallway. He dropped the iron poker, which at some point had found its way back into his possession, on the parquet floor. It hardly made a sound above the wind that wailed past him to sift and search through the cabin's empty spaces. Quick to retrieve his make-do weapon, Smiler hurried back outside and grappled the door shut behind him. He stood for a moment, his back against the door, and clutched his shoulder. Callie lifted the woollen throw from around her shoulders and held it above her head to shield herself from the weather. She squinted her eyes against the insistent shards of rain that found their way beneath the throw and mouthed to Smiler *Are you okay?* In reply to which he sucked rain from his bottom lip and nodded.

They bowed their heads against the driving wind and dashed across the veranda together, the wooden boards slippery underfoot. Callie's face stung and the woollen throw whipped about above her like a phantom scarecrow. She kept two of its corners bunched in her fists, not altogether sure why she continued to hold on because soon, she knew, it would be a sodden, cold mass weighted down and clinging to her back. Her feet pounded on the veranda steps, each board shuddering beneath her weight and urgency, then she rushed onto the waterlogged lawn where mud squelched between her toes. It was a cold unpleasantness that she imagined might include fleshy earthworms flooded from their burrows below. She kept on moving though, her feet slapping and churning more mud. More worms.

Looking ahead, the lake beyond the garden was a profound dark stretch under a heavyweight sky concealing a complacent moon. Not a single streetlight, headlight or house light could be seen nearby or in the far-off distance, which emphasised the cabin's absolute remoteness and made Callie imagine a whole pressing void of blackness above them. A black dreadnought universe that bore meagre snatches of light, none of which shone here, right now, in this place. She felt unusually small in her surroundings, as well as unimportant. Mislaid. The only source of light was the undying pink of the lightning that strobed the clouds. The entire sky looked like a contracting womb, gripped with electric spasms and heavily pregnant with rain. Each lightning flash showed the lawn, ghastly grey, and the Bentley, a gleaming behemoth, before them. And the body, the body was still there. An unmoving dark mound, face-down on the grass, not five metres away.

Callie turned to check that Smiler was still following. He was. His hair and clothes were pasted to his skin and he looked rigid with cold. Or fright.

'I don't like the look of this,' she said, her voice a hoarse cry that competed with the wind. It was a redundant statement, but she'd needed to say something to expel some of the tension that had her innards wound tight. She stopped and waited for Smiler to catch up and cast a look back to the cabin, which was sitting in unmoving darkness. 'And where's Pollyanna? Why isn't she watching?' Callie had no idea what she was accusing the girl of, but the fact Pollyanna's white face wasn't at the lounge window troubled her. Greatly.

Smiler shrugged and opened his mouth to say

something, but lightning flashed, making the whole sky sizzle with a blinding electric burst. At the same time the body on the lawn moved. They saw it was a man. A large man. Whatever words Smiler had previously thought to say were lost to a consequent clatter of thunder loud enough to make him and Callie cower, arms raised, as if the sky might break apart and fall on their heads.

'Oosh,' Callie said.

The man on the floor lifted his head and looked in their direction. His eyes lacked cognisance and his face was swollen and bloodied. He slid his hands over grass and mud, stretching his arms to either side as though to gain leverage to push himself up. But he didn't. He became still again and just lay there, seeming to lack the strength and coordination to crawl let alone stand.

Callie let go of the throw and grabbed Smiler by the arm. 'Shit, shit, shit! He's alive!'

Smiler looked at her in wide-eyed bemusement. 'Isn't that a good thing?'

'I dunno. Maybe we should reserve judgement. I mean, *look at him!* He's pretty fucking big.'

'He's pretty fucking beat up too!'

'Okay,' Callie said, making a decision based far too much on empathy for her liking. She hunkered down beside the man and buried both of her hands deep into his right armpit. 'Let's get him inside.' Smiler was quick to secure his other side, then together they heaved. The man tried to help by drawing himself up onto his knees, but it felt to Callie as though his body had absorbed half of the sky; he was leaden. Helping him to the cabin would be an enormous task. She looked across at Smiler, whose own expression was grave, and braced herself. They waited a few moments, allowing the man to catch his breath, then heaved him to his feet. He staggered backwards at first, but they managed to hold firm till he was steady. Then Callie threw an arm around his waist for better support. Smiler did the same.

As they shuffled forward, the man limped and rested heavily on Callie, his arm draped across her shoulders weighing against her neck and pushing her head forward so she was forced to look at the ground. The smell of his aftershave was faint above the sharpness of the rain-infused air and it reminded her of someone or something, but she couldn't think who or what. Some nostalgia, she imagined, lost to her in the freakishness of the moment. Or maybe it was nothing more significant than the smell of a past co-worker or the waft of a stranger in some shopping mall or departure lounge. The man stood a good half a foot taller than she and Smiler, and she imagined in good health he would be quite intimidating. His shirt clung to him like a second skin and she could feel that beneath it his body was taut and muscular. Each time he took a ragged breath his ribs swelled hard against her and he shivered uncontrollably. She gripped him tighter in a gesture of encouragement, but he gave no outward sign that he was at all encouraged.

The dark, skulking shape of the cabin wasn't far away, yet at that moment it could have been as distant as the mountains beyond the lake. They struggled on, trudging and wading through the mud, exhausted and freezing. Thunder roared above them with bone-stiffening loudness and rain continued to wash down in biblical torrents. Callie and Smiler eventually got the man to the edge of the lawn then push-heaved him up the steps onto the veranda. After a manic grapple with the wind and the door, all three of them clambered inside the cabin and shuffled awkwardly down the hall in a sideways chain, each of them grunting and panting and making pools of water on the parquet. In the lounge Callie and Smiler guided the man to the couch where they flopped him down, both proclaiming their relief with pained groans.

'That's my exercise for the year,' Callie said, out of breath, while scrunching her fists and flexing her arms. Water dripped from her fingers and when she wiped her hands down her sides, her dress felt like dolphin skin. Already a chilblain sensation was sweeping over her entire body as her skin reacted to the warmth of the room. Weak with exertion, she felt she might collapse to the floor and not get up for a week.

Smiler was looking at her while tugging on his bottom lip with his thumb and forefinger. 'What do you reckon?'

But before Callie had time to answer the overhead light snapped on.

Pollyanna was by the stairs, her hand lingering on the light switch. 'Reckon to what?' she said, her eyes baby deer wide and hair a wilder tangle of copper than before.

'How'd you get the light to work?' Callie asked, bemused.

Pollyanna made a face as if to say *are you really that stupid?* 'The usual way.'

'Power's back up,' Smiler said. He looked as relieved as Callie should feel. Yet she felt only suspicion.

'Who's that?' Pollyanna asked. She was looking at the back of the couch, unable to see the latest arrival from where she was sitting.

Callie looked at the man and choked on her own breath. He was sprawled on the couch and in the new light, she could see him properly. Despite the bruising and swelling to his face, which otherwise might have spoilt the instant familiarity, his eyes were recognisable beyond any shade of doubt. They were the kind of blue that made you look twice. The kind of blue that would get you in trouble. The kind of blue she most definitely knew. '*Thurston!* What the hell are you doing here?'

'Whoa.' Smiler turned to her, pale-faced. 'You

actually know who he is?'

'Of course! It's Torbin Thurston. *Look!*' She jabbed her finger in the man's direction as if Smiler mightn't have already taken a look.

But Smiler was no more enlightened. 'Torbin who?'

'My God, you've never heard of Torbin Thurston? He's only a famous bloody film producer.'

'Really?'

'Really!' Callie found herself smiling despite the bad shape Thurston appeared to be in, relieved to have an ally at last. Someone she knew. Someone she could trust. Between them, she thought, they could sort this mess out.

His eyes locked on hers, but they were glazed with a vacant unknowingness, like he had no idea who she was. 'Where am I?' he said. His throat sounded scratchy, like the words had barbed hooks.

'Hey, it's me.' Callie perched on the arm of the couch and put her hand on his shoulder. She gave it a gentle rub, then squeezed. 'It's *me*. Callie. Callie Crossley.'

At first he didn't seem sure, but then a sudden recognition made his entire body sag with what she took to be relief. *'Cal?* Where am I?'

'Listen, Thurston,' she said, taking his hand in hers. 'Do you know what happened? Do you know how you got here?'

'No.' He shook his head and looked down at their hands, entwined. Hers were an ugly shade of purpled white; blotchy from the cold. His were similar, only his knuckles were raw and bloodied. 'I can't remember. I was…'

'Uncle Dean?' Pollyanna had moved to the front of the couch and was regarding Thurston with a look of abject horror.

'Who the hell's Uncle Dean?' Callie asked.

'He is!'

Thurston tried to ease himself up but the effort proved too much and he ended up half sitting, half slouched. He massaged his forehead and sucked air in through his teeth in response to some wave of pain that ripped through him. 'Sorry, kid,' he said, 'you must be mistaking me for someone else. I'm Thurston. Nobody's uncle.'

But Pollyanna didn't appear to hear. 'Why did you leave me here? On my own.'

Thurston closed his eyes and sighed. He rested his head against the couch's cushion. 'I don't know who you are, man. I didn't leave you anywhere. I've never seen you before in my life.'

'Liar. This is your cabin and you brought me here in your car with Aunt Roxanne and Sarah Jane.'

'What?' Callie was stunned. 'Since when the hell did you know who owns this place?'

'Since the first time I came.'

'But I already asked you. Why the fuck didn't you tell me?'

Pollyanna shrugged. 'What's it to you?'

'What's it to *me?*' Callie jumped to her feet, rage twitching inside her; a red seedling about to sprout. 'Yesterday I was tied up and bundled into the boot of a car then brought here by God knows who, so *actually* it has every-fucking-thing to do with me, you difficult little shit!' Her face had flushed and she imagined blood was bubbling beneath the surface of her cheeks. She scrunched her fists tight by her sides and counted to five.

'She's right, Poll,' Smiler said. He'd moved close to the wood burner and was standing on the hearth as though the ashes at the bottom the grate would generate enough heat to dry the back of his jeans. 'You should have told her when she asked. You should have told *me* when I asked! Why have you never told me that before?' He looked hurt.

Pollyanna didn't answer, but looked on the verge of apology; her head lowered and eyes awash with something like guilt.

Callie sifted through her memory bank, trying to find a Dean; a colleague, an ex-boyfriend, a childhood friend, a family friend, an old neighbour, a bar tender, a super fan, anyone. But none was readily available. 'Okay, okay,' she said, holding her hands up to gain everyone's attention. 'So, what you're saying is that your uncle owns this place?'

Pollyanna glared at Thurston. 'He's not really my uncle, that's just what we called him. He was having an affair with my aunt.'

'That's what *we* called him?'

'Me and my cousin. Sarah Jane.'

'Roxanne's daughter?'

'Yeah, I used to stay at their house a lot. That's how I ended up coming here. Aunt Roxanne brought us with her because Uncle Stevie had gone away for the weekend and she'd arranged to meet up with *him*.' Something about the way she was eyeing Thurston chilled Callie. There was an indisputable truth simmering in the awfulness of her black eyes. Even if it was a mistaken truth, Callie could see that the girl truly believed Thurston was the person she'd known as Uncle Dean.

Thurston sighed; a forced, impatient sound. 'Hey, I don't know what your problem is, kid, but I'm telling you I'm not Dean. I don't know who you are.'

'Liar,' Pollyanna said, without blinking, without breaking eye contact. 'You told me and Sarah Jane about Whispering Woods. About how the trees talk and how there'd been a murder here…'

'What?' Callie's veins felt like her heart was pumping ice thaw through them. She recalled her dream. *Listen to the trees, Callie Crossley. Hear them in your head and*

*you'll have the answers. You'll know why you're here.
You'll know why I'm here.* 'Trees, talking? A murder?
What? Just *what?*'

'I dunno.' Pollyanna shrugged. 'He never finished
telling us the story. Aunt Roxanne made him stop.'

Everyone was looking at Thurston now.

'Are you serious?' He covered his eyes as though the
light hurt them. 'Is talking trees a euphemism or
something?'

'You would know,' Pollyanna said. 'Can't you hear
them?'

'All I can hear is *you.*'

'What happened to your aunt and cousin?' Callie
wanted to know, more confused now than when she'd
first arrived at the cabin. 'How come you were left here
alone?'

'How should I know? Ask him.' Pollyanna spun her
chair round and wheeled it over to the window where
she picked up a packet of cigarettes off the sill.

Thurston held a hand up, like *don't even bother.*

'Tell me what happened,' Callie said to Pollyanna.
'Tell me what you do know.'

Pollyanna shook a cigarette free and Smiler was
already on hand to light it with a blue Zippo. She took a
long draw and shrugged. 'That first night me and Sarah
Jane went to bed and argued. We often did.'

'About what?'

Again she shrugged. 'All sorts of things. She was a
difficult person to get along with.'

'What did you argue about on that particular night?'

Pollyanna, now swathed in smoke, gestured to
Thurston with a tip of her head. 'Him.'

Thurston opened his eyes and regarded her with a hard
stare.

'What about him?' Callie urged. 'Why did you argue
about him?'

'Sarah Jane fancied him. But she wouldn't admit it.'

'Then what happened?'

'Nothing.'

'It must have.'

Pollyanna huffed. 'After arguing we fell asleep. I woke up a bit later and it was thundering, like it is now, like it always is, and Sarah Jane wasn't in her bed. I didn't bother going to look for her because it was the middle of the night and I thought she must have gone to the toilet, so I just went back to sleep. Next time I woke it was morning and I was on my own. They'd all left me. Aunt Roxanne. Sarah Jane. And *him.*'

Pink light sparked at the window and thunder rumbled not long after, shaking the floor and furniture as though it was crashing about above them in the tower room. The light flickered and Callie look up. The room was then plunged into darkness. A deep black which was the true face of the cabin, Callie thought. Everything they could see when the lights were on was nothing more than a guise to mask something insidiously worse. She felt as though the cabin in this darkness was breathing and almost had a voice. The blackout only lasted a couple of seconds then the light came back on. When it did, Callie saw that Thurston was glaring at Pollyanna and his eyes, she noticed, were every bit as cold as the night. She wrapped her arms around herself and shivered.

11

The man who was allegedly called Torbin Thurston slept on the couch and didn't wake till sunlight was streaming through the large window. As he stirred his brow creased and he was quick to shield his eyes with his hand. Callie was sitting opposite him in the worn leather armchair. An empty mug rested in her lap and shadows caused by a sleepless, uncertain night rested beneath her eyes. She became tense as Thurston gained consciousness, feeling discomfited by the appeal in his familiar blue eyes.

Who are you?

Did she really know? Because suddenly he seemed as unknown to her as the cabin's tower room, which lurked above them like speculated cancer, its malignancy unknown, as yet unchallenged. When he swung his leather-shoed feet to the floor and sat up, groaning as he did, nobody rushed to his aid, or thought to say anything. Pollyanna was watching from her favourite spot by the window and hadn't moved in hours. She was like some sun-starved reptile conserving energy. Callie wasn't even sure she'd blinked. Smiler had remained sitting on the dusty, ashy hearth and was onto his ninth cigarette of the day. Hours ago he'd stripped to his underpants before lighting the wood burner. He'd sat close to the intense heat for so long his hair looked too dry. Frazzled to yellow straw. Callie had taken her dress off and was wrapped in a white bath sheet, which was secured above her chest and gaping open mid-thigh. Her black designer dress was slung over the back of the couch as though it was little more than a charity shop cast-off.

'Cal, what's going on?' Thurston reached up to apply pressure to both sides of his head, above the temple. His eyes, tourmaline-blue, stayed with her as though she was the only other person in the room.

For Callie the initial relief of having him there had faded to unsettled obscurity; Pollyanna had caused that to happen with talk of *Uncle Dean*. She remained seated in the armchair, allowing paranoia to build. 'If this is a little project of yours, Thurston, I won't be happy. At all.'

He jerked forward and gripped the edge of the couch; an unexpectedly quick movement that marked some indignation. His knuckles turned white. 'A project of *mine?* What's that supposed to mean?'

Callie had never made or seen Thurston angry before. His forehead had creased into several deep lines and his attractive mouth had tightened to a cruel sneer. She wasn't the type to shy away from an argument, but right now Torbin Thurston exuded a dangerousness that made her throat constrict with apprehension. His show of defensiveness was understandable, if he was indeed who he said he was, she supposed, but there was something about the way his eyes blazed that greatly unsettled her. She looked down at the mug in her lap and began to feed its ceramic smoothness round and round in her hands, aware that the cabin was throbbing all around them as though it had a heartbeat of its own. She wondered if anyone else could hear it or if it was just in her head. She imagined the oppressive darkness in the tower above them rolling and turning in rage, churning up dormant sleeping things that couldn't see, yet saw everything. And suddenly she felt like everyone and everything was waiting for her to reply. Even the trees in Whispering Woods and the birds in the ash tree. She shrugged and tried to look offhand, again meeting the intensity of Thurston's glare. 'I dunno, I was thinking maybe an experimental film,' she said. 'You know, cameras recording us off the cuff, that sort of thing.'

Thurston shook his head and laughed at the suggestion and all sense of danger passed, just like that. His eyes were normal again. He smoothed a hand over his lightly stubbled jawline. 'If there are any cameras I can assure you they've got nothing to do with me, sweetheart. Not my style.' He shuffled further forward, so he was sitting on the lip of the couch's cushion and looked to the lake beyond the window. To no one in particular, he said, 'Where is this place?'

It was Smiler who answered. 'Whispering Woods.' He flicked ash onto the hearth behind him and was regarding Thurston with an aloofness that didn't seem befitting of him.

'But of course you knew that already,' Pollyanna said.

'Jesus, kid, not this again.' Thurston rocked forward and hoisted himself to his feet. He stood still. The pain of having moved had tightened his expression. 'I'd hoped you and Uncle Dean were a bad dream.' He took a step forward and his left leg buckled beneath him. As he collapsed to the floor his shoulder hit the edge of the coffee table and there was a bone-splintering crunch. Callie leapt from the armchair and went to him. Wrapping an arm around his torso, she helped him back to the couch.

'Came over all dizzy,' he said, by way of explanation. He clutched at his chest, seemingly unfazed by the hit to his shoulder.

'You need to take it easy.' Callie sat next to him, so close their legs touched. Then she rested her hand on his thigh; a bold gesture that seemed to raise no eyebrows except her own. 'Can you remember what happened yet?' Her hand felt like a brick, awkward and heavy, on the end of her arm. She wanted to move it but couldn't.

'I dunno,' he said, shaking his head. 'I was having a quiet night in. At home. Alone. I was watching a film when Betsy started barking at the front door. There was no one there when I opened it, so I did a scan of the CCTV out front. I even checked the back but couldn't see anyone anywhere. Betsy kept on barking though, so I put my shoes on and went outside and…and that's all I can remember.' He raised a hand to his head where his fair hair was matted around a thick line of black, hardened blood that ran about six inches long, around four inches up from his ear. He winced when his fingers touched it. 'Some bastard must have hit me over the head.'

A round of slow clapping made everyone look to the window. Pollyanna was sneering and her black eyes held all the intensity of dark matter. 'You're very good at this kind of thing,' she said. 'Aren't you?'

'Excuse me?' Thurston lowered his hand from his head and gave Callie a sideways glance.

Callie slid her hand away from his thigh.

'Acting,' Pollyanna said, wheeling closer. 'Faking stuff.'

Thurston sighed and rolled his eyes back to show his impatience. 'Are we *seriously* going to do the whole Uncle Dean thing again?'

'What did you do to Aunt Roxanne and Sarah Jane?' Pollyanna demanded to know. 'Did you kill them like in that story you told us? The one with Old Mally Murgatroyd.'

'Who's Old Mally Murgatroyd?' Callie looked between Thurston and Pollyanna before settling her gaze on Smiler, who she was pleased to see looked just as clueless as she felt.

Thurston's jaw worked tightly. 'Fucked if I know!'

'It was very clever with the eye,' Pollyanna said. 'You had me fooled. I thought you were actually blind. You pretended you were a sergeant in Afghanistan too. But it was lies. All of it.'

Thurston breathed heavily and his eyes presented

danger again. 'I've had enough of your shit, kid.' His voice was a low, warning growl. 'So just back off and shut the fuck up.'

Callie touched his thigh again, a gesture that was meant to calm him, but he didn't seem to notice. The room was throbbing again, antagonised by his anger.

'Just leave it, Poll,' Smiler said, fidgeting on the hearth and looking nervous, as though analysing his responsibilities and contemplating what he was meant to do if the argument got out of hand.

'Why?' Pollyanna said. 'Whose side are you on?'

'I'm just sick of all the arguing.' He slid his tenth cigarette from the packet of Superkings at his side and gripped it between his lips without making eye contact with her. 'It's just, I don't care if he's a film producer, your long-lost uncle or frigging, I dunno, Jesus reincarnate, I'd just like us all to work together to find a way out of this.'

'You don't believe me.' Pollyanna flinched as though he'd struck her. Her voice was now low, having lost its edge of fiery belligerence to hurt disappointment in a slip of a moment. 'You don't believe that he's the one who brought me here, do you?'

Smiler closed his eyes, his face a maelstrom of desperate unhappiness. He took his time lighting his cigarette, but his lack of immediate response was enough to make Pollyanna flee from the room. Moments later her bedroom door slammed shut.

'Shit,' Smiler hissed, slamming his palm against the hearth tiles. He got to his feet, a graceless effort made worse by underpants wedged between his arse cheeks, and flicked the unsmoked cigarette into the wood burner. 'I'd better go and talk to her.'

'Hey, wait.' Thurston pointed a loose handed finger at him as he passed by the couch . 'Aren't you that kid, the one off that programme? *Only Me?* Joey Whatshisface.'

'Miles Golden.'

Thurston's eyes became wide at the confirmation. 'What the hell happened to you? Pressure of fame get too much?'

Callie jabbed him in the arm with her elbow, but Smiler didn't seem to care what Thurston thought. He wandered off towards Pollyanna's room without another word, his head held low.

'That was bloody rude,' Callie said.

Thurston raised his eyebrows, looking somewhat surprised by the reprimand.

Callie shook her head. What was the point?

Outside the day was fine. A post-storm stillness hung in the air like the aftermath of some personal tragedy. The ravens chattered in the ash tree, their deep caws provoking thoughts of graveyards and death and overall sombreness.

'How are you feeling anyway?' Callie said.

'Like I had a run-in with Lennox Lewis.'

'Looks like you put up a fair fight.' She eyed his busted knuckles.

He flexed his hands and made a noise, halfway between a laugh and a grunt.

'Hey, I'm sorry for being weird with you before,' Callie said. 'Yesterday was a crazy day and I just don't know who I can trust anymore. I suppose I got a bit paranoid.'

Thurston smiled in forgiveness. Whenever he smiled his eyes narrowed to a squint, making him look somewhat untrustworthy. Unscrupulous even. Callie had noticed this since the first time they'd met, but had always thought he was intriguing enough to take a risk on. Yet now, as quiet amusement shaped his eyes and mouth, she was no longer sure.

'Don't worry about it,' he said. Then adding fuel to her doubts, he winked.

'Where hurts most?' she asked, unsure whether to be pleased or offended by his cockiness. 'Your head?'

'Funnily enough my chest feels ten times worse. Like someone stabbed me with a hot poker.'

'Want me to take a look?'

'Yeah, okay.' Thurston kept his eyes fixed on hers and began to unbutton his shirt. Some deep remembrance stirred within Callie. Of a certain way he'd looked at her before. Of teasing or longing, she couldn't tell.

'Freya will know something's up,' he told her. 'When she goes over to my house and sees I'm not there she'll realise something happened.'

'Then when she rings me and I'm not around…'

'She'll call the police.' Thurston's fingers halted on the fourth button down and his gaze dropped to Callie's mouth. She squirmed. He had the ability to make her feel incredibly foolish. His eyes were definitely mocking, she decided, and she wondered how she had ever considered him a friend. Well, that was an exaggeration. She hadn't. Not really. He was her friend's boyfriend, which made him a friend by association, that was all. He was someone she felt awkward around because he highlighted an aspect of herself that she'd rather ignore. She licked her teeth self-consciously and nodded. 'Let's hope so.'

'Hmmm.' His fingers started moving again and his eyes were back on hers.

When his shirt flapped open, revealing his bare chest, Callie clamped a hand to her mouth and gasped. Thurston, surprised by her reaction, looked down. He jerked backwards in shock and cried, 'What the fuck's that?'

A large gash beneath his left pectoral had been crudely sewn together with thick, black twine. The edges of the wound were red and puckered, and a general swelling of the area signified potential infection.

'Who would do this to me, Cal?' he said, gripping her arm. 'Who would fucking *do this?*'

But Callie had no answers. Nor any words.

12

Callie tried calming Thurston, stroking and soothing him with her hands and her voice. For her efforts, at least he wasn't shouting anymore. But he trembled in some catatonic state of shock. All the initial commotion had brought Smiler dashing back to the lounge. He stood in the doorway watching, horrified. Not daring to come closer.

'Are there more blankets anywhere?' Callie asked, noticing him there.

Smiler nodded and pointed to a wooden chest by the fire, but made no attempt to fetch one. He seemed so young all of a sudden, rendered useless in the unfolding crisis. His stooped demeanour signified a complete lack of confidence and assertiveness, so Callie couldn't stir irritation enough to feel mad at him. She left Thurston and went to the chest to get a blanket herself. They were all scratchy and smelled of mothballs and camphor wood. None of them pleasant. But it couldn't be helped. She chose a particularly large grey one and laid it on top of Thurston after buttoning his shirt up to keep the wool fibres off his wound; the wound she had no idea what to do with. It was like a macabre statement, inherently worse than the one she was left with: DEAD TO ME.

While Smiler continued to linger in the doorway like a remnant of the cabin's past, Callie sat with Thurston for a while longer. Eventually she squeezed his arm and said, 'Don't move from here. I'm going to go out and get help.'

'No.' His hands came out from beneath the blanket and he pawed her arms. 'Don't go.'

In any other scenario Callie might have been flattered

that Torbin Thurston, successful film producer and owner of Blue Bolt Productions, wanted her to stay with him. But she couldn't feel flattered. Only fearful. Because whoever had sliced his chest open, it seemed they were making some bold but unclear threat that couldn't be ignored, which in turn made her wonder what was to come next. If Smiler and Pollyanna had been at the cabin for some time now, as they said, then it seemed that things were suddenly happening quick and fast. Coming to some terrible, revelatory head perhaps. She took Thurston's hand in hers and clasped it. 'I have to,' she insisted. Already she worried that his constant shaking might be some feverishness brought about by the onset of infection and not just shock. She needed to fetch a doctor or an ambulance, as well as the police.

A shadow swooped across the room. A fleeting flash of greyness. Callie's attention was drawn to the window. A raven had settled on the sill. Watching. Its eyes showed an unsettling intellect and she thought, perhaps, it might even be gloating over some exclusive knowledge.

Do you know who did this to Thurston? She wondered. *Did you see?*

The bird began to flap its wings against the window, as if in answer, and it jabbed at the glass with its beak, creating a ruckus surely meant to intimidate. Another raven arrived and attacked the window with just as much aggression as the first. Both birds were huge, frightening in their display of unprovoked frenzy.

Thurston lifted his head from the cushion to look. 'What are they doing?'

Callie looked at Smiler for an answer, but he was staring at the ravens with such horror she could tell their behaviour wasn't a normal occurrence. She jumped up and dashed to the window. 'Get away!' she cried, slamming the pane with her palm. 'Go!'

The ravens regarded her coolly for a moment then took to the air, croaking their annoyance. When they were mere specks in the sky and their caws could no longer be heard, the lounge became weighted with a sentient quiet. As though the cabin was listening. Waiting.

But for what?

'I have to get dressed,' Callie said, feeling a sense of urgency, as well as an upwelling of survival instinct that strengthened her nerve.

But for how long?

She went upstairs and Smiler, who had been reduced to a frightened man-child and who looked like he'd need instruction for whatever was to happen next, followed. She'd much rather he had stayed downstairs with Thurston, but allowed him to accompany her to the red and white room.

'I'm worried about him,' she said, pushing the door inwards. Hinges creaked; a long mournful sound that would be even more terrible at night, she thought. Inside the room the air was cold and unfriendly. Callie rubbed gooseflesh on her arms to flatten it, but it was stubborn enough to stay.

'Who did that to him?' Smiler stayed in the doorway, pulling on his bottom lip with restless fingers.

'I've no idea,' she said. 'No idea at all.'

The double bed was red-sleek and still as indeterminably offensive as it had been the first time she'd seen it. She gave it a wide berth and moved to the window, picking up a blue checked shirt from a pile on the floor. 'We have to leave,' she said. 'We have to go and get help.'

'I understand what you're saying,' Smiler said, clearing his throat. 'And I'll go with you wherever you want to go. It's just, I can guarantee that we won't find any help.'

'How do you know?'

'Because there is none.'

'I can't believe that.' Callie started to unbutton the men's shirt and looked out of the window at Whispering Woods. The morning sun made the wooded area no less ominous. Spiky branches reached up as if to puncture the sky and a gossamer layer of grey mist lay low amongst the undergrowth.

'I'm on your side.' Smiler's voice was bereft of any spirit, as were his eyes. Callie could see he wasn't far from some emotional breaking point. 'I want to leave as much as you do.'

In that moment she didn't doubt it. She puffed her cheeks and sighed. 'I hope so. I really do.'

'It's true. And since I'm being honest, I may as well tell you that I'm pleased you're here. I know it sounds selfish, and maybe it is, but you've given me a sliver of hope. Just by being here. You're probably the best chance I have of getting out.'

'Wow. Thanks for the vote of confidence,' Callie said, unable to hide her sarcasm. 'But who do you think I am? A bloody miracle worker?'

'I hope so.' Smiler sounded strained. He was on the brink of some emotional overload that was about to spill over. 'I might not be physically wounded like Thurston, but *I* need your help as well.'

'Okay.' Callie felt she had little choice but to take the lead. To play mother. After all, she was in the best shape physically and mentally. It was down to her. *No pressure then.* 'We'll work it out.' By no means was she convinced by her own assertion. She just needed to sound proactive for his sake – and her own.

Smiler continued to frown and began picking at the flaky paint on the doorframe. Callie could tell that something else was bugging him. 'What is it?' she asked.

He shook his head. 'Nothing.' Then seemed to think

better of it. 'It's just, er, I dunno, I'm not too sure about Thurston.'

Callie was surprised by his awkward admission, though not terribly so. 'What about him?'

'I dunno.' Smiler scrutinised a piece of paint he'd peeled off the doorframe a little too much, as though it was actually interesting, and Callie expected it was to avoid looking at her. 'I know Pollyanna must be mistaken about everything she's said about him being Uncle Dean and whatnot, I mean he's your friend, you know him better than any of us. But there's something else, something I can't put my finger on. I…I don't know. There's something about him.'

Isn't there just.

'Listen, leave Thurston for me to worry about,' Callie said, attempting to reassure him with a smile that felt empty. 'Now give me five minutes to get dressed, then we'll get going, okay?'

He turned to leave but quickly turned back, his eyes glimmering with an idea. 'Oh hey, what size shoe are you?'

'How come? Have you found a secret stash?'

'No, but I can find out what size Pollyanna is. She must have some shoes. Maybe they'll fit you.'

As much as Callie wasn't overly fond of the idea, she raised a thumb to him. Any shoes would be better than none. He flashed her a quick smile then he was gone and she was left alone in the red and white room. Never had she been more horribly aware of something. She dropped the bath sheet to the floor and shrugged into the blue checked shirt, needing to be back downstairs already. Needing to be outside. As she fastened the buttons as quickly as she could with fumbling fingers, something in her peripheral view caught her eye. A grotesque red swan on the canvas above the bed. But when she lifted her head to look at it more directly, she saw there was nothing more than the random splashes of paint that she'd seen the day before. Trusting her eyes but not the room, she looked down at the shirt's buttons again and tried to see the canvas as she'd seen it with the swan. But there was nothing swanlike about any of it. A rash of gooseflesh spread up her bare legs with an icy chill. She had a deep, intrusive feeling that someone was watching. It took all her effort to move again, to snap out of her trancelike fear. She had a rummage in the piles of clothes and found a pair of black thermal leggings. They'd have to do. She pulled them on and looked out of the window at Whispering Woods.

Do you have something to say? she challenged; willing, daring, wanting the trees to speak. To enter her head and impart their almost certainly baleful wisdom. *Because if you do then say it to me now, you bunch of weather-bitten bastards!*

She yelped then because she heard a female voice. Not inside her head, but somewhere else in the cabin. Close by. Out on the landing. Or in the room next door. A woman. Maybe the same voice she'd heard the previous night, just before Thurston had arrived. This time she couldn't make out any of the words. It was a hushed, insistent chatter as of someone in a hurry.

Hoping to confront whoever it was, Callie ran from the room. The landing was empty except for its own gloom. Her stomach flipped. Had Smiler been lying to her all along? Did he have someone in his room? A key to the tower room? She burst through his door and found him sitting on the bed, dressed in different jeans and a t-shirt, facing the tower door.

'Callie?' He jumped to his feet, his expression too guilty. Or maybe he just looked alarmed.

'Who's here with you?' she said, her fists pulsing. Blood roared in her ears.

'No one.'

'I heard someone.'

'When?'

'Just now.'

'But there's no one here.' Smiler looked about the room to emphasise his point.

'I heard a woman,' she insisted.

'In here?'

'In here.'

'You can't have.'

'I did.' She charged over to the tower door and rattled its handle. It was still locked.

'Seriously, Cal.'

'Don't call me that.'

'Callie.'

She dropped to all fours and moved folds of an ancient valance sheet to peer beneath the bed. There was no one there. A colony of dust bunnies scattered. She sneezed and rubbed her nose. 'Where is she?'

'I don't know who you mean.'

Undeterred, Callie stormed over to the window. She shoved it open and leaned out, but there was no one there either. Just the ash tree and its ravens. Several sets of eyes watched her. The ravens were uncharacteristically quiet. Each of their beaks was long and thick, likely implements for breaking windows, she thought. And gouging out eyes. She clapped the window shut and turned to Smiler, who was busy wringing his hands together and trying, it seemed, not to look guilty. Which made her think he wasn't.

'Maybe you heard Pollyanna,' he suggested. 'These wooden buildings distort sound, make it travel.'

'It wasn't Pollyanna, it was a *woman*.' *And I've heard her before*. Again Callie eyed the tower door.

'You can't honestly think someone's up there?' he said. 'I'd have heard something too. But I didn't. I heard nothing, Callie. *Nothing.*'

'There was a woman,' Callie insisted. 'I heard a voice. In here.'

Or am I simply losing my mind?

Maybe it was the trees.

Ha de fucking ha!

'Really. You can't have,' Smiler said. There was an element of pity in his eyes now.

'Right, I'm going,' she said. Her rage had burnt out and her voice was depressingly flat. She felt depleted. Beaten. 'I guess it doesn't matter. Are you coming or not?'

Downstairs Pollyanna had emerged from her room but was sulking by the window. She glanced up at Callie and Smiler as they came down the stairs. 'What's going on?'

'We're going out to find help,' Callie said, rolling up her shirt sleeves, which were much too long.

'No, I meant what was all the shouting about?'

'Nothing. Doesn't matter.'

'Well where are you going?'

'Anywhere but here.' Callie stood behind the couch, frowning as Thurston tried to sit up. The top half of the left side of his face was bruised and the rest of his skin kept a spectral greyness like the fog that was currently haunting Whispering Woods. The cabin, Callie thought, had infected him with its poison already and in a moment of warped clarity she had a crushing feeling they were all doomed: all four of them to live out the rest of their lives right here. Because deep down she somehow knew that when Smiler had said there was nowhere beyond the cabin and its woods he was telling the truth. There was no way out.

Whispering Woods. Once it gets into your head it won't let go.

'I'll come with you,' Thurston said.

'You're total idiots,' Pollyanna said. 'But I think it's a great idea, you both should definitely go.'

Callie pushed against Thurston's shoulder, forcing him to lie down again. 'You're in no fit state to go anywhere,' she said. 'Apart from hospital. You need to stay here and rest while me and Smiler go and find help.'

'I don't see why *you* have to go,' Pollyanna said to Smiler.

'Because Thurston's not well,' he said, gripping the back of the couch. 'He'll have to stay here. With you.'

'Shit, man.' Thurston groaned and rubbed his forehead agitatedly. He looked up at Callie and said, 'If you're set on leaving me here, can't you at least take her with you? Tip her in the lake on the way back or something?'

Despite herself, Callie couldn't resist a small smile. 'Sorry.'

'Well, if you aren't prepared to put yourself out,' he said with a wink, 'promise you won't leave me here with her indefinitely. I don't think I could take it.' He fidgeted, trying but failing to find a more comfortable position. 'She might convince me I'm Captain Dean.'

'It's sergeant, you mong!' Pollyanna said. Her eyes were as black as furnace backs and genuinely frightening.

Even so, Callie laughed. 'Okay, I promise.' She held Thurston's gaze for such an amount of time that it toed the line of a boundary she wasn't comfortable about crossing. She looked away and coughed. Blood pumped behind her eyes, a burning intensity. She closed them and saw the hook of a swan's head and neck. A white swan on blue. A fleeting image which disappeared and gave way to amber-red.

'Why don't all three of you go?' Pollyanna said, her show of anger directed at Smiler in particular. 'Get lost in the woods. Or fall off a cliff. I don't want you here anymore. *None of you!*'

'Aw don't be like that,' Smiler said, his eyebrows crumpling in genuine upset. 'I won't be long.'

'Like I care.'

'Course you do.'

'Don't.'

'Do.' Smiler went to her and hunkered down so he was at eye level. He took hold of her hands and squeezed. 'I *won't* be long. I'll be back before you know it.' He stuck out his tongue then, forcing a reluctant smile from her. 'Oh,' he said. 'How big are your feet, Poll?'

'Why?' She looked intrigued for the briefest of moments, then her face became a scowl again. 'Screw you, Miles Golden! She's *not* taking my shoes as well.'

13

'Woods or road?' Smiler said. He and Callie were standing on the narrow access road to the rear of the cabin, both of them wearing shirts belonging to a man neither of them knew. A base layer of fog sat around the bottoms of the trees, not spilling out much onto the access road. It had thickened since Callie had looked out of the red and white room's window. Earlier it had been a thin veil of steam-like whiteness, but now it was a dense greyness that would easily swallow legs and feet. At the front of the cabin, the lake had been framed by a vignette of mist and the mountains were no longer visible. Callie had a creeping feeling the world was shrinking, that more fog would roll in till nothing existed except the cabin. She *had* to get out before she was suffocated by Whispering Woods.

'Hmmm. Woods or road.' She scrunched her toes in Pollyanna's red Converse, which were a size too large but not entirely uncomfortable, and looked right to where the access road stretched on for some quarter of a mile before bending out of view amidst Whispering Woods. 'What difference does it make?'

'About an hour.'

'In favour of the woods?'

'Yeah.'

'But if we go through the woods we lessen our chances of seeing anyone who might be passing by on the road, right?'

Smiler looked almost amused. Almost. 'I guarantee that won't happen.'

'All the same, I'd like to make sure it doesn't.' It was a half-arsed excuse, because really she believed him. She would do anything to avoid entering Whispering Woods. Even a three-hour detour if that's what it would take to keep her from amongst those dreadful trees.

'Hey, it's up to you,' Smiler said, looking more relieved than perhaps he'd intended. 'You're calling the shots, I'm just the guide.'

'Road it is then.'

They started walking and there was a chillness to the air that cut straight through the brushed cotton of Callie's shirt. For a moment she considered going back inside to put on an extra layer, but decided against it; wary that the cabin might reel her further into its possession if she did. What if next time it wouldn't let her back out? Cold or not, this was where she needed to be. Outside. Breathing fresh air. Hugging herself, she listened for any hint of traffic. There was none. All she could hear was the insistence of the ravens back at the cabin; their calls carrying on the light breeze that breathed through branches and brought the treetops to life.

'Do you think it'll rain again?' Callie said after they'd been walking for a while. Part of her hoped it would to drown the fog, but another part of her hoped it wouldn't because she wasn't kitted out for it.

Smiler looked up to the sky, which was already churning up lint-coloured clouds to stifle the sun. He sucked on his bottom lip. 'Hard to tell, it changes so fast here.'

Here.

Callie contemplated the vagueness of the word with a deep, resonant sense of despair. 'Wherever that may be.'

Smiler acknowledged her pondering with a sad smile. He looked worse today, she thought. Thurston's impromptu arrival seemed to have taken some personal toll on him. He seemed a little duller on the outside and deader on the inside. The natural light outside the cabin emphasised his vitamin-starved skin and socially-starved eyes. Callie worried for him. She worried for them all.

They followed the dirt track for just under a mile before coming to a T-junction. A white homemade sign with black painted lettering pointed to the right. It read: The Lake. There was no sign, similar or otherwise, to indicate what was left but Smiler had already turned that way and was following a newer, wider, less potted road. 'Come on,' he said, signalling with his hand. 'This is us.'

'Won't anyone be at the lake?' Callie said, faltering. She could glimpse its black expanse from where she stood. 'Like fishermen? Or maybe there's a boathouse?'

Smiler turned to face her but continued walking, backwards. 'Might have been at one point,' he said. 'But the lake's totally deserted. I doubt there're any fish in it to be honest. I mean, they'd have to be GloFish or something.'

Frowning, Callie jogged to catch him up. 'So this way leads to the village?'

'Yeah.'

'Good.'

'Hmmm.'

On either side, trees crowded them and Callie realised with dawning dread that the road to the village cut straight through the woods. The very thing she hadn't wanted. She was still being forced to enter Whispering Woods, it was like some preordained trickery that was always going to happen no matter what. Her mouth became dry and she focused on the muddy road: the beaten track that wouldn't accommodate cars with low suspensions and body kits. It wasn't even a proper road.

Where the hell am I?

She thought about the Bentley. The driver must have driven this way. It was the only route in. But where was he now? In another part of the country? Long gone. Or hiding in the woods? Concealed by fog that was standing about like old, stagnant disco smoke.

'Who'll be missing you?' Smiler said, breaking through her thoughts and causing a sting somewhere deep inside her chest.

'I'm not sure.' Callie breathed in hard. Her dry throat stung with the intake. 'My agent Sam Dent-Worth, maybe. But when I fail to answer his calls for the umpteenth time he'll probably think I've taken a last minute flyer. I've done that before, so he won't be overly concerned. I've got a couple of close friends, but I don't speak to them all that often. I'm always busy. We're all too busy. So it might take a week or two for them to notice that something's not right. Apart from that, though, there's no one to miss me. Not really.'

Smiler raised his eyebrows. 'Whoa, that's sad.'

'Tragic,' Callie said, without a scrap of irony. She was looking past him into the trees. A long strip of white polythene had caught her eye. It was snagged on a branch and for a moment looked like the dismembered neck and head of a swan. A random gust of wind took hold of it and it became no more than a torn bin liner, billowing and flapping. 'I have a much older brother who lives in France. He leads a humble life on a sheep farm with his wife and two girls. He won't notice I'm gone, not for a while.'

'I'm guessing you don't have a husband or boyfriend?'

Callie shook her head and laughed. The laugh had a bitter edge to it. 'Nope. Absolutely no one would be too put out if anything was to happen to me. If I was to die.' She realised at once that this sounded self-pitying. But she wasn't sorry. If she couldn't indulge herself in a time such as this, she wasn't sure when she could. Besides, it was true.

'What about your fans?'

'Oh I've no doubt my fans would mourn their loss on

social media if I wind up being worm food in Whispering Woods,' she said. 'And that's really sweet. But it's a different kind of mourning, because none of them know the *real* Callie Crossley. They don't see me on a day-to-day basis or know what my faults and bad habits are, the things that make me human. Mostly my fans fall in love with the characters I play on screen. The characters who in no way represent my self because they're all larger than life optimists who spout witty comments as easily as breathing air. But I'm not like that. I'm serious a lot of the time and I have down days just like everyone else. First thing on a morning I'm absolutely bloody awful to be around and, as you know, I swear like a trooper. I comfort eat a lot. I drink alcohol almost every night. And sometimes I cry myself to sleep at night because it scares me that life is passing me by and I feel like it's never lived up to my expectations. The expectations that movies helped create in my head when I was a kid. I know, I'm like a walking contradiction, right? A total mess. Most days I feel like I've lost my way though, you know?'

'Oh I know,' Smiler said, without having to pretend to.

Callie rubbed angrily beneath her eyes with the shirt's cuffs. She felt foolish. Annoyed with herself for opening up so much. 'Sorry,' she said, blinking back tears. She focussed on the dirt at her feet, trying to channel her self pity into the ground, because if she didn't she'd break apart. 'I didn't mean to offload on you like that, I dunno where it all came from.'

'Hey, don't worry. I'm here anytime.' Smiler smiled; it was a gesture which seemed to back the sincerity of his offer.

'So what about you, Mr Popular?' she said, needing to direct conversation away from herself. 'I bet you have a lot more people giving a shit about you. In fact, I bet there're girls all over the world wondering where you are.'

Smiler looked across at her and she thought he had more colour. There was an element of quiet surprise about his face. Or perhaps it was nervous suspicion. Callie wondered what nerve she'd hit. 'If I ever get out of here I'm way past those days,' he said. 'Being here has changed something fundamental inside of me. I could live the humble life now, no word of a lie. A farm, a wife, two kids and a whole load of sheep sounds perfect to me. Your brother has it all sussed. He's the lucky one.'

Callie considered this and found herself agreeing. 'You know, I think you might be right.' She kicked a stone with the toe of Pollyanna's shoe and watched it bounce ahead some five metres. When she caught up with it, she booted it into the trees. It was eaten up by the fog and she thought it might as well never have existed because its absence had made no noticeable difference whatsoever. There were plenty more stones for passers-by to kick or ignore. But that was a stone, not a person. So what about Smiler? Why hadn't there been anything on the news about the disappearance of the Golden Boy? And why was there a distinct lack of search parties scouring the country? 'In all seriousness,' she said, trying not to scrutinise too much in case she offended him with her suspicion, but needing to read his expression all the same. '*Shouldn't* someone be missing you by now?'

Smiler wellied a stone of his own into the woods and grunted. 'Apparently not,' he said. 'The media had their fill of me before I went missing. My fans, sorry *ex* fans, probably think I'm rotting in jail somewhere and the authorities, well, they'll most likely think I'm living in some subway or dosshouse, doped up to the eyeballs, lamenting my guilt. Or fwapping off to the memory of what they think I got away with, more like.'

Callie stopped walking and gawped at him. 'And that would be the memory of what exactly? Why would people think you're in jail?'

He stopped too. 'You mean, you don't know?'

'Er, I don't believe so.'

'Seriously?'

'I'm sure I'd be sure if I did.'

Smiler closed his eyes and tilted his face to the sky. 'I should have known!'

'I feel like I should too.' Callie waited to be filled in.

'I thought you were being nice to me because you didn't believe the vicious slander.' When he opened his eyes again they were glossy with tears. Of frustration, not sadness. 'But that's not true. You're being nice to me because you don't frigging know. You have no idea!'

'So you and Pollyanna keep telling me,' Callie said, with an unappreciative scowl.

'I'm sorry, I didn't mean it like that.'

'Well, aren't you going to give me an idea?' She began to feel more than a little uneasy. The fog had crept a little bit closer while she hadn't been paying attention to it and Smiler was right in her face. Too close. She edged away.

'I'd rather not talk about it right now if that's okay,' he said, beginning to walk again, his shoulders hunched. 'It kills me every time it gets dredged up.'

'Well, as long as it doesn't kill me to not know.' Callie could barely find the will to move her feet to go after him. Who was he? What had he done? It was the fog and the trees breathing down her neck that got her walking again. But she lagged behind by a few paces.

'I was acquitted, just so you know.' He stopped and waited so she had to catch up. 'And I'll carry on professing my innocence till the day I die. The whole thing makes me feel sick. Sick! I swear to God, Callie, I didn't do anything.'

'Well, if you say.' Callie cringed at her own words. Was it too weak a response? Condescending even? Was he about to flip his lid and go berserk? She was stranded in the woods with some bloke she didn't know who had apparently stood trial for something which, if she was a betting person, sounded pretty bad.

Come on life, give me a fucking break!

'I don't speak to either of my parents,' Smiler said, as though offering voluntary information about his personal life might smooth over everything he'd said before. 'They won't know or care that I'm missing.'

'Oh?' Callie tried to look interested, but really her mind was still on the acquittal and what might have preceded it.

'Yeah, they tried to leech all of my money before I turned eighteen. They were always more interested in my career than they were in me. I was like some cash cow. And I don't have any brothers or sisters.'

'How about a girlfriend? Surely teen eye-candy of the decade must have a girlfriend.' Callie tried smiling to ease the tension that was as thick as the fog.

'No.' Smiler kicked another stone. It bounced twice on the road then disappeared amongst weeds on the grass verge. 'We broke up. She said she couldn't stand the fact I was so famous. She'd started to accuse me of sleeping with every fangirl I met. Eventually it got to the point where I couldn't interact with any other female without her busting my balls over it.'

'Some people just can't get past their own insecurities, I suppose.'

'I told her I'd be going on an *Only Me* tour around the UK. That's when she gave me an ultimatum: her or my career.'

'Ouch. It's a shame it didn't work out,' Callie said, immediately not liking the way his eyes had darkened. 'But hey there's always Pollyanna, ey?'

'What?' The darkness in his eyes multiplied tenfold and Smiler no longer resembled the indecisive man-child she'd thought she'd struck a rapport with earlier.

'Bloody hell, calm down,' she said, trying to laugh off her remark but sounding entirely too nervous. She upped the effort and lightly punched his arm. 'It was a joke!'

He looked down at his arm, not in the least bit amused.

'It's just, the way she looks at you,' Callie explained. 'I know a crush when I see one. I bet she has Joey Chaplin posters all over her bedroom wall.'

'I hardly think so,' he said. 'She's just a kid.' He flushed so profusely his ears turned red. Callie would have preferred to think he was embarrassed, but she could see plainly that he was furious.

14

The village at the edge of Whispering Woods was unkempt in a forgotten-about, overgrown kind of way, as though its residents had evacuated long ago, never to return. There was no sign of structural damage to suggest some natural disaster had occurred, nor any kind of damage or vandalism indicative of mass panic or rioting. It seemed as though everyone had just got up for work and school one day, left home after breakfast and not bothered coming back again.

A light fuzzy mist hung around the outskirts of the village like a spectral gathering. The place was both quiet and eerie, reminding Callie of the setting of some zombie apocalypse video game. She imagined for a moment that she and Smiler were survivors of an airborne virus that had wiped out civilisation, leaving nothing but walking corpses and mutant dogs in its wake, all of which had a taste for fresh meat and were hiding around the next corner.

Now you're being silly!

Dull green moss fur coated stone surfaces and hardy weeds grew through the cracks in pavements. Dead leaves had accumulated in gutters, creating mounded strips of mushy brown gunk. A busy stream divided the village in half, but a stone bridge linked the gap like an Elastoplast of cobblestones, healing some age-old rift. The blatant lack of people and traffic noise unsettled Callie. There wasn't even any birdsong. The only sounds were the steady rush of stream water and the creak of a metal sign, which swung back and forth outside a pub called The Whispering Maid at the other side of the bridge. The Whispering Maid was a traditional looking public house with whitewashed walls and black Tudor beams. Its downstairs windows were grids made up of small bullseye squares and its door, presumably once black, had turned a graduation of mossy green from the bottom upwards. The swinging sign showed a painting of a young woman with blonde hair who looked remarkably like Callie. She was cupping a hand around her mouth as if to impart a secret. Hanging baskets to either side of the sign had most likely over-spilled with vibrant colour at one point; fuchsias and petunias to buffer the maid's secret amongst the buzzing of bees. Now the aged baskets held nothing but decrepit brown tangles of dead stalks, the flowers killed by autumn or knowledge. Callie thought it was hard to say in a place such as this. She looked at Smiler. He was gravely serious. She expected he was still mulling over his own past.

'I'm beginning to notice a theme,' she said. She started across the bridge, expecting him to follow. He did. 'There's a fascination with whispering. Even the local had something to whisper about.'

Smiler trudged along beside her, rubbing his arms as though he felt a chill. 'Everywhere has secrets. And a place called Whispering Woods was bound to have its fair share.'

'Hmmm.'

At the other side of the bridge, directly in front of them, was a post office with a massive sun-bleached poster in the window that showed a smiley brunette holding a suitcase: an advertisement for discounted travel insurance.

Looks like the whole fucking village jumped all over that *deal.*

Callie cupped her hands against the window, to one side of the poster, to peek inside. The shop's interior was dirty-white, like the poster model's teeth and eye whites.

It was deserted. Nothing at all remained except dead flies that littered the inner sill.

On the pavement, a freestanding post box had turned washed-out red in the same sun that had faded Smiler's eyes. Further down the street, right next to the village butcher's shop, Callie saw a telephone box of the same colour. The sight of it made her heart speed up.

'Doesn't work,' Smiler said, adopting a deadbeat tone to thwart all hope she might have.

Not dissuaded, already she was hurrying towards the booth. 'Maybe today it does.'

'It won't,' he insisted.

'It might.' She pulled open the door. Its hinges were stiff, making her entry cumbersome. Then a dry dustiness of age and disuse caught at the back of her throat, making her cough. She picked up the phone receiver and held it to her ear. A loud and impenetrable silence filled her head. She spoke into the mouthpiece, 'Hello? Hello!' just to be sure. But all she got in return were her own words coming back at her through the earpiece.

Shit!

Smiler was waiting for her outside, leaning against an empty bicycle rail with a thoughtful look on his face.

'Where *is* everyone?' she said, letting the door of the telephone booth slam shut behind her. Each small glass pane rattled harshly in its metal frame. She looked about in case the noise had roused anyone's attention. But if it had, nobody showed any interest. The street was still dead. Smiler didn't answer, but she hadn't really expected him to. So instead she asked, 'What's in all the houses?'

'Nothing.'

'Nothing of interest? Or *nothing* nothing?'

'See for yourself.' He led the way to the nearest house – a small mid-terraced cottage – and opened its door without knocking. Callie followed him inside, into the cottage's reception room. There was no furniture or décor and the walls, ceiling and floor were painted white.

'Are all the rooms the same?' she said.

'Yeah.' Smiler spoke quietly, yet his voice boomed in the emptiness. 'It's the same story in all the other buildings too. None of them escaped the whiteout, as I call it.'

A tight ball of panic, grapefruit-sour, rose up from Callie's stomach, reaching her throat in an acidic chokehold. She felt like she needed to sit down, but there was nowhere to sit except the floor so she remained standing. 'You're absolutely certain?'

'Yes.'

'You've checked every single one?'

'Yes!' He looked more than a little impatient about her insistence. 'More than once. But we can do the rounds if you like. You can see for yourself.'

So they did. They went inside every house, shop and public building, including the post office, Delia's Flowers, Wayburn's Family Bakery, Stephenson's Butchers, David Rosenthorn's Funeral Home, Tea Time Café and The Village Fishery. Inside all of them there was just whiteness. Every room in the village little more than a white cell, even The Whispering Maid. There were no bar stools or beer mats or optics hanging on the wall. Not even a bar itself. It was an empty, rectangular room that echoed loudly with every footstep, highlighting their aloneness. There was nothingness all around them and Callie found herself despising white. Back out on the street the everyday drab colours of concrete and stone were refreshing and characterful in their variety, so many shades of browns and greys that weren't white. Weren't mocking them with some inferred sterility.

A narrow pavement on the bankside across the road followed the course of the stream, disappearing behind a cluster of sycamore trees which were rendered faded by a blurring of fog.

'What's that way?' Callie asked, pointing.

'An old church.' The mention of which gave Smiler no amount of enthusiasm.

'Did the person with the white paint fetish get in there too?'

'I dunno,' Smiler said. He fingered his chin worriedly and looked at the sycamores as though they were a group of antisocial thugs waiting to lynch them. 'The door's always locked. But we can take a look if you really want.'

Callie was almost out of optimism but her curiosity wasn't yet sated, so they set off along the path towards the church. The sky was fuller and darker now and the wind had more bite. She wondered if they'd need to shelter in one of the village buildings if the sky unloaded more rain like the previous evening. She hoped not. Where the cabin had a menacing perceptive air about it, the village was utterly dead and soulless. If they were forced to stay in one of the white rooms for any considerable amount of time, Callie feared that she and Smiler would fade to white and be lost forever.

Her thoughts turned to Thurston. How was he holding up? What if she couldn't find help? What then? Would they all have to stay at the cabin till help found them? If at all. And would Pollyanna drive them all crazy with talk of Uncle Dean? Callie's fingers brushed the shirt fabric on her arm. *Is this yours Dean? If so, who and where the hell are you?* There were too many questions filling her head; questions with no easily identifiable answers. She thought about bouncing some of them off Smiler, but decided it would be pointless. He wouldn't know the answers any more than she did.

The church's tower poked above the tops of balding trees; a black conical spire with a crucifix balanced on top. It was an architectural parody of sorts, because you couldn't possibly look at it without seeing the resemblance to a witch's hat: a ginormous pagan accessory misplaced in the countryside and dressed up as Christian. Callie and Smiler left the path and picked their way through the churchyard. A cold breeze swept across the open, grave-marked stretch, bringing with it a fine mizzle from the fog. Callie shivered. The grass slid across her ankles like strands of wet corpse hair. It was an overgrown mess and tall clumps of it formed tangles around gravestones. Gravestones that looked like they were dissolving with age. Callie read some of the inscriptions as they walked. Most were indecipherable, lost to the past, while others bore names but no dates or epitaphs. The brooding quiet of the village was extended to the churchyard, but it was broken by the hoarse cry of a raven. Callie could see two of them perched on neighbouring gravestones at the far side of the churchyard. Immediately she felt tense.

'I don't remember seeing those before,' Smiler said, looking decidedly paler.

'Creepy little shits have probably been following us.'

'I meant the gravestones they're sitting on. They're new. They weren't there last time I was here.'

'When was that?'

'Last week maybe,' he said. 'Or the week before that.'

'Shall we go and take a look?'

His eyes widened. 'Must we?'

'Are you scared of the birds? Do you think they might attack us?'

Smiler clapped his upper arms and turned his back to the graveyard so he was facing the church instead. 'The birds don't bother me as such. It's just, something feels off. I mean, who put those gravestones there? And why has their appearance coincided with yours and Thurston's arrival?'

Callie gave an impromptu hiccup of laughter, which betrayed her own feelings of unease. 'Do you think if we go over there we'll find they're marked out for me and Thurston?'

Smiler rolled his eyes, but his intended derision was overridden by a total lack of confidence. 'No. I don't know. It's just, the more I think about this the more I don't think it can end well.'

'Hey don't go all pessimistic on me, Golden,' Callie said. She then turned her back to the gravestones, afraid that if they did go and look it would seal some terrible preordained fate. That her name would be there in gold serif font simply because she'd had the audacity to look. 'Let's go and check the church, then get the hell out of here.'

Smiler didn't argue. They made towards the squat, stone building that was sleeping beneath the witch's hat. The two ravens took to the sky and circled overhead, cawing as if in protest that they were heading the wrong way.

'Ever get the feeling this place is run by ravens?' Callie said, looking up.

'I get *lots* of irregular feelings about this place and that's just one of them.'

When they had passed the church earlier it was small and compact. Now it appeared to have doubled in length. It looked to have been constructed in a time when buildings were made to withstand the elements, to last a millennium or longer. In a time so far removed from modern society it was structurally charismatic in a mystical way. Its stone walls were mossy and emitted a cold dampness that Callie could feel without even touching them. She shivered. She felt almost afraid of the building itself. Every stained glass window they passed was unremarkable because there wasn't enough light to showcase colours and patterns with any real clarity. A dark figure on the front-most window might well be Jesus rising up, Callie thought. Or a tree reaching for the sky. The figure's limbs were outlined black and spindly, but the inner colours were too dark to determine just what was going on.

At the front of the church Callie climbed two shallow steps to a heavy wooden door. She gripped its iron handle fully expecting it to be cold and was taken aback by just how cold it was. It was a deep coldness that bit into her bones. She turned to Smiler for some reassurance. When he gave none she said, 'Shall I give it a go?' knowing full well that she would anyway. He shrugged his despondency so she pushed the handle down. Its mechanism clunked and the door cracked open an inch. She gave it a firm shove, swinging the door fully open. Then her breath caught. She saw no white, only blackness. Not a bleak congregation of sunless shadows, but a vast black that contained swirling colours. Bands of silver specks and clusters of purple and blue lights pulsated.

A rapturous happiness washed over Callie in cold but not unpleasant waves and she wanted nothing more than to give herself up to this magical display of glittering black. She felt like she was standing on the doorstep to the entire universe. But when she tried to step forward she felt something restraining her. Smiler was clutching her arm, pulling her backwards. She groaned and tried to shrug him off with vigorous backward elbow thrusts. 'Callie!' she heard him say. But he sounded distant, like he was nothing more substantial than a dream. Yet still he was tugging at her arm.

'No!' She struggled, ripped free and stumbled forward. Then she could feel his hands grabbing fistfuls of her shirt as she fell down and down into the black.

15

Pollyanna stayed by the window, watching Thurston. Only, he was Uncle Dean but with shorter hair, a recently shaven face and two blue eyes. Shortly after Callie and Smiler had left he'd dragged himself off the couch, making no announcement as to what he meant to do, and with all the finesse of a drunk had staggered outside. She could see him now inspecting the Bentley. Inside and out. His shoulders were hunched as if to accommodate the wound on his chest. They were plenty wide enough, she thought, to span the width of Hell's back door. Not the front, though, because that would be a cavernous rift too big even for him. He lurched around the car, his left leg causing him trouble, and he touched paintwork and pulled open doors, carrying out the same searches in the same places over and over again. Pollyanna wasn't sure what he was looking for, but his mouth was pulled taut in a grimace that showed he was having no luck. It was the same mouth that had recounted the tale of the unfortunate motorist and his family, and of Old Mally Murgatroyd and Whispering Woods.

She didn't believe he was a film director any more than she believed he'd been an army sergeant. So who was he really? A good-looking sociopath who preyed on vulnerable and promiscuous women, selling them stories of heroics and materialistic wealth? Or whatever it took to reel them in. Pollyanna knew these things happened outside of soap operas. For real. She supposed this was the most likely theory.

She thought about Sarah Jane and Aunt Roxanne, of what might have happened to them. It wasn't that she missed her cousin all that much. Most of the time Sarah Jane was nothing more than a self-interested bully who thought the world should revolve around her. In fact, if Thurston confessed to having bludgeoned Sarah Jane to death before burying her body beneath the ash tree outside, arguing that she'd deserved it, Pollyanna didn't suppose it would take much to convince her to accept what he said. After all, she'd thought of killing her cousin many times. It had been a careful, complicated relationship that the two girls tolerated, encouraged by the will of two very close sisters; Pollyanna's mother was Roxanne's twin. Pollyanna, therefore, couldn't accept that her aunt had deserted her. Couldn't believe that she would have left her here all alone. Unless of course she was dead, which was looking the likeliest possibility. And it seemed to her that the man outside held the answer.

When Thurston came back into the cabin, at last satisfied that Callie and Smiler could indeed identify an empty engine bay when they saw one, he eased back down onto the couch. The shadows beneath his eyes were like thumb-smudges of charcoal.

Pollyanna feigned too much interest in her cigarette. She blew on the lit end and watched as flakes of ash crumbled down the front of her dress, leaving a talc-like residue. 'What did you do to them?' she said, her voice controlled.

'What did I do to who?'

'Aunt Roxanne and Sarah Jane.'

Thurston rested his head against the back of the couch and closed his eyes. That was the extent of his response.

'Whatever you did to Sarah Jane, I don't much care,' Pollyanna said, as if that small pardon might coax the truth from him. 'But I'd like to see Aunt Roxanne again.' She picked at some loose skin next to her fingernail and noticed that the skin on the inner section of her left forefinger and middle finger were stained yellow above the knuckle with nicotine. If Thurston intended to answer, he made no show of doing so any time soon. She squeezed her right fist into a ball. 'You have to tell me what you did to her!'

Thurston opened his eyes. He looked dangerous and unpredictable, like a wolf deciding how hungry it was. He said nothing.

'Where is she?' Pollyanna insisted. She began fiddling with a cigarette packet, flipping it round and round. Again and again. The *tick-tick-tick* noise it made against the arm of her chair gave the room more tension than it needed.

'I. Don't. Know.' Thurston tapped the side of his head with the middle knuckle of his right hand. 'Why can't you just get it through your thick skull that I don't know who your fucking aunt is?'

'Because you're a *liar!*'

Lurching forward, he bared his teeth. 'Why don't you tell me all about you, *Polly?*' The way he shortened her name sounded like a curse.

She flinched. 'Because we haven't finished talking about you.'

'But apparently you already know all about me.'

'Only the lies. Tell me who you really are!'

Thurston grinned; an unfriendly sneer that made his eyes cruel slits of blue. 'You want to know who I am? Okay, I'll tell you.' He nodded self-assuredly. Master of lies. 'I'm Torbin Thurston, but no one calls me Torbin.' He flicked his right hand in the air, a show of flippancy. 'I always thought it too pretentious. My mother calls me Torby. Everyone else calls me Thurston. Including my dad. I never served in the army and nor have I ever professed to have done so. I've never faked blindness either. That would be weird. I have no association with the name Dean and I don't know anyone called

Roxanne. Or Sarah Jane. I'm the founder of Blue Bolt Productions and over the years I've produced twelve films. Three of them were indie award winners. I was born and raised in Durham, but these days my home is in Devon. I have no siblings. Or living grandparents. I left school with nine GCSEs. My favourite subject was geography. My preferred drink is water. Gin if we're talking alcohol. Is that enough?' He edged back in his seat. 'No? Okay, let's see. I never got bullied as a kid. I had my tonsils removed when I was fourteen. My favourite food is steak. Medium rare. I'm thirty-five years old and I've never been in love. If I could be an animal, any animal, I'd be an eagle. My favourite colour is blue. Dark blue. I have no idea why the sky is blue. I also have no idea where we are right now. Or why I'm here. My life in a tiny nutshell. Is *that* enough? Or would you like me to continue?'

Pollyanna lit a new cigarette and watched him through a thin veil of smoke. When she'd said nothing for a few minutes, he said, 'Come on, your turn. Tell me who you are. Convince me that you're not trying to set me up.'

She started at the accusation, then laughed. An uncertain, confused laugh. 'Trying to set you up?'

'You're sitting there like that, but how do I know you can't walk? How do I know whose daughter you are or what your motivation is? How do I know...' He sighed and squeezed the bridge of his nose. 'Just tell me your fucking story, kid.'

16

Callie fell backwards, her body responding to the fierce pull of gravity. She thrashed the air with her arms, fighting for balance and groping for something to hold onto because she knew the fall would be skull-clatteringly hard. As it was, she collapsed against something that held her upright.

Smiler!

He staggered but caught her, his hands firm on her shoulders. 'It's okay,' he said. He was out of breath and panted the words in her ear. 'I've got you.'

She murmured some confused response, unable to remember making a conscious decision to leave the magnificent black that had consumed her. The black that had felt like a luxurious velvet mouth, savouring her and rolling her about on a star-spangled tongue that ruminated old and forgotten words that nobody knew. An ancient language of nature and creation, too massive for human perception. Had she heard any of the words spoken just now? She wasn't sure. Probably not. Her mind would surely be blown. And yet here she was now, standing on the pavement outside as if the church had spat her out. Perhaps she *had* heard but failed to understand those silver verses read aloud from an ageless golden tome. Written from the memory of all that had ever been. Translated from the dreams of all that had ever lived.

She blinked rapidly. Tried to focus. Turned to look at Smiler, to see what he looked like after their foray with the stars. She imagined his skin might glisten with cosmic dust and his eyes would shine with lightning. She thought that maybe the glittering black had stripped away all that had turned bad about him, making him beautiful again. But this wasn't so. If anything, he along with everything else around them had dulled, as though the world's contrast button had been messed with. Or as though staring into the universe's euphoria of rich black, which had bequeathed billions of untouchable electric dots of colour in a visual display that would have explained life itself had she stayed longer, had altered her vision, partially blinding her. Drunk on wonder, Callie's head swum. What had just happened? Had she fallen into herself? Was that where she was now? In some deep part of her own psyche, seeking to cure what she had become.

But no. That couldn't be the case because she could see Orion hanging low in the sky. His usual stance just to the side of Smiler's head. Then she noticed other pale stars above the church, bedecking an anaemic moon's darkening décolletage. It was dusk.

'How can it be almost night already?' she said, continuing to gaze upwards.

Still gripping her shoulders, Smiler shook her. 'We need to get going,' he urged.

'But, what just happened?' Callie had come over all lightheaded, like she was breathing thin air at high altitude. She couldn't comprehend how time had moved so quickly. How it was that she'd entered the church during daylight hours what seemed like just minutes ago, yet the sun had completed its arc of the sky and night was now creeping forth, enveloping the churchyard in menacing obscurity. 'I don't understand.'

'Neither do I.' Smiler eyed the church, his expression one of awestricken terror. 'I don't know what happened in there, it was...I dunno, it was...' He struggled to find words to describe it. 'Dark,' he said at last. 'Only, not a terrible dark. Just a dark like I've never seen before. It was *full*.'

'It was amazing,' Callie said. Her whole body tingled with the memory. 'It seemed to amplify all sense of *me*.'

'So much blackness.'

'Like being caught up in a riptide, only I knew I couldn't drown because there was no water, and it felt kind of nice so I didn't want to fight it. Does that even make sense?'

'Yes.' Smiler nodded but by no means showed as much enthusiasm as she did. 'That's exactly how it felt.'

'I'd like to do it again.'

'I'm not sure.'

'But it was so peaceful, how could you not?'

He considered this. 'Do you think that's what it feels like to be dead?'

'Maybe we are.'

'We can't be.'

'Why not?'

'We need to go.' He squeezed her shoulders again before letting his hands drop to his sides.

'You didn't answer the question.'

'We have to get back to the cabin,' he insisted. 'Now.'

'But we haven't found help.'

'After everything you've seen, do you really still hold out hope of finding someone to help us?' Smiler pulled his shirt sleeves down over his hands and shivered.

'Of course. What else is there to do?'

'We need to get back.'

'Why the urgency?'

'I'm worried about Pollyanna.'

'Why?'

'Because we left her with Thurston.'

'If you have such a bad feeling about Thurston, then how come you left her alone with him in the first place?' Callie scoffed.

'Because I thought we wouldn't be long,' he said, eyes downcast in disappointment at his huge misjudgement. 'I thought I could change your mind. I thought I could make you see how hopeless it is trying to find help.'

'You thought you could manipulate me?' Callie was furious.

'No!' He held his hands up. 'I didn't mean that at all. I just wanted you to see the village. I wanted you to understand. But now it's almost night time and that's not good. Not good at all. The last thing we should be doing is wandering around this place in the dark.'

'Why?'

He focussed on a window of the church, purposefully resisting eye contact. 'There's, er, something I haven't told you about.' He brought his hand up to his mouth to chew on the edge of his cuff.

'Oh?' Callie scowled and put her hands on her hips; trying to display more annoyance than she could muster.

'When I said there are no other people here,' he said, 'well, there aren't. But there *are* other things.'

Other things?

'Oh piss off, Golden,' she said. 'Is this a ploy to hurry me back to the cabin?'

'Not at all, I swear to God.' Something about his face told her he wasn't lying and a sense of fear was quick to fill the space between them like a plague of daddy longlegs, tingling bare skin with the same dread-feel as lanky appendages.

Other things?

There are other things.

A new chill penetrated Callie's skin, her bones absorbing most of the cold but it left its sting in her flesh.

There are other things.

She shivered and looked about the churchyard, but saw nothing different.

There are other things.

The ubiquitous feeling of complete vulnerability that

she'd had since arriving at Whispering Woods stepped up a notch, rendering her nerves as fragile as blown glass. Even the floating galaxies and unsaid truths of the church's wondrous innards were fading fast, already in danger of joining last week's dreams in a blur of irrelevance.

There are other things.

'What other things?' she said, finding her voice at last; although it was strangely monotone.

'Things that live in the woods.'

For a moment Callie couldn't breathe. What was this new torment? 'But you said earlier that we could cut through the woods!'

'Yes, during the day,' he said, as if she should know that already. 'These things are nocturnal.'

'What things?'

'Things you wouldn't want to encounter. Things I don't want to have to tell you about. Not if I don't have to.'

'But you *do* have to.'

Smiler shook his head. 'No I don't. Not yet. I don't want to spook you.'

'Too late for that.' A raven cawed far away. The noise carried on the wind like an eerie death-call straight to Callie's ears. She shivered and wrapped her arms around herself, wishing she was back at the cabin. Subsequently she felt depressed that she thought of the cabin as a safe place right now.

'Still, I'd rather not go into too much detail,' Smiler said.

'But I'd rather you did so I know exactly what it is that I need to avoid.'

'Believe me, you'd know.'

There was another caw. Much closer this time. Callie and Smiler both looked up and saw a hunched black silhouette on the church roof.

'Come on, let's go,' Smiler said. He took Callie's hand and tugged her arm gently. 'We have to get back to the cabin.' When she didn't move he started off without her, towards the church gates.

Callie gawped after him. 'But will it be safe to walk back now?'

'Possibly not.' He carried on walking in the direction of the village and its bordering woods anyway.

Reluctant to be left alone in the dark and unsure what else to do, Callie went after him. 'But what if we keep going that way?' she said, pointing behind them to the far side of the churchyard. 'What if we turn around and follow the stream?'

'We'd end up back at the village. The stream runs in a loop.'

'What about the road? If we follow the road, it'll take us somewhere eventually.'

'Same difference. It leads straight back to the village.'

'Impossible.'

'But true.'

'What if we cross the stream and head out over the fields and meadows instead?'

'Already tried it.'

'And?'

'I've never found anything.'

'You mustn't have walked far enough.'

Smiler cast a glance over his shoulder, admonishing her with narrowed eyes and thinned lips. 'I walked for two days solid. Ended up right back at the village.'

'Then you must have gone off track. Doubled back on yourself.'

He stopped walking and turned on her, his eyes almost as dangerous as Torbin Thurston's. 'Don't patronise me, Callie Crossley. You think I only tried the once? You think I'd quit that easily?' He kicked a stone. It bounced off a gravestone and left a chalky mark beneath the E in someone's name. 'Go ahead and try it, though, if that's what you want to do,' he said, waving a hand to indicate the stream that ran somewhere beyond the two new gravestones. 'But I'm going back.'

Callie crossed her arms over her chest. 'I thought you said you'd go wherever I wanted to.'

'I thought you'd have more sense!' His face softened then, as though he instantly regretted the rebuke. 'Besides,' he said. 'I'm tired. And Pollyanna needs me. And it's really not safe out here.'

Callie had seen the ferocious need in Smiler's eyes. The need to get out. He wanted to escape this place perhaps even more than she did. But the things he'd kept hidden from her – a potentially dangerous past and a knowledge of nocturnal things in the woods – caused new uncertainty to fester. Even if she hadn't started to doubt his intentions, her clothes and shoes weren't suitable to endure bad weather if another storm kicked up. She felt she had no choice but to accompany him back to the cabin.

'What about the lake?' she said, falling into step beside him. 'Have you tried crossing it?'

'I've tried building a few rafts but was never able to get it right. They either fell apart before I launched them or start sinking so that I didn't dare go far in case I drowned.' He looked away then, shame evident in his boy-ish eyes. 'I can't swim.'

Callie nodded; an idea forming. 'Okay, so that's what we'll do. We'll build a raft together. I'm sure between us we'll manage to craft something sturdy enough. Something that all four of us can get onto.'

Smiler's top lip twitched with the bare bones of a smile. A miniscule sliver of hope. 'You think?'

'Why the hell not?' she said, forcing a smile of her own, which was nothing but fake.

Neither Callie nor Smiler was filled with elation at the

thought of the task that lay ahead of them, but both were quietly determined as they walked the rest of the way back to the village. They had a plan at least. A solid one. Building a raft was the best option they had. And it was an escape route Smiler hadn't yet fully explored. For now, they just had to make it back to the cabin. Safely.

17

Pollyanna feigned a bored look of resignation and huffed like she was greatly put out. 'Alright,' she said, tapping her fingernails on the arm of her wheelchair and hoping to annoy. 'I'm Pollyanna Figg. Most people call me Pollyanna, which is fine because I never thought it pretentious. Smiler calls me Poll. Nobody ever calls me Polly. I hate Polly.' At this she gave Thurston a particularly hard stare. 'I was born and raised in Easington and still lived there, before I came here. I've got one sister. Younger. No living grandparents. I started going to drama school when I was five. When I was eleven I auditioned for a part in the long-running soap opera *Northern Way.*' She rolled her eyes at Thurston's lack of reaction. 'But you've probably never heard of it, you being down south these days. Anyway, I got accepted to play the part of problem-child Ava Tunstall.' She made quotation marks with her fingers when she said 'problem-child' and Thurston raised an ironic eyebrow. She ignored him and went on, 'They had big stories planned for Ava Tunstall and it was going to be the beginning of my acting career on screen. But the accident happened just two weeks later.' She looked down at her legs. 'And I never got to be Ava Tunstall.'

Thurston opened his mouth to say something, but judging by his expression Pollyanna imagined it would be something filled with empty condolences, so she spared them both the embarrassment and went on, 'My preferred drink is Dr Pepper, though I can barely remember what it tastes like. I don't drink alcohol.' She took a draw on her cigarette and smirked with defiance as smoke billowed back out of her. 'Because I'm too young. I got bullied often at school. I still have my tonsils. And appendix. And adenoids. But my top wisdom teeth give me gyp. My favourite food is anything but tuna. I'm fourteen and have been in love. If I could be an animal, any animal, I'd be a spider because I'd have eight legs and most people would be scared of me. My favourite colour is grey. Any shade. I know the sky is blue because of the way molecules interact with the sun's light. They disperse the blue light more than the red. I know that we're in Whispering Woods right now. But I don't know why. So there you have it, *my* life in a tiny nutshell.'

Thurston looked marginally amused, and perhaps he would have looked more so if not for the greyish pallor that spoiled anything his face might offer beyond a frown. 'Well, Pollyanna Figg,' he said, his eyes managing to maintain a smile. 'I guess that's us introduced.'

Pollyanna chewed on the corner of her bottom lip and regarded him in quiet contemplation. After a while she said, 'You really aren't Uncle Dean, are you?'

Thurston shook his head. 'Whether that's good news or bad news for you, kid, sorry but no I'm not.'

'But don't you think it's odd that you look like him?'

'Very.'

She looked towards the lake, her expression troubled. Clouds were gathering above it, preparing another storm. She wondered how big it would be and wished Smiler would hurry home.

'Do you mind if I ask what happened?' Thurston said. His eyes were on her wheelchair, indicating his curiosity, yet his body language showed a modicum of discomfort, perhaps even shame for having asked.

'Whether I do or not, you just did.' Pollyanna continued to stare out of the window, unsure if she would answer the question as he'd expected her to.

Unsure if he deserved to learn the more intricate and emotive details of her life. He held his hands up and started to verbalise an apology, but she shook her head in pardon and cut him off, deciding it wouldn't change anything if he did know. 'I went over Sarah Jane's,' she said, smoothing down the fabric of her dress, beneath which her wasted white legs protruded. 'She had a trampoline in the front garden that we used to mess about on. When Aunt Roxanne and Uncle Stevie weren't watching we used to take turns to jump off the garage roof onto it. On that particular morning, I jumped first.'

She closed her eyes as memory served her the details: everything down to the small frivolities that should have meant nothing and would have been lost to surplus detail if it had been an ordinary day, but because of the accident her mind had held onto the way her Aunt Roxanne's washing had flapped about on the washing line: a white sheet and a white duvet cover with a repetitive pink rosebud pattern. The way the mucky-white of the painted brick garage had dazzled her eyes in the sun. The way the air was thick with the aroma of freshly cut grass, which she'd known would make her sneeze as the day wore on. The way her own and Sarah Jane's arms and legs were bared to the sun. The way she'd squealed with glee as she left the garage roof. The way her bones had sounded when she hit the floor. The way Sarah Jane had screamed. The way the black of her yo-yoing consciousness had glittered. But most of all, the way the pain had felt. And then the fear.

'The canvas was split,' she said, opening her eyes again. 'I went straight through and hit the concrete patio beneath. Broke my spine in three places. Haven't been able to walk since.'

Thurston sucked in air through his teeth.

'But hey, that's life,' she said, shrugging her bony shoulders and trying to appear more stoic than was probably convincing. She didn't want him to know that she'd tried and failed to make peace with the situation at least a million times over. Didn't want him to know how vulnerable and angry she still felt. 'Life served me up a great big shit sandwich that day,' she said. 'Someone else took the part of Ava Tunstall. That was me finished.'

Thurston mulled over potential responses before finally going with, 'Weren't there other roles you could've auditioned for instead?' Then realising he sounded every bit as condescending as he'd hoped not to, he shook his head as much as to say that he didn't expect an answer.

But Pollyanna didn't mind. It was a valid question. 'I lost interest. Didn't care much about anything anymore. Not for a long while. After I'd spent months adjusting to life in a wheelchair, I *did* come round to the idea of acting again though. Just before I ended up here as it happens. I'd heard that a new character was to be introduced to *Tyne Line*. A girl with spinal injuries, much like my own. It felt like it was meant to be. I mean, the very idea that I might get to play a part in such a popular show was really exciting. It gave me a new goal and purpose in life.' She breathed in wearily and rolled her eyes. 'But then, as I said, *this* happened.'

'Shit, that's terrible. I mean, such a shame.' And there was nothing but sincerity that Pollyanna could take from his remark.

'I'm sure you'll get there eventually,' he said. 'You seem like you're pretty independent and strong-willed.'

This prompted a laugh from her; a genuine sound that lit up her eyes and turned her into a normal, fun-loving fourteen-year-old for the briefest of moments. 'What you mean is that you think I'm a pain in the arse.'

'Well, yes. I do.' He laughed too. 'But what I meant is that I'm sure you'll figure something out.'

'Hardly.' She became sullen again. Her shoulders hunched and she picked at the hem of her dress. 'This place continues to serve me up shit sandwiches. It won't let me go.'

Thurston looked around the lounge, as if directly acknowledging her supposed captor. Shadows had changed position and it was impossible to tell if they were slow dancing to the sun's pace or if they were playing independent mind games. The cabin itself was quiet. Resting, perhaps. Watching, most like.

'You talk like you think this place is alive or something,' Thurston said.

'Maybe it is.'

18

Thurston lay on the couch, slipping in and out of nightmares. Each time he woke his arms and legs thrashed out at some invisible assailant. He felt increasingly feverish to the point where his whole body ached and his shirt was damp with sweat. Sometimes it was easy for him to imagine that he was lying on his own couch, in his own home. But then reality would settle on him like a cold blanket and he'd remember where he was. Sometimes Pollyanna would ask if he was alright, but mostly she sat by the window unspeaking. Waiting for Smiler to return.

The pain in Thurston's chest was still a constant low throbbing, perhaps even more so now he was aware of the crude black stitches that cinched the wound there. Even in his dreams the stitches plagued him. One time they were glistening black worms that had been woven into his skin. They squirmed and tugged, but when they couldn't break free tunnelled down through his flesh and muscle with bitey chomping teeth till their bodies got fat and they reached his heart: a juicy red apple with slick pulmonary arteries. Another time the stitches were leeches, binding the jagged edges of the wound like gleaming, pulsating laces. They drained him of his soul as well as his blood and left his body nothing more than a desiccated flap of leather. Most frightening was when the stitches were lengths of hair as thick as nylon, stripped from the mane of the last in a line of four giant obsidian horses. Black figures with blank faces looked down from the first three mounts, but Death sneered at Thurston from atop the fourth with glowing red eyes. Even when Thurston snapped out of the nightmare he could still see the eyes wherever he looked; scorched onto the ceiling, burnt onto the sky, charred onto the wood panelled walls that encapsulated him.

When the atmosphere's molecules were scattering more red light than blue to make a pink sunset sky, Pollyanna baked potatoes. Neither she nor Thurston ate much. By the time the sky was black they couldn't see anything outside, only the reflection of the lounge and duplicates of themselves.

'Do you think they'll be okay?' Thurston said.

Pollyanna was hunched close to the window. His question made her spine straighten. 'I dunno.'

Thurston shuffled about to find a more comfortable position, but couldn't. 'How well do you know Smiler?'

'As well as I've known anyone, I suppose.'

'Is he a decent bloke?'

Pollyanna nodded without needing to ponder the question. She tapped the end of a cigarette with her bony finger. Ash broke away and fell to the floor.

'And he knows the area well?' Thurston persisted.

'He should do, he's been here a while.' She took a draw. Tobacco and paper crackled to ash.

'How long's a while?'

'How big's Titan in square yards?'

'What's Titan?'

'Saturn's largest moon.'

Thurston's eyes narrowed. 'How should I know?'

'Exactly.' Pollyanna flashed him a grin, which he couldn't help but reciprocate. The kid had character.

They listened to the wind pick up speed. It blasted the cabin with handfuls of leaves and other debris. Callie and Smiler's absence had grown into something impossibly large in the empty spaces of the cabin. A momentous feeling of uselessness shared between Thurston and Pollyanna made the air thick with dread.

'How well do you know Callie Crossley?' Pollyanna

said.

Thurston rolled onto his side. He kept his head on the cushion and looked at her. 'Not massively. She's a friend, but not a particularly close one.'

'But you like her?'

'Yeah.' He smiled then. 'But not in the way you're probably thinking.'

Pollyanna mirrored his smile, only hers was sly. 'Whatever.'

'Yeah. Whatever.' Gripping the end of the chair arm, Thurston began to pull himself up. 'Anyway, I'm thinking I should go out and look for them.'

'You can't!' She jerked forward in her seat at the suggestion.

'Why not?'

'It's dark.'

'I'd noticed.'

'You can't go wandering around Whispering Woods in the dark.'

'I'm touched.' Thurston lightly touched his chest and winked. 'I thought you of all people would be pleased if I got lost.' He was working for a smile, but instead got a scowl.

'It's not a case of getting lost,' she said. 'There are things out there.'

'What things?'

'Bad things.'

'Sounds scary.'

'They are.'

He was standing now, waiting for his body to adjust to the strain of having done so; his hands poised and ready to grab the couch if he came over wobbly. 'Are they bad things from the stories that Uncle Dean filled your head with?'

'No.' Her mouth tightened at the apparent insult of being considered childish. 'I've seen them myself. They come out of the woods at night.'

'What are they?'

'Sort of like wolves, only not. They're pretty big and not normal. There are two of them.'

'Some local probably has a couple of malamutes that roam free.'

'They're definitely not dogs.' This time she looked at him like he was silly.

'How can you be sure?'

'Because malamutes don't walk on their hind legs any more than normal wolves do.'

19

Bare branches were black crackles against a deep violet sky. An eerie calm to the incoming night amplified Callie's and Smiler's careful footfalls on dead leaves and loose dirt, revealing their whereabouts despite their best efforts to sneak. It was as though the woods had captured them in a bubble of weather-resistant stillness and was revelling in their fear and exposing them to whatever might be searching. Callie still wasn't sure. The as yet unidentified antagonists that Smiler had merely warned her about had grown and gained shape in her mind till she had by now half-convinced herself that there was a bunch of demented ex-residents of the village who had taken to the woods decades ago after being infected by contaminated drinking water, and who now looked like the monstrous set from *The Hills Have Eyes*. She imagined she and Smiler might be bludgeoned over the head at any moment and dragged off to a den somewhere, where they'd be tortured in horrific ways. Of course, that was ridiculous. Logic told her so. Still, the idea of being back at the cabin was idyllic right now.

They stuck to the middle of the dirt road, maintaining a hasty pace. Whispering Woods bore down on them on both sides and the deserted village was by now a difficult sprint behind them. Callie thought she and Smiler might as well be the last two people on Earth, because even though she knew Thurston and Pollyanna were just a few miles down the road, covering those few miles safely while walking a perilous stretch of land amongst unseen danger seemed an impossible goal. They were a whole universe away, which meant that her little pocket of existence as a human being, right now, was shared only with Miles Golden. The ex teen star. The acquitted felon. Which might be laughable, she thought, if not so hideously terrifying.

Callie wished the wind would pick up, to mask their progress from whatever it was that Smiler said sought them. But the wind owed them no allegiance, it simply held its breath and waited; the silence unnatural. Disconcerting. When she could bear the suspense no longer, she said, 'Tell me what's in the woods, Smiler.'

She felt him bristle against her arm. When she looked at him, his face was cast in shadow. He held a forefinger to his lips and shushed her.

She wasn't deterred. She needed to know. 'What's in the woods, Golden?' This time her tone had a hardened edge and everything including the moon stopped to listen.

'Forget about it,' Smiler said, in a hissed whisper.

Callie stopped walking and put her fists on her hips, a flash of anger taking the edge off the palpable feeling of dread she'd allowed to build. 'Just tell me!'

Spinning round, Smiler grabbed her by the arm, his fingers too harsh, his grip too tight, and urged her onwards. 'Okay, okay, I will. But keep walking,' he said. 'And be quiet!'

Too late. Somewhere off to their left a branch snapped. It sounded like dry bone splintering underfoot and it echoed through the black woods like an explosion. Smiler's hand tightened even more on Callie's arm, but she didn't notice. She grasped for his free arm with both of her hands and held on, her heart a deafening pulse in her head. 'What was that?'

'Shhh.' Smiler tugged, urging her on. She didn't resist and soon they were walking faster than before in an awkward huddle of entangled arms and clutching hands. Neither of them could hear much above their own panicked breathing, but when there was another crunch of breaking wood, closer than before, Callie's throat tightened and she made a startled squeaking noise. Both of them stopped to listen.

Quietness ensued.

There are other things out there.

Their fingers squeezed hard enough to leave bruises on each other's skin and Callie wondered if she'd ever be able to move her legs again. Fear had rooted her feet firmly to the ground.

There are other things out there.

Clouds had moved overhead without them having noticed, draping the moon like thick gauzy voile. They stood staring into the moving stillness of Whispering Woods. Everything at ground level was depicted in murky shades of grey and black, so it was impossible to make out what was tree and what was shadow.

There are other things out there.

Callie's chest hurt. She worried her heart might do something dysfunctional and debilitating. She willed it to keep working. No way could Smiler carry her back to the cabin if she flaked out.

There are other things out there.

'Now's about the right time to tell me,' she said. The whites of Smiler's eyes glinted and she could feel his quick breath on her cheek. She didn't think he'd answer, but he licked his lips and whispered the word 'Wolfmen,' as if it was code for something she should already know.

'What?'

'At least two of them.'

Callie stumbled for words. Stumbled for clarity. 'Are you taking the piss?'

'I swear to God.'

'There's no such thing.'

'I knew you'd say that.' His voice was a frustrated hiss. 'That's why I told you to forget about it, but you just wouldn't let it go.' His fingers were still tight on her arm and she could feel him trembling.

'So, what?' Her stomach churned. 'You expect me to believe there are werewolves out there?'

'Wolfmen,' he corrected.

'What's the fucking difference?'

'They walk on hind legs and don't turn into men.' His eyes glinted again. 'At least, I don't think so. But maybe they do. I dunno.'

'Ha-fucking-ha!' Callie nipped his forearm, a sharp tweak between thumb and forefinger that made him suck air in through his teeth. 'When we get back to the cabin you're dead meat, Golden.'

'*Why?*'

'For being a total dickhead.'

'Hey, I'm not!' he whisper-shouted. 'I'm being serious.' He jabbed a finger at the blackness of the woods. 'There are two great big fucking *things* out there. In the trees. I'm telling you. So. Shut. The fuck. Up!'

Neither prompted the other to move, but they started creeping forward again. Both needed the sanctity of the cabin. Right now.

'If there really are wolfmen out there, then why the hell didn't we stay at the village till morning?' Callie said, incensed that either she was being taken for a fool or led to certain death.

'Because we need to get back to Pollyanna.'

'Fuck Pollyanna! What about *us?* I'm worried about us.'

'Well I'm sure we'd stand more of a chance of making it back in one piece if you'd just be quiet.'

Callie's lips pinched. She wanted to argue, but knew he was probably right. She wanted to slap his hands away, but knew she'd regret it. Regardless of what she thought of him, she needed him to lean on to make it along the wooded road, which seemed to stretch on forever. Otherwise she thought she might just freeze with fright and take root alongside the trees. Woodland smells of turned earth, fungi and the decomposition of old leaves pervaded her thoughts, making her think of the cabin. She wondered if the cabin was made from trees felled in Whispering Woods. Wouldn't be at all surprised if it was. Whispering Woods was all around her and inside her, suffocating her with its oppressiveness. She had an overpowering urge to flee in the opposite direction. To go back to the church. But she was closer to the cabin now, closer to the lake: perhaps their only escape route. And closer to Thurston. Because despite what Smiler thought about him, Callie couldn't quite allow herself to think that Thurston might be connected with Uncle Dean. He couldn't be.

Could he?

A shimmying noise above made Callie and Smiler jump, but they realised with some small relief that the wind was picking up, making the treetops chatter. The susurration continued to develop, however, till it was a chorus of voices all talking at the same time. Callie looked at Smiler with dread, but he didn't seem to notice that anything was different.

'Can't you hear that?' she said.

'Hear what?'

'The trees.'

'It's just the wind.' He sounded mildly vexed at her insistence on talking.

Couldn't he hear the furore of whispered words being shaken from the branches? The voices that were filling her head with an avalanche of nonsense, like lyrics from a forgotten lullaby being regurgitated in a mixed up order. She wanted to close her eyes and scream for them to stop, but she couldn't. She had to stay quiet, but on and on and on they went...*Do you know any stories? Suppose that depends. Lived here as it happens.*

Something really awful. Take a guess. Suppose that depends. Why does anyone do anything? Suppose that depends. All except the small boy. But why? But why? But why? But why? That's just how it is, sweetheart.

Another mile down and Callie wasn't sure her nerves could withstand much more. Her emotional state had surpassed any physical sense of feeling, she didn't even care that Pollyanna's shoes had bitten the skin off her heels. She looked across at Smiler but couldn't see his expression because dark shadows of trees raked across his face. She felt lightheaded for the umpteenth time that day, like she was having some kind of out of body experience. But on she walked. Down the horrible road that led to the horrible cabin which was surrounded by horrible woods, while the onset of deepest night chased at their heels. And all the while the trees kept talking. Teasing her with the notion of something that had happened here. Something significant. *Something really awful. Suppose that depends. Why does anyone do anything? Take a guess, sweetheart.*

'By the way.' Callie looked at Smiler again, still not really seeing him. She needed to speak, however quietly, before the trees drove her mad. 'I think the cabin is haunted.'

'What makes you say that?' She saw a flash of white. His eyes.

'I've heard someone talking. A woman. The one I heard in your room, maybe. I heard her downstairs too. And I felt someone touch me when there was no one there.'

'And you chose now of all times to bring it up?' Smiler still sounded vaguely annoyed. Not what she'd expected. 'As if things aren't shit-scary enough right now.'

'I've been thinking,' she said, ignoring his complaint. 'What if it's Pollyanna's aunt?'

Smiler was quiet but she knew he was looking at her.

'What if Roxanne Miller is dead?' she put it more plainly.

'Then why would she communicate with you and not Pollyanna?'

'I don't know, maybe I'm more susceptible to hearing ghost-talk.'

'Isn't it possible you imagined it?'

Ha! Callie almost laughed. *If only you could hear what the fucking trees are saying!*

They walked without speaking for a while, Callie trying to ignore Whispering Woods as it moved and whispered all around them. When the cabin eventually came into view like some nightmarish mirage in the far distance, shapes in the treetops moved in a black scattering that flew closer. Soon the ravens were circling overhead, cawing tale-telling stories that would be enough to worry the too distant morning with pangs of grating darkness had it cared enough to listen.

Little bastards are ratting us out!

Callie quickened her step and Smiler matched her pace. They let go of each other and broke into a jog. The finishing line was so close, yet still so far away. Gravel skittered noisily beneath their feet and their jogging turned into a full-blown run. Soon Callie's legs no longer felt like her own. She was working them, pumping her feet up and down, but couldn't feel them.

From in the distance or maybe close by, from somewhere distinct yet everywhere and nowhere, came a terrible sound. A sound they'd hoped not to hear. A long, harrowing howl.

No! No! No!

Callie's scalp prickled.

Then there was a second howl in answer to the first, in what Callie could only interpret as two animals' communication through a primal language of hunger and teamwork, cunning and stealth. She was panting now, not even trying to control her breathing because she didn't care how loud she was. It no longer mattered. The wolfmen knew exactly where she and Smiler were. Perhaps they had all along; stalking them this far, heightening the anticipation of the thrill of the kill having allowed them to hope they could make it back to the cabin. But now their paws thundered heavily through the woods.

Now the chase was on.

20

The night air nipped with insistent vicious teeth, making Thurston's skin hurt. He imagined the fluid in his spinal cord was simmering with fever and his blood was boiling around muscle and bone. He'd made it as far as the veranda but begun to wonder what the hell he thought he was doing. He felt weak and woozy, and shivered so much with hot and cold chills that his teeth knocked together. Even his eyeballs hurt. How did he hope to find Callie and the young actor in this state?

For a moment he thought about going back inside, back to the relative comfort of the couch, though he quickly dismissed the idea. Not because the cabin bothered him, but because Pollyanna would think he'd chickened out, given all she'd told him about the wolves-but-not-quite that walked on hind legs.

Chrissakes, what a load of shit!

But that's what you got when a couple of kids with nothing better to do made up stories to scare each other.

The light from the lounge cast a glow as subtle as slug trail across the lawn and the Bentley glistened like a giant beetle. Thurston looked to the end of the garden where the lake lay silently in wait. For what, he didn't know, but he could see its foreshore looked slick with hostility and hungry for something. He didn't believe in bipedal wolves any more than he believed trees could talk, but Thurston could tell that the night was bringing something bad. He could feel it on his skin as a looming premonition. The woodland air was charged with the decay of many dead things; an underlying reek on a breeze that should have been fresh. He tipped his head back and looked up at the starless sky, imagining just for a moment that he was at home. Standing in his own garden with Betsy, his Kerry blue, at his feet. Clouds had worn thin in places and he saw the perfect circle of the moon behind. It was a phosphorescent white coin that he thought would fit neatly in his palm.

It had to be bloody full!

He lumbered down the veranda steps, leaning heavily on the rain-slimy bannister, onto the gravelled path that led along the side of the cabin and round to the back where the access road was. His legs felt weak with the exertion and his stomach had tightened, readying to vomit in protest if he didn't ease up. He imagined Pollyanna was watching him from the lounge window. Resisting the urge to turn to see if her black bug-eyes were staring back, he clenched his teeth and hobbled down the side of the cabin. Out of sight.

Above the *shhh-shhh* of gravel beneath his feet, Thurston couldn't hear anything besides the distant subtleties of the woods; branches relaxing, trees sighing, ravens repositioning. The night was altogether too quiet, in a brooding kind of way, as though it was holding a secret about to be revealed. A secret that would have the potential to ravage friendships and blur the boundaries between sanity and madness. Because Thurston could feel the threat of death hanging thick in the air. It touched his skin and he breathed it in. It filled his lungs and he felt the stitches in his chest tighten. The red eyes of Death came back to him in a flash of clarity, all too real. Had his dream been an omen? He rested against the back wall of the cabin to catch his breath, cursing his eagerness to come outside and play the hero. He was in no fit state to be any such thing. Pain played his nerve-endings like a jagged violin bow, zinging to his detriment. All he wanted was his own bed and a whole load of painkillers. And Betsy curled up next to him, her wet nose nuzzling his neck.

Poor Betsy.

He hoped Freya would take care of her till he got home. Whenever that might be.

Freya.

The thought of his girlfriend made him frown with guilt. She was twenty-one, he was thirty-five, and apart from Thai food, an adventurous wanderlust and Benedict Cumberbatch's Sherlock (albeit for differing reasons), they had nothing in common. Subconsciously the considerable age gap had always fed Thurston's ego, but right now, with some startling new insight, he was able to acknowledge his own shallowness. He felt deeply ashamed. Freya had long blonde hair, a lithe body and a youthful sparkle in her eyes, the kind of natural effervescence that couldn't be recaptured or bought back once it had dulled with time. Thurston had been swept along by her infectiousness and she said she was in love with him, but he had never reciprocated the sentiment. Not even falsely.

He pushed off the cabin's back wall and hobbled onto the narrow dirt track that separated the cabin from the woods. The nearest trees were jagged giants, arms outstretched to the sky. To the left the road ran to a dead end. He presumed Callie and Smiler must have gone right, unless they'd cut through the woods. Which he had no intention of doing.

Just ten minutes. I'll walk for ten minutes and if there's nothing I'll go back. Then at least I can say I tried. At least I can say I did something.

It frustrated Thurston to be so incapacitated. He was independent and self-sufficient; it didn't sit well with him to rely on others. So when Callie and Miles Golden had failed to return by sunset, the pressure to do something – anything at all – had grown till he couldn't stay on the couch a moment longer, even though moving around made him feel sick with pain.

He clutched a hand to his chest as he limped along the road, his mind more willing than his feet. With his fingertips, he could feel the stiffness of black twine through his shirt and found it hard to concentrate on much beyond the gruesome wound someone had inflicted on him. He wanted to take the stitches out. Felt repulsed by them. Sickened by the symbolism, whatever it might be. Sickened by the vulgarity of the way he'd been handled. Whoever had done this, whoever had seen fit to disfigure him, would pay the price. Of that he was sure. It was the thought of revenge that spurred him on. He hissed angrily with each pained step.

Branches ruffled further ahead and a furore of raven-squabble broke out. Thurston stopped to listen. He looked up and saw a mass of blackness take to the sky. He wondered what might have disturbed them, then blanched when he heard a different noise. Urgent footfalls. A slapping of feet on earth. Coming towards him. Someone in a hurry. No. There was more than one set of feet. He strained to see past the dark but saw nothing but a patchwork of black shadows against blacker night, fringed by nearby trees. His whole body became rigid and he thought that if he moved again his joints might shatter. But he had to. He had to move. Because what if it wasn't Callie Crossley and Miles Golden running towards him? Or what if it was? Why were they running? He pitched himself, ready to run in either direction. Then the night smashed like glass all around him with the onset of a howl.

Christ Almighty!

He edged backwards, his feet stuttering on gravel, his eyes still focussed ahead. Then came another howl. This time from somewhere else. Somewhere closer.

Oh man!

Movement up ahead made him freeze again. Two figures. Running fast. Blonde hair. Miles Golden and…

Callie!

Blood roared in Thurston's ears and he wasn't sure if that's all he could hear or if there was a thundering of large paws churning up undergrowth. Wolves on hind legs.

No fucking way!

Callie was some way behind Smiler. Her arms were bent and fists punched the air with forward thrusts as she tried to catch up. Branches snapped and crashed somewhere amongst the trees, too close for comfort. Thurston waved his arms, beckoning to Callie, but he froze in horror when something barrelled out from the trees behind her. Everything else ceased to exist then, everything except Callie, Miles Golden and the dark hulking figure that moved like an animal. On all fours. It was the size of a grizzly bear but looked decidedly canine. Larger than any malamute or wolf had a right to be. Thurston hoped that Callie wouldn't turn round to look, because if she did, if she saw what he saw, he thought she would surely melt to the floor. His own legs were just about holding out, staying solid.

Animalistic grunts of excitement and exertion were loud above everything else. Thurston imagined the sound would be hot and deafening to Callie. He stood and watched, helpless to do much else but will her to run faster. The thing behind was closing in and would soon be able to swipe out and bring her down.

'Run, Callie. *RUN!*' he screamed, finding his voice at last.

Which prompted Smiler to turn his head, to look back. Thurston heard the young actor yelp, then watched as he veered off to the right and ploughed straight into the spiky blackness of Whispering Woods.

'Smiler!' Callie screamed his name with such terror attached to it that Thurston stopped breathing. But when the beast swerved and followed Smiler into the woods,

leaving Callie on the road, unpursued, he began waving his arms again and urged, 'Come on, Cal! *Run!*'

He could see her face now. And her confusion. She carried on coming towards him, her feet pounding the ground, her breaths coming hard and fast. When she reached him, she slowed to a canter and Thurston picked up a jog to move alongside her. He slung an arm across her shoulders and she gripped his hand. Thurston thought he might well pass out with the pain. They hurried to the cabin. Thurston misjudged the back corner and slammed his shoulder against the wall. Callie managed to stop him from falling to the ground and they stumbled along the side of the cabin together then up the veranda steps, in a bundle of grasping arms and shaky legs. There were no more sounds to suggest they were being followed, but this didn't ease their panic. Thurston pulled open the door and they spilled into the cabin, into the musty hallway. Both breathless. Fighting for air. Thurston's throat felt raw, as though he'd drunk fire. He leaned against the door and breathed. It was all he could do. Callie slid down the wall. She sat with her knees pulled up to her chest, then her face crumpled and she began to cry. Thurston pushed himself away from the door and hunkered down next to her. 'Shhh,' he told her, stroking her hair.

She looked at him but didn't seem to see.

'Come here.' He gathered her into his arms.

She didn't resist and rested her chin on his shoulder. 'You saw it, didn't you?' she said. 'You saw it.'

'Shhh,' he said again, gripping her tighter, knowing that neither of them would sleep much that night.

'What was it?' She pushed away so she could look at him.

Thurston frowned. He'd rather not dwell on the thing out there. Whatever it was. He'd never seen anything like it and he didn't want to ever again. 'I don't know. I really don't know.'

'And…Smiler. What about Smiler?'

He shrugged. He didn't have the answers she sought and right now he had a new problem. A problem all of his own. A problem that filled him with quickening dread. Now that he was in the hallway, safe but exerted, he was aware of something most alarming: he didn't have a heartbeat.

21

'I have to go back out.' Callie paced about, raking her fingers through her hair. She couldn't keep still. Couldn't get Smiler out of her head.

'No,' Thurston said. He looked on the verge of collapse, clutching at his waist with both hands. His face retained a film of feverish sweat and his skin was the colour of wallpaper paste. A grazed swelling on his eyebrow extended down to make the area around his left eye puffy and darkened. His lips drew back as he spoke, 'You can't. It's too dangerous.'

'But I have to.'

'What happened?' Pollyanna's voice was an unexpected addition to the gloom of the hallway. She appeared in the doorway like a spectral shadow and looked between Callie and Thurston. Her eyes conveyed a quiet dread as she asked the question that reinforced Callie's guilt, 'Where's Smiler?'

Callie made for the door resolute in her decision to go back out, but Thurston was surprisingly quick to stop her. He put his large hands on her shoulders and held her firm. 'No, Cal,' he said, his voice a strained bark. 'What the hell do you expect to do out there?'

'I don't know,' she said, both surprised and discomfited by his strength. 'But we can't just leave him.'

'There are at least two of those *things* out there,' he reminded her. 'Even if Golden managed to get away, he's likely to be hiding up a tree or something.'

'So?' Callie shook her head, perplexed. 'What do you suggest we do?'

'Wait.'

'For what?' She shrugged away from his hands, angry at him for trying to undermine her both physically and mentally.

'Morning. That's all we can do.'

'But what if he's hurt?' Pollyanna said, her black eyes wide, childlike and needy. 'What if he needs help now?'

'There's nothing we *can* do to help.' Thurston's own eyes showed vexed frustration. He'd moved and was blocking the door with his body now. 'It'd be suicide to go wandering back out in the dark. Even if *I* was well enough what good would that do? Those things are easily three times as big as me.'

Callie closed her eyes and massaged her forehead with anxious fingers. She knew that what he was saying was true, but his logical reasoning didn't make it any easier to accept that they were in no position to offer help to Smiler. She shook her head despairingly and turned, unable to face him anymore, unable to face anyone, and slouched through to the lounge. Her limbs felt heavy, her heart heavier still.

'So that's it then?' Pollyanna called. 'You're just going to leave him out there to die?'

Callie sat down on the couch and buried her face in her hands. She felt drained to the point of numbness. 'Thurston's right, if we go outside we're as good as dead.' *Then it would mean that what Smiler did would have been for nothing. He saved us. He saved* me. Her eyes became hot with tears. She readily accepted that she bore some responsibility for what had happened to Smiler. If she'd believed him when he'd told her there was nothing in the village, they might not have made the trip. If she'd run that bit faster, he might not have had to take a diversion into the woods to save her sorry arse. If she'd insisted that they stayed at the church, they might have been safe. *If, if, if.* All useless hindsight that didn't change a thing.

The couch shifted as someone sat down next to her. She didn't turn to see. Knew it was Thurston. Then she felt his hand on her back. Warm. Sturdy. The more vulnerable side of her, she thought, would like to seek refuge in his arms and stay there till morning. Like a child, shedding all responsibility. But the fiercer part of her wanted to push him off and to tell him to get the fuck away. He seemed so calm. Too blasé. He didn't share her guilt. It wasn't his fault.

That's right, it's not his fault.

Her shoulders sagged and she chose neither to crumble into him nor to slap him away. Instead she allowed his hand to rub warm, soothing circles on her back.

'Why don't you try and get some sleep?' he said.

She did look at him then. 'How the hell can I sleep with all this going on?'

He looked sorry for the clear inanity of his suggestion. For inciting such a backlash. Seemingly at a loss for what else to say or do, he touched her hand; an overly intimate response that forced her to maintain eye contact. Then, as if obliged to say something, anything, he said, 'We'll look for him in the morning. Together. Or I can go out and you can stay here, in case…well, you don't have to go.'

What he meant was that he didn't expect Smiler to be alive, she thought, and that if they found any dismembered body parts it might be too distressing for her. 'Of course I'm bloody going,' she said, scowling at his implied doubt over her strength of character. This second rebuke prompted him to move his hand back to his lap and for this Callie was sorry.

In the ensuing silence the cabin offered no comfort. It stifled their lungs with its fetid smell and coated their skin with a grimy chill. Pollyanna had moved to her usual spot by the window, but nobody had seen her get there. She was motionless and didn't speak. In fact, nobody said anything else. All three of them held onto their own thoughts, all of them eager for morning. Thurston stayed close to Callie and managed to doze on and off, in short bouts of closed-eye stillness with his neck cricked to one side. Having little to no emotional bond with Smiler, Callie wasn't surprised by the ease with which he let go. She watched him each time he slept and was confounded by the confusion of emotions that welled up inside her; a love-hate blend mostly dominated by anger. But her anger at him, she knew, was a direct result of being angry with herself. This anger also extended to Smiler and Pollyanna. And the trees. The bloody trees. She closed her eyes and was convinced she could see the red that was running through her own veins. She heard voices, the memory of the trees talking in the woods. She tried to remember what they'd said. Tried to make sense of their words. *That's just how it is, sweetheart. How what is? Lived here as it happens. Right here? Something really awful. Like what? Take a guess. I couldn't possibly. Suppose that depends. On what? Why does anyone do anything? Suppose that depends. Exactly! All except the small boy. What boy? But why? But why? But why indeed! It doesn't make sense. That's just how it is, sweetheart.* She clutched her head and stifled a sob.

When, eventually, the lake could be defined as a separate entity to the night, and the lazy sun was approaching without haste, Callie stood up. Thurston's weary but alert blue eyes opened and he watched her. She could tell he hadn't really been sleeping because of the instant level of awareness in his expression, which in turn made her wonder if he'd known she'd been watching him. 'All this sitting about's driving me nuts,' she said, feeling awkward as well as the need to explain herself. 'I'm going to take a shower. It'll keep me busy till it's time to head out.'

Thurston lifted his eyebrows, such a minute tic it was hard to tell if it was in direct response to what she'd said. Then he closed his eyes and resumed apparent restfulness. Pollyanna didn't react at all. She carried on staring at the outside world as though nothing within the cabin existed.

Callie trudged off to the bathroom, where she turned the shower on and waited till steam billowed above the plain white shower curtain, hitting the ceiling and spilling out into the rest of the bathroom, before stripping her clothes off. The showerhead was affixed to white tiles above a standard white bathtub and along the same wall was a toilet and small frosted window. The window had no blind or any other covering, but Callie didn't care. Peeping Toms were the least of her worries. On the wall opposite the bath was a sink and large mirror. The bathroom was basic but functional. In need of a good scrubbing. Dirt was ingrained in the grouting on the wall and floor tiles and mould spores decorated the ceiling above the window wall. Callie hung her clothes on a peg on the back of the door and stepped into the bath, careful not to let the grubby shower curtain touch her. Jets of water covered her face with a rush of hotness that stole her breath. A metal soap holder, screwed to the wall at elbow level, held a bar of soap that was sitting in a pool of white scummy water. Callie left the soap where it was and just stood beneath the water, allowing the heat to thaw her bones and ease her aching muscles. She stayed there thinking, till her skin was red and her thoughts were even more so with the pounding of her own blood and the sound of someone else's words. *Something really awful.* The trees in her head. *Take a guess.* Bony black silhouettes. *Lived here as it happens.* Moving and swaying. *All except.* The hush-a-hush-hush of leaves. Blowing. *The small boy.* And the snarling, chasing something. *Something really awful.* Something worse than hate. *But why?* Desire. *Suppose that depends.* The pounding of paws on earth like a rapturous heart. And the howling. A longing, needing, wanting. *But why? That's just how it is, sweetheart.* No! I want... I want... I want... *Take a guess.* All of the time. All of the time! *Why does anyone do anything, sweetheart?* Obsession? *As it happens.* Yes.

When she imagined the sky might be some shade of sugared almond and she felt sick with a sense of vertigo because of her own thoughts, Callie turned off the shower and pulled the curtain open. Beads of swirling steam clung to the cold air, creating droplets of water on the porcelain sink and toilet. She reached over for the fresh towel she'd left in the basin and saw that the mirror above it was opaque with condensation. As she wrapped herself in the towel, her body pricked with gooseflesh. Not because the morning chill overpowered the shower's effects, but because she heard a voice right there in the room with her. Clear. Real. 'How can she be here, Dean? She can't be!'

Dean!

Uncle Dean?

It was the same voice that Callie had heard coming from Smiler's room the day before, only this time it was uncomfortably close.

'Who's there?' she said, doubting her own sanity.

No answer.

The trees?

A sharp burst of water spurted from the showerhead and landed on the enamel by Callie's feet with a heart-thumping jolt. Ghost fingers touched her scalp. She pulled the towel tighter around her body and listened to the ceiling fan that continued to burr with a normality that somehow seemed to negate the voice she thought she'd heard. But she *had* heard it. She knew it. Slowly, tentatively, she stepped from the bath and for reasons unknown felt compelled to wipe the steam away from the mirror. The film of damp greyness she now thought might be concealing a parallel world of dead things, because the mirror was some portal. A window for the cabin's victims to reach back through. With an arm outstretched, she leaned forward and took a deep breath.

This is silly. You're being silly.

Her hand was shaking, her nerves shot.

Using her palm, she cleared away the excess moisture in one quick swipe.

And that's when she saw a woman with long black hair staring straight back at her. Callie had never seen a ghost before and reeled at its ordinariness. Her wet feet slipped on the floor tiles and she floundered for a moment, trying to regain some balance, but gravity brought her down hard, smacking the back of her head against the edge of the bath. Then everything glittered black.

When she came round, Callie reached for her head and groaned. For a fleeting moment she could have been in her own bed with a stinking hangover, but the red-black pain from the crack of enamel against her head pressed against the backs of her eyes with a ferociousness that snatched away the thought before it was fully formed. Her elbows hurt and coccyx throbbed. She was on the bathroom floor. In the cabin. And she'd seen a ghost. The fluorescence of the ceiling light shimmered like stardust and she worried she'd slip out of consciousness again. Securing the towel, which had come loose during her fall, Callie sat up and leaned against the bath panel. Hardly daring to look but needing to, she saw that the mirror was now clear, reflecting only white tiles and ceiling.

The woman was gone.

Elsewhere in the cabin a door slammed, making the bath panel tremble behind her. Urgent footsteps made

Callie sit up straighter. A familiar voice was then calling her name. She scrabbled to her feet and caught sight of her own haunted face in the mirror. *'Smiler!'*

22

Callie flung open the bathroom door and fled through the cabin. She clutched the back of her head with one hand, to lessen the thudding soreness that resonated through her skull after each crashing step, and gripped the towel fold at her chest with the other. When she got to the lounge door she came to a sudden halt, mouth agape. Smiler was in front of the wood burner. Every part of his skin and clothes was caked with dry mud.

'Holy shit, Golden!' Rising hysteria made Callie feel like laughing, but she found she couldn't even summon a smile. 'You're alive!' She hadn't known what to expect, what state she might find him in. Perhaps better. Probably worse. But he was standing and moving and that was great. And all of him seemed to be intact.

The whites of his eyes appeared whiter than usual, contrasted against the mud mask. But his teeth were just as yellow when he smiled at the sight of her there. He lifted his arms as if to validate his present state of being alive and said, 'Just about.'

Thurston was standing behind the couch, his hands gripping the leather so hard his knuckles were white. 'Looks like you got off pretty lightly, all things considered.'

Smiler was taken aback by this criticism or doubt or whatever it was. He gawped at Thurston for a moment then shrugged. 'I guess luck was on my side.'

'How did you manage to stay alive? All night. Out there.' Thurston's face displayed all the cynicism that his tone implied.

'Frigging hell, what's this?' Smiler's fists tightened at his sides and his eyes glowered. 'I gave them the slip and found a hollow tree to hide inside, is that okay?'

'Pretty convenient.'

Dried mud cracked on Smiler's brow. 'It certainly didn't *feel* convenient.'

'Did you stay in the tree all night?' Pollyanna asked, trying to sound casual in an indifferent kind of way. Her eyes betrayed her awe, however, and it was astoundingly clear to everyone else in the room that Smiler was something of an idol to her. Much more than a teenager's saccharine dream of cherry lips and dripping honey. Ever since he had arrived at the cabin he had wasp-stung her heart with a fervour that neutralised her acid tongue with many imagined alkali kisses and gave her a reason to wake each day. She hadn't moved from her place by the window. Would probably rather stick pins in her eyes than let him know or think that she cared. But the fact she was too preoccupied to light a cigarette only proved her painful secret: she was in love. And love such as this was like dying.

Smiler's hands relaxed and he reddened beneath his mud-layer. 'Yes. But I wouldn't recommend anyone else try it.'

'Why not?' Thurston wanted to know.

'Because.' Rubbing his neck, Smiler's demeanour prickled as he attuned to Thurston's continuing disparagement. 'It was uncomfortable as fuck.'

'Didn't it talk to you?'

'The tree?'

'The tree.'

'What's your problem, man?' Smiler stormed to the foot of stairs, passing close to Thurston while continuing to hold his gaze. 'I don't need this shit.'

'Hey, where are you going?' Callie wandered further into the lounge but stopped again when she became altogether too conscious of her nakedness beneath the towel.

Smiler's expression softened as he spoke to her, 'For a lie down. I didn't get any sleep.'

'Join the club.' Thurston huffed and moved round to sit on the couch.

Callie threw Thurston a look of disdain, then said to Smiler, 'Good idea. We should probably all grab a few hours. We've a raft to build later.'

'A *raft?*' This time Pollyanna seemed keen to spew some negativity, but Callie cut her short with a tired, 'Don't fucking start,' before tramping back to the bathroom to get dressed.

The bathroom was empty. The woman gone.

How can she be here, Dean? She can't be!

Callie hurried back into yesterday's clothes, not wanting to linger for too long. All of the steam had dissipated and the chill had returned to the room with biting freshness. She was too afraid to look at the mirror again but could remember the ghost-woman's face all too well. She tried to recall if she'd known her from somewhere, but couldn't think where and suddenly didn't want to in case the thought alone could rouse the dead. And who knew how many spirits the cabin might keep.

By the time Callie went back to the lounge Pollyanna and Smiler had disappeared and Thurston was alone on the couch. 'You look like shit,' she told him.

He smiled – his eyes squinting in that guileful way – but even so, he looked deeply troubled about something. 'You've looked a lot better yourself, sweetheart.'

She tried to laugh in response but it was a pathetic effort. 'Go and get some rest,' she said. 'You may as well use the spare room upstairs.'

'Nah.' He shook his head, his eyes not leaving hers. 'You take it. I'll sleep on the couch.'

'If you're trying to be a gent,' she said, putting her hands on her hips, 'you'll take the spare room and let me have the couch.'

'What's wrong with the spare room?'

'Nothing,' she lied.

'As long as you're sure.'

She wasn't sure what he wanted her to be sure about – the spare room being okay or her being okay about the couch – but she said that she was and watched as he went upstairs. He didn't say another word, his broad back serving as conversational closure.

The night had been chased away by a blasé sun that showed no other intention than to idle low in the sky. It would be a dull day, made worse by the fog which had thickened at the horizon and rolled closer. Callie was tired, but wasn't sure it would be enough to allow her to sleep. The world was closing in around her and the memory of being chased along the access road by whatever was out there in the woods made the idea of going back outside terrifying. However, the idea of being cooped up in the cabin with its ghosts and damp was also terrifying.

She lay on the couch and could smell Thurston. A faint residue of his aftershave, Hugo Boss. Turning her head, she buried her face in the cushion and breathed him in, feeling disturbingly comforted by the normality of his sweet and sour tang despite an underlying feeling of weirdness that was prompted by something else. Something deeper. Eventually she fell asleep.

Two bodies lay by her feet in a splatter-gore of red on cream vinyl. Her heart felt swollen and so did the thing between her legs. She held a knife to a little girl's throat. The little girl's brown eyes were wide and she begged for her life over and over. Callie found no mercy, only excitement in this. Voices filled her head, mesmeric and insistent. She didn't think she'd heard them before and yet she knew they had never not spoken to her. Words generated by the wind, perhaps. Spoken in some leafy tongue, translated inside her head. Something outside thrashed against the windows; branches rustling, whispering, ordering. The trees. Of course. It was always the trees. Callie applied pressure to the blade and felt metal slice into warm flesh. Her groin gushed hot and thick then and she opened the little girl's throat like jam roly-poly while a little boy cowered in the corner. Watching. She felt no ill will towards the little boy. He reminded her of her. And she thought then how masculine her own hands looked. And how nice the jam roly-poly would taste. And how the little boy might think so too.

Then she was out in the woods. Alone. Mulchy ground beneath her feet felt like the rotting flesh of dead animals. The trees congratulated her; bowing, curtsying and waving in a condescending line-up. They told her this was the end. And she was at peace with this decision. Two large black birds looked on. Overseers of the execution. She stepped up onto a tree stump then found herself looping a length of rope over a branch and circling the other end around her neck. It was thick and scratchy, but her belly felt sickly full with little girl and she knew this had to be done. It was the only way. She closed her eyes and jumped.

The tightening noose made Callie jolt upright. Awake. Her hands went to her throat and she dry-heaved at the thought of what her belly had been filled with. She was breathing raggedly and thought for a moment she was still within the dream because she could hear voices. The same voices she'd heard in the woods. The trees' nasty, vindictive chanting. Whispering. Filling her head. *Did it with a filleting knife. Right there in front of the little boy. Can you imagine that? Why do you always have to be so bloody horrible? Left the boy here and went out into the woods. That's just how it is, sweetheart. What happened to the boy? Stayed here. How long for? Hard to say.*

Where is he now? I don't know! It's him, isn't it? Who? Uncle Dean. What's that supposed to mean? You've been staring at him all day. Shut your stupid face. Else what? I'll kill you. Can you imagine that? What happened to the boy? That's just how it is, sweetheart.

Callie leapt off the couch, covering her ears with her hands, and without really thinking scarpered up the stairs. She couldn't be alone. Not with the voices. She paused outside of Smiler's door, her heartbeat loud in her ears, and raised her hand to knock. Then stopped herself.

Miles Golden? Really!

What the hell would she say to him? What could he do? So she went to the next door along and opened it without knocking, before she had time to change her mind.

23

In the red and white room Thurston was lying on top of the slippery sheets like some erotic nightmare. Shirtless and bruised, with a bloodied wound bound with black twine.

Did it with a filleting knife. That's just how it is, sweetheart.

He opened his eyes and looked at her as if he had expected she might come.

Callie felt a twinge of guilt for seeking solace here. 'Sorry,' she told him.

'For what?' When he shifted the satin beneath him made no noise at all, his feverish skin gliding over its smooth coldness.

Callie stayed in the doorway, aware that she was shaking visibly. *You've been staring at him all day.* She wrung her hands together. *Shut your stupid face.* And squeezed her eyes shut. *Else what?* Her head was filled with satin redness. *I'll kill you.*

'Hey, what's up?' Thurston propped himself up onto his elbows, his face showing concern.

'I'm scared.'

'What of?'

Now she felt foolish. She could hardly tell him about the voices. The trees. What they'd said. 'Nothing,' she said. 'I had a nightmare.'

'Come here.' He patted the bed next to him. 'Come and lie down.' Bizarrely, the invitation sounded like a threat. But she did, she went to the bed and climbed onto the horrid satin and lay on her back. 'Sleep with me,' he said, but the way he said it was without sexual proposition.

The curtains were pulled and everything that should be red in the room was dark grey. The only red Callie saw was in her own head. And there were no voices anymore, just the sound of Thurston breathing. Right next to her. She concentrated on the ceiling. Slow seconds and eventually minutes passed where she was aware of nothing but him. Even the tower room above them ceased to exist.

'So tell me about this nightmare,' he said at last.

'It was dark.' She turned her head to look at him. His face was close to hers. Closer than she'd thought. 'It's this place. It reaches in. Can't you feel it?'

'I feel something.' He looked up at the ceiling, as though to find what it was that she found so captivating there, his breaths calm and deep. 'So you really did come here because you're scared.'

'Why else?'

'Because you're lonely.'

His arm touched hers and the contact was electric.

'I'm a pro at being alone,' she said, forcing a hiccup of fake laughter that made her cringe. She wanted to lead him away from the things she thought should remain unsaid, because she wanted him. Badly. Always had. But the only reason Torbin Thurston would ever indulge her in that respect, she thought, would be to indulge himself.

'Me too,' he said.

Before she had time to process what he meant, he told her, 'This room is fucking awful.'

Callie laughed then; a genuine, effortless sound. And when Thurston pulled her closer, so she had no choice but to lie with her head on his shoulder, it didn't feel awkward. Not even when he started to stroke her hairline with his thumb. She closed her eyes. The room around them buzzed with white silence and the noiseless red of the sheets throbbed beneath her.

'What if this is it?' she said after a while, when she

thought her nose might bleed from the pressure in her head, when she thought the bed might try to absorb her and all that she was.

'If this is what?'

'All we have for the rest of forever.'

'How could it be? The world would miss us.'

'Doubtful. Look at Smiler.'

Thurston stilled his thumb and seemed to give her last point some serious thought. 'Would it be such a bad thing?'

'Staying here forever? Yes.'

'Even with me?'

'Wow,' she said, dryly. 'Serious?'

'No.' He huddled her even closer so that her mouth touched his chest, her lips on dried blood, and he laughed. 'I'm flattered that you think I'm such an egotistical arsehole though.'

'No,' she said, unmoving. 'I don't think that.'

'Course you do. And that's okay. I was thinking only earlier that I need to change.'

'Oh?'

'Somewhere along the way I forgot to be me.'

'Sounds too deep.' Callie breathed in. Hugo Boss. And allowed herself to imagine, just for a moment, what it would be like if he belonged to her. She licked her bottom lip; a subconscious effort that tasted like rust.

'I've had a wake-up call that's all. I'm not happy.'

'Who is? This place has a knack for sucking the shit out of all optimism, so that's hardly a ground-breaking revelation.' She sighed. 'But here's some news you really won't thank me for: if we're here forever, we'll never be happy again. Ever.'

'Swings and roundabouts, sweetheart.' His breath hot on the side of her face. 'My life outside the cabin is pretty fucking miserable too. I need to shake it up. Change it.'

'Shut up!' Callie sat up and turned to look at him. 'What the fuck makes Torbin Thurston so unhappy?'

'I don't do enough good in the world. And I need to see more of it and have some fun.'

'So go to Vegas with Freya. Or Machu Picchu or Chichen Itza for some ancient culture. Or take her to the Arctic Circle to see the Northern Lights, then spend a few nights together in an ice hotel wrapped in reindeer skins and drinking vodka from ice glasses.'

'Sounds great.' He hesitated for a moment. Callie thought he was giving her suggestions some consideration, but then his mouth twisted to the side and he said, 'But I don't love her, Cal.'

'*What?*'

'Never have.'

'I thought you were nuts about her.'

'Things were great in the early days, but she's just not the one for me. The whole relationship is just...*wrong*. She keeps hinting that we should get married, but I just don't feel the same way about her as she says she feels about me.'

'Aren't you just going through a funny patch or something? Bachelor's nerves? Temporary cold feet?'

'Absolutely not, I'm not opposed to getting married and settling down. In fact, things would be a hell of a lot easier if I did love her, but the truth of the matter is that I really, desperately don't.'

Callie lay down again and stared at the ceiling, unblinking. In shock. 'Well. This is awkward.'

'Sorry.' He touched her arm, urging her to look at him. 'I know she's your friend. But it's true.'

'And why are you telling me all of this?'

'I thought you were my friend too.'

'Well, yes. Okay. So as a friend I'm going to give you some advice.'

'Okay.'

'Don't make any rash decisions.'

'I won't.'

'Good.'

'I already decided a while ago.'

They lay quiet then and may as well have been in separate rooms. Thurston's shock admission had created a chasm that not even the red wanted to fill. Callie turned on her side and faced away from him. She lay still, concentrating on her breathing until eventually she heard him snoring gently. It was only then that she allowed herself to sleep.

She was back in her own house, surrounded by her own things. An enormous swell of happiness, wedged somewhere in her chest, seemed to create a glowing edge around everything. She was lying on her own couch, wearing her own clothes, eating her own food, drinking her own wine. And when she finished the last mouthful of wine in her glass, Thurston came in from the kitchen with a brand new bottle of Rioja to top it up. He was wearing a pair of lounge pants, which meant he must be staying over, and as he bent to fill her glass he kissed her on the lips. Smooth. Hungry. Everything she'd wanted. The sound of the doorbell rang through the house, a rude shrillness that spoilt the moment. Callie started to ask if Thurston wouldn't mind answering the door, but saw he wasn't there anymore. So she went through to the hallway herself. She found that instead of skimmed biscotti walls, wood veneer surrounded her on all sides. A claustrophobic box of stale stink. A coffin she might live in. *The cabin.* She was back in the cabin. And the voices. She could hear the whispering of the trees. *Why do you always have to be so bloody horrible? You've been staring at him all day. Who? Uncle Dean. It's him, isn't it? I don't know! Can you imagine that? Where is he now? Hard to say. What's that supposed to mean? I'll kill you. But why?*

That's just how it is, sweetheart.

She threw open the door and found Pollyanna standing out on the veranda. Her hair was plaited down her back and she wore a denim pinafore with red flowers embroidered on the breast pocket. She looked healthy. More alive than usual. And she was standing, her legs fully supporting her. 'Hey, Caroline,' she said, grinning that sly grin of hers. 'How's tricks?'

Not for the first time Callie thought she knew the girl from some other time, some other place. But couldn't think when or where.

'We're not so different, you and I,' Pollyanna said, when Callie failed to reply. 'I mean, sometimes I think I can't be who I am. But I must be, mustn't I? Ha, you should see your face! What a conundrum! I love puzzles.'

On some ephemeral level Callie knew she was dreaming, but was convinced that there was some clue to be gained from Pollyanna's cryptic babble. 'What are you talking about? Who are you?'

'You really don't know, do you?' Pollyanna feigned sad eyes and her small mouth clenched into a pout. 'Would you like me to tell you?'

'Yes!'

'Well, alright then, let's see. I'm...' Pollyanna's eyes grew wide, fearful, and she shook her head in disbelief when her lips clamped shut as though someone else was controlling them. She began to claw at her mouth with desperate fingers and Callie watched as thick black twine punctured through the skin at both sides of her mouth, from the inside out. The two threads of twine then proceeded to snake up and down like tiny black adders, piercing Pollyanna's lip line, top and bottom, and working with a scary synchronicity till her mouth was completely sewn shut. Pollyanna made desperate panting noises and picked at the stitches with her fingers till blood seeped down her chin. Then she was screaming; a horrible muffled sound that came mostly from her nose. Callie pitched forward. She had to help, had to undo the stitches so she could find out what it was Pollyanna had been about to tell her. She began to dig and tear and pull at the tight, wiry sutures with her nails till her hands were covered with Pollyanna's blood. Till the bottom half of Pollyanna's face was nothing but an open wound filled with teeth.

Callie awoke hot and sweaty. Her fingers felt wet and sticky. Instantly she was aware that she was touching something small that had hard nodules, like ridges of bone. When she looked at her hand she saw a length of black twine curled around it and her fingers weren't visible at all. They were inside something. Inside Thurston! Recoiling in shock, she pulled her hand away and saw that his chest was a slick black glistening wound in which she had been delving.

Oh God!

She looked up at his face and saw that he was watching her, his eyes bewildered blue. 'Cal, what are you doing?'

'I'm so sorry,' she said, struggling to find words. Meaningful ones. 'I was dreaming. I didn't mean to. I didn't know. You never said. But…what is it? There's something inside you. Inside your chest.'

'What are you talking about?' Thurston had turned white, in some developing state of shock. 'What's inside of me, Cal? *What?*'

'I don't know.' She covered her mouth with her bloodied hands and stifled a sob. 'There's something there. Someone has sewn something inside you. Right there. In your chest.'

Thurston bolted upright. At first he touched his raw flesh with gentle fingers, but then he rammed three inside, knuckle-deep. There was an unpleasant, wet sucking sound and his face screwed up as his fingers searched the gory, hot cavity of his own chest. He hissed through his teeth and blinked away tears of pained horror. Callie tried to stay his hands but he slapped hers away and kept probing his innards till he found a long, thin object which scraped against one of his ribs as he pulled it out. He held it in the air and made a wretched sound of revulsion. Callie reeled backwards.

What the hell?

An instant sourness in her mouth made her gag, but she managed to swallow it back down with a whimper.

Inside Thurston, someone had sewn an old fashioned iron key.

24

Thurston sat forward with the key clamped in his bloodied hand. He swung his legs round and put his feet on the floor. Callie reached out to stop him from standing, but froze when she saw his back. Two birds were perched together on an ornamental branch in a frozen state of blue-black ink. Their beaks were large, slightly curved, and a spark in their eyes seemed to imply intelligence and wit. Other branches snaked upwards behind the birds, in an intricate filigree of space-filling decoration. In its entirety the artwork covered most of Thurston's back.

Callie traced her finger along the line of the left bird's wing, making Thurston's skin break out in gooseflesh. 'Why ravens?' she asked, feeling strangely subdued by this uncanny coincidence.

'I like them.'

'But why?'

Thurston's head turned and she saw that he was chewing on some newfound agitation. He opened his clenched fist to show her its contents, and said, 'I just pulled a frigging key out of my chest, Cal. What does it matter what tattoos I have?'

'Because I think it's relevant.' She contemplated the ink birds again, not sure why she'd felt inclined to touch them. They were the ravens from her dream. The ones that had watched as she'd pulled the loop of rope over her head. As the trees had mocked her. Just after she'd left the little boy in the cabin. *Did it with a filleting knife. Right there in front of the little boy. Can you imagine that? Left the boy here and went out into the woods. What happened to the boy? Stayed here. How long for?*

Hard to say. Where is he now? I don't know! It's him, isn't it? Him.

'*How* is it relevant?' Thurston pushed himself off the bed and stood. He was unsteady on his feet but turned to face her. She could no longer see the nightmarish tattoo on his back, but was faced with the wet, openness of his chest instead. He stood with his shoulders severely stooped, as though his pain threshold wouldn't allow him to stand up straight.

Callie felt nauseous, about her thoughts and what this might mean. 'Because an infestation of ravens live in the tree outside the cabin.'

'So?'

'So it can't be a coincidence. It's like another piece of the puzzle.'

'No, Cal, it's just a fucking tattoo I had done years ago.' He staggered sideways as though struck dizzy, but reached down for the bed and managed to regain some balance.

'Where the hell do you think you're going anyway?' she said, suddenly angry with him. 'You should be lying down for goodness sake. We need to get you cleaned and stitched up again.'

'No.' He stayed where he was, stooped over the bed in a hurt, broken stance, and held the key up. His eyes glinted maniacally and he bared his teeth. 'I'm going to see what I can stick this fucker into.'

Callie jumped to her feet, her breath exploding outwards in an almighty gasp. *That's it!* 'I think I might know what it's for!'

'Really?' Thurston stepped back and seemed to trip on his own feet. Unable to right himself again, he crashed to the floor with a heavy thud; the sound of cushioned bones on wood reverberated dully. Callie held her breath. The entire cabin shuddered. Seconds later the door burst open and Smiler was standing on the landing, bleary eyed and dirty. 'Everything alright?' He looked from Callie to Thurston and upon seeing blood on both of them decided that it most definitely wasn't, so asked instead, 'What the hell happened?'

'Quick!' Callie said. 'Give me a hand to get him up.'

Spurred into action, Smiler rushed into the red and white room, forgetting his misgivings about the place, and grabbed Thurston by the underarms to hoist him up from behind. But Thurston was heavy and reluctant to move. His eyes rolled back in their sockets and he groaned. Smiler's face turned red from the strain. Callie took hold of Thurston's hands and pulled upwards, encouraging him to get back on the bed. Eventually they got him to his feet and as they eased him down, she couldn't help but think that his blood had formed some vile coalition with the sheets, which were showing up dark red like old congealed blood, now that weak light was stealing in through the open door.

Once he was settled onto his back, Callie snatched a clean t-shirt from the pile of clothes on the floor and pressed it against Thurston's chest. 'Here, hold this,' she said, placing his hands on top.

Smiler was mesmerised and couldn't take his eyes off Thurston. There was so much blood, so much mess. 'What happened?' he asked again.

Callie took the key from Thurston and showed it to Smiler. 'We found this. Inside his chest!'

'Really?'

'Really.'

'That's pretty messed up.' Smiler touched his head, stupefied. 'What's it for?'

'We don't know.' Callie twiddled the key in her fingers. It was dark with Thurston's blood. Tacky with it too. 'But here's what I'm thinking, supposing it unlocks the door to the tower?' Smiler and Thurston exchanged a look that she didn't even try to interpret in full. 'I just have this feeling,' she insisted.

Thurston was shivering now and his lips trembled when he spoke. 'Where's the door to the tower?'

'Next door. In Smiler's room.' Callie folded the duvet over, covering him with it.

'And why are you so convinced that will open it?'

'Because no one has been up there. The door is locked and there is no key. It's the only place in the cabin that hasn't been explored.' She looked at Smiler then and could tell she had almost convinced him. 'Pardon the pun, but I think this is the key to the answers we need.'

'Okay, let's try it then.' Thurston moved his arms to his sides and braced them to push himself up.

'It might be a whole load of excitement over nothing,' Callie said, placing a firm hand on his shoulder. 'You stay here, I'll go and check.'

'But it's only next door.'

'Last time you didn't make two steps from the bed before you tried to face-plant the floor. And besides, you're too bloody heavy for me and Smiler to keep lugging about the place.'

Thurston inhaled loudly to mark his frustration, but eventually conceded with a nod. 'Let me know how you get on. The suspense is killing me.' He touched her hand then and she wished he hadn't.

At the door, Callie looked back and had a disturbing thought that the bed might swallow him while she was gone. The shiny, slippery redness of the duvet enveloped him like an exposed, greedy stomach. She hated the constant symbolism the room kept projecting into her head. Hated that it was the place Thurston had opened up to her. Hated that it had devoured the knowledge that he didn't love Freya. Hated that it had turned his admission into something terrible and seedy while revelling in her guilt. She also hated that her thoughts about Thurston were so ambiguous, but as real as his blood, which had congealed black around her nailbeds. *It's him, isn't it? I don't know! You've been staring at him all day. How long for? All day! But why? It's him. It's him. It's him!*

Callie turned away, afraid of the thoughts that weren't her own, perhaps even more afraid of the ones that were, and followed Smiler to his room. As she walked her legs felt like they didn't belong to her. Like she was floating and none of this was really happening. At the tower door she inserted the key into its lock. Anticipation fizzed in the air. She could feel Smiler's tense eagerness beside her as if it was a real thing of substance. Even the stag's eyes gleamed with expectancy and she imagined it nostrils might be quivering and that it might snort at any moment. Everything rested on this moment. If Callie was wrong and the key wasn't a match, she and Smiler would have to haul their arses outside and get to work building a raft. But somehow that no longer felt like the right solution. There was a simpler way out of this, she knew it. And this was it. All she had to do was…

Plick-plick, plick-plick-plick.

'What's that?' She turned to face the window. The curtains were drawn, so she couldn't see what was tapping the glass.

Plick, plick-plick, plick-plick.

'Shall I go and look?' Smiler said, making no attempt to.

Plick-plick, plick-plick.

'Maybe it's just a branch.' But Callie wasn't convinced.

PLICK-PLICK-PLICK, PLICK-PLICK.

The window imploded with a splintered crash. As glass rained to the floor the curtains billowed inwards and a large black bird flew inside. It came right at them, cawing a terrible warning. Then more ravens followed; a stream of angry black plumage that raged into the room.

Beaks snapped and claws pinched at any soft tissue they could find. One raven tore at the skin on Smiler's neck, stirring fresh blood, while others pulled his hair and tried to get to his eyes. He held his arms up to shield his face and screamed for Callie to open the tower door.

Callie swiped her arm up to dislodge a bird that was tangled in her hair. It beat up and down more furiously, its wings whipping her face. Instinctively she knew then that the key would open the door, because the ravens were guarding something. Something up there in the tower. A secret about to be revealed.

Shut your stupid face.

She turned the key.

Else what?

The lock mechanism made a satisfying clunk and the door pulled open.

I'll kill you!

Callie pushed Smiler inside and bustled in after him, swatting at ravens that tried to follow. Something wedged in the door as she pulled it closed. She gave a sharp yank and there was a head-hurting screech. Then something fell to the floor by her feet with a soft, sickening thump. Sheer darkness surrounded them, accommodating all too well the eerie sound of birds' beaks hitting the other side of the door in a frantic tirade. Callie stood still. Unable to move. Needing to keep the door pulled shut, just in case they knew of a way to open it and come after them.

Eventually all went quiet on the other side of the door and Callie and Smiler were left with nothing but the sound of their own frenzied heartbeats in the dark. And then voices. A new tirade of voices in Callie's head. *Do you know any stories? There used to be a man. How did he do it? Did it with a filleting knife. Can you imagine that? Sounds like the picnic was better off that way. But why? Not everyone hears the trees anyway. But why?*

That's just how it is, sweetheart. Where is he now? She won't hear. Where? I won't tell. But why? I'm sorry. I think we've all heard enough. 'Yes, enough!' Callie cried, close to tears, close to hysteria.

Smiler didn't argue.

With the threat of the birds gone, the threat of the unknown grew. Callie became aware only now of the overbearing smell wafting down from the tower, as though the cabin's foul dankness originated in this place. In its rawer form the smell had a meatiness to it, like old blood and decaying flesh. Of something dead or dying. Something waiting in the dark. Oppressively possessive. Like the red that swathed Thurston. *I'll kill you.* And the trees of Whispering Woods. *Can you imagine that?* Whatever it was that wanted them dead was breathing and existing in this same dark space as them. Churning the words that the trees spoke. Perhaps even creating them. Callie and Smiler had to go up. They had no choice but to venture to the top of the cabin. To face whatever truth lay in wait for them. *That's just how it is, sweetheart.*

25

Callie reached for Smiler. Her hand closed around his arm. He flinched at first, then his hands were clutching at hers. It wasn't hard for her to imagine other hands reaching out, which prompted a new sense of dread of being touched by unseen, unknown things that dwelt in the dark. Phantom hands fingering and teasing the air around them, ready to whisper-brush exposed skin in mocking caresses of hard-edged deathly promise. Or less subtle hands that were very much real and intrinsically more dangerous.

'Do you have your lighter?' Callie said. Her voice sounded gut-wrenchingly loud in the quiet space and she imagined it was being explored and devoured by the dark and everything in it.

'Yes!' Smiler's hands left hers and she heard him patting down the pockets of his jeans. There were a few hisses and failed sparks, then an orange flame lit his face and hand, though not much else. Darkness dwarfed the lighter's tiny glow.

'Hold it next to the wall,' Callie said, moving his arm because he didn't do it quickly enough. 'See if there's a switch.'

He held the lighter close to the grubby unfinished plasterboard to his left and moved it about in circular motions, trying to make the most of its ineffective light. It hardly made a difference, so Callie began to pat the wall blindly, her hands instantly made gritty by what she imagined was cobweb residue and dead skin. Without much searching, her fingers found a switch. *Too easy.* She flicked it down but nothing happened. She was about to relay her disappointment to Smiler and anything else that might listen when a dull creaminess broke through the darkness, somewhere above. *Energy saving lightbulb.*

A wooden staircase, leading up, was dingily illuminated by the bare bulb that dangled from the ceiling at what was presumably the mouth of the tower room. The bare wood boards of the stairs looked dirty from years of use and disuse and the plasterboard walls where Callie and Smiler were standing, came to a sudden stop at the foot of the stairs, after which point the walls were exposed brickwork all the way up to the second floor.

Callie looked at Smiler and took a deep breath. 'Ready?'

He didn't reply, but when she stepped forwards he moved with her. His arm was pressed against hers and she could feel how tightly coiled he was. She was the same, her body so tense it almost hurt. They stepped onto the first stair together, but then Smiler stopped. He took a deep breath. Callie waited. And the cabin listened. 'What about Thurston?' he asked.

This was perhaps the last chance Smiler saw to turn around and go back, and Callie could tell he was contemplating taking it. But her resolve was stronger. 'What about him?'

'Won't he wonder where we are?'

'I expect so.' Callie began to climb again; the boards dry beneath her feet like old bone.

'He asked us to let him know about the door.'

'And we will.'

'When?'

She made a cough that didn't leave the inside her mouth, an involuntary reaction to dust stirring, and paused till he moved to catch up. 'After we've found whatever there is to find.'

Three stairs further up and Smiler sneezed. Loudly.

They both stopped to listen to what might have been roused, but heard nothing so continued on. Creeping upwards. Slowly. Callie's hand trailed a dirty wooden bannister that felt loose and seemed too makeshift to have been intended as a permanent fixture. In fact, the whole staircase looked like an unfinished project. A refurbishment gone astray.

'What about the ravens?' Smiler asked, when they were almost at the top.

'What about them?'

'Won't they find Thurston? Will he be safe?'

'I closed his door as I left.'

There was an ensuing silence that was laden with Smiler's disappointment.

'In any case, none of us are safe,' she reminded him.

At the top of the stairs a great staleness of stagnant air that hadn't been breathed in quite possibly forever filled their lungs. Both of them coughed. The cabin's tower was a stark wooden frame with layers of dust and no natural light because its windows had been blanked out with what looked like black sugar paper held in place with duct tape. All of the room's shadows were stationary but ample enough to evoke a sense that they kept things within that moved jaggedly and quickly between two worlds – this one and another much worse. The room was bare except for a prevailing feeling of gloom, as weighty and portentous as the lake outside, and a large wooden chest that had been placed in the middle of the vast floor space, most definitely deliberately.

'I bet it's locked,' Smiler thought aloud. His voice ruptured the tower's loaded quietude, goading any lurking evils to materialise. None did. But the light behind flickered. Neither of them moved.

'No,' Callie said. 'We're meant to see whatever's in there.'

Smiler rubbed his neck where the raven's beak had pierced his skin. The superficial wound had begun to scab over, but his fingers made it bleed again. He carried on poking as though that was the only thing he could do. When Callie said nothing further, he felt obliged to say, 'Shall we take a look?' Which was a redundant question because he knew they had to.

Still, neither of them moved.

The cabin revelled in their indecisiveness, growing stronger as their nerve weakened.

'Are you scared of what we'll find?' Callie asked, unsure why. Another pointless question.

Smiler's face slipped easily into an age-inducing frown. 'Too many bad surprises.'

She reached for his hand and gripped it, squeezing his fingers between hers, then together they crept to the chest.

Beneath the dust of however long it was rich in colour, some Indian rosewood perhaps, and the size of a decent blanket box. It was an expensive looking hand-crafted piece with black iron studs running vertically down each of its sides. Two black handles at either end made it portable and a large black clasp at the front gave the option of security. However, no padlock was in place. As Callie had predicted, they were to be allowed easy access to its contents. Investing himself in a joint discovery, Smiler huddled down next to Callie and gripped a corner of the lid. Callie lifted the clasp and together they swung it open. Inside, the chest was filled with shadows. Callie reached in and felt something at the bottom, her fingers tracing hard edges. She pulled out a small rectangular object that was wrapped in red linen.

It had to be red.

She unwound the material and let it fall to the floor, then stared with a certain amount of trepidation at the black leather-bound book in her hands. Gilded text on its front cover proclaimed it to be a **JOURNAL**.

Callie closed her eyes and breathed in long and hard. 'Here we go.' She ran a finger over the embossed letters. A marrow-deep chill prickled its way up through bone to the surface of her skin, causing a rash of gooseflesh. She caught Smiler's eye for a brief moment and saw that he shared her apprehension. This was it, they were about to unveil the truth. Her fingers trembled and she opened the book.

Oh God.

She stared blankly down at deeply-pressed pencil handwriting which declared that the journal belonged to: *Sarah Jane Miller.*

'Pollyanna's cousin,' Smiler acknowledged with no hopeful expectation.

The girl who went missing.

Callie read the name over and over in her head. It seemed more personal written down. She could imagine an actual girl attached to it. The Sarah Jane Miller that Pollyanna had mentioned was no longer just some urban myth. Callie looked about the unfurnished tower room and a great wave of sadness washed over her. 'Do you think she was kept up here?'

'But when and who by?'

Callie shrugged. 'I guess we'll find out, won't we?' She skimmed through the journal's pages and saw that most of them were written on. Hundreds of pencilled sentences constructed by a girl who neither she nor Smiler knew, but a girl who most likely held the answers not only to the cabin's mystery and her own disappearance, but Callie's, Thurston's, Smiler's and Pollyanna's cryptic involvement as well. 'Let's show Thurston. He needs to see this.'

'What about the ravens?' Smiler now seemed reluctant to go back down, as though Sarah Jane Miller's journal was not the breakthrough he'd expected and he needed time to think, to process what it might mean. He was visibly unsettled and the mention of Thurston seemed to add to his anxiety.

'Well,' Callie said, 'we can't stay up here forever.'

With the threat of her statement feeling all too real, like a dare that had to be exacted, she and Smiler went back downstairs. They found Smiler's room free from ravens, except the one Callie had decapitated with the door. The curtains billowed at the window, but the ash tree outside was bare. Above the bed the stag had resumed its lacklustre death-stare. Nothing about the room held an immediate sense of malevolence or threat. The ravens had tried but failed to stop them finding the journal, which meant that Callie and Smiler had achieved one small victory. But at what cost, they had to wonder. The cabin still breathed all around them, watching. Waiting to make its next move.

In the red and white room Thurston was where they'd left him. The bed hadn't eaten him. But there was a sour smell that Callie hadn't noticed before. Too much blood and fevered sweat.

'Where've you been?' Thurston asked.

Callie sat on the bed next to him, close enough to feel his heat. She felt a strong urge to touch his face, to test his fever with the back of her fingers, but refrained. 'In the tower.'

His blue eyes flashed with vexation and he pushed himself up. The red duvet fell to his waist, but the t-shirt serving as a bandage clung to his chest, tarry with blood. 'You said you'd let me know.'

'Yeah well, we ran into a spot of bother,' Callie said. 'I'm surprised you didn't hear. But that's by the by, it really doesn't matter.' And she meant it. The ravens' attack was far less important than the journal; the book in her hands that felt so warm with the promise of knowledge it might burst into flames.

Noticing it, Thurston said, 'What's that?'

'We found it in the tower. Inside a chest.' Callie looked down at his chest and the corner of her mouth twitched up, but her eyes lacked any humour. 'Ironic, huh?'

'Hilarious.'

'Hmmm.' Callie showed him the book's cover and, in case he hadn't figured it out, said, 'It's a diary.'

'Whose?'

'Pollyanna's cousin's.'

'Sarah Jane Miller?' Thurston pushed himself further up so his back was resting against the wall, overt curiosity seeming to counteract his pain and his eyes losing their glazed look of malaise. 'Have you read any of it?' he wanted to know.

'Not yet.' Callie opened the cover and flipped to the first page of writing. 'But I'm dying to. Shall we?'

Smiler was still in the doorway, his intrigue offset by the apprehension in his eyes. He folded his arms over his chest and nodded.

26

Sunday 4th October 2009

Dear Dorian,

I've decided to write down all of my thoughts and feelings. Everything has changed and you're the only one I can trust. From now on I'll tell you **EVERYTHING.**

First, let's see though. I need to get this right in my head, so I know who I'm talking to. I expect you have dark hair, almost black but not quite, and very, very pale skin. I like that combination a lot. It's very ~~ethreal~~ ethereal. So I think that's how you must look. And your eyes must be blue, because that's my favourite colour for eyes to be. I imagine you look like an angel, but without wings. Because wings are too fussy. And angel wings are white. Like swans' wings. And I don't like swans. At all.

I suppose you could have black wings and that would be ok. But I don't think you have any at all, do you? Of course not. That would be silly. And besides, your feathers would get everywhere if you did. I could always stuff my pillows with bits of you and make writing quills. But no, you definitely, definitely don't have wings.

Maybe you have horns though? Just little ones beneath your hair, so no one can see.

Maybe.

*I'll think about that some more and then you can tell me for sure later whether you do or not. But for now, now that that's us sort of acquainted, I need to tell you something. Something really big. Something massively exciting. Something truly **AWFUL**...*

I'm in love!

At least that's what I think it is. It's horrible and awesome all at the same time. My skin feels tingly and lately my name sounds different whenever anybody says it. Like I'm somebody new and I'm discovering myself for the first time ever. The old Sarah Jane Miller is nothing more than a discarded chrysalis shell blown to the gutter and the new Sarah Jane Miller is a cinnabar moth, ready for the darkness she's bound to dwell in because of this love.

Ah Dorian don't get me wrong, it's not all bad living and breathing varying shades of darkness. In fact, it's like I want to live forever feeling this way, like I'm dancing in the sky with moon halos burning pearlescent colour into my eyes. Yet in the same breath I also don't want to live a moment longer. It's too painful. I ache. I yearn. And I've run out of space in my head for much else to fit in except Dean.

*Because that is his name. **Dean**.*

Uncle Dean.

Dean. Dean. Dean. Dean. Dean. Dean. Dean. Dean.

I feel sick when I think about him. Not because I don't want to be in love or because I'm scared, but because I know he can't be mine. He's too old and I'm too young.

And besides, I think he's in love with my mother.

It's like some Shakespearian tragedy, isn't it Dorian? And that's maybe what I'm in love with. I love tragedy.

I don't know when I'll see him again. It all depends on Roxanne, I suppose, and whether she'll take me along with her. Next time she might leave me with Dad!

But if I threaten to spill the beans, she'll have to take me. Won't she?

*She **WILL NOT** keep me away from him!!!*

*I've already decided not to tell anyone at school about Uncle Dean, not even Lucas Adams who sits next to me in English Lit. On Friday he told me he'd snogged some girl from the fifth year behind the science block, like I should be impressed. Well so what?! I saw Uncle Dean with no clothes on!!! But no one else deserves to know that. He's **MY** secret. And as long as he's in my head and nobody else can see him then he'll stay there and there'll always be a part of him that won't be able to get out. So that means I own a tiny piece of him and I won't ever give it back. Not even if he asked very nicely.*

I'm going to google Whispering Woods today to see if I can find out where Uncle Dean's cabin is. Then I'm going to pack my bags and run away. I expect to hitch rides for most of the way, because it was an ~~epicly~~ epically long journey. I bet long distance lorry drivers will be glad of the company, but I won't mind walking either. No matter how long it takes.

Then when I get there I'm going to climb up the side of the cabin and into the tower. And that's where I'm going to live. Forever. And I'm going to take you with me, Dorian. I can't wait.

Monday 5th October 2009

Demonic Dorian,

I've decided I'd like it if you do have horns. But whether you do or not, today was shit.

Jade Tucker and Kyra Richmond tripped me up in the assembly hall this morning. Everyone saw. Including Kieran Stock. He laughed his head off, although I didn't really care as much as I once would have – he's nothing but a stupid little boy! In fact, everyone at school is stupid. Mostly Jade Tucker and Kyra Richmond though. I hate them. And they'll be sorry they tripped me.

For the rest of the day I imagined I had the ravens from Uncle Dean's ash tree with me. They surrounded me like a big force field of building black thunderhead and nobody did anything else to me, so I think they'll protect me from now on. I'm sure Uncle Dean won't mind that I've borrowed them. I'll take them back when I go to his cabin.

Speaking of which, I've been planning on what to take with me. So far my list is as follows:

Money from money box (and whatever I can pilfer from Roxanne's purse)
Snacks from kitchen cupboard (mainly chocolate to keep my energy levels up)
Dad's big flask (which I intend to fill with coffee to keep me awake)

Plasters (in case I get blisters on my heels from all the walking)
Toothbrush
Change of underwear
Cigarettes from Dad's secret stash

That's all I've thought of for now. Oh and you, of course.

xxx

Shitting hell, Dorian, there's been a delay with my plan. After tea I googled Whispering Woods but couldn't find anything that matched where Uncle Dean's cabin might be. Nothing at all! I wonder if it's a secret place? Like maybe nobody talks about it or refers to it by its proper name since those murders happened. A bit like High Hopes, the house in Amityville. It was renamed and painted a different colour so that people who are obsessed with murders and ghosts and other peoples' tragedies wouldn't keep nosing about. Maybe Whispering Woods is now known as something completely different and only its truest residents, like Uncle Dean, know the truth.

So there's nothing more I can do for the moment. I'll just have to wait and ask Uncle Dean next time I see him. I don't want to quiz Roxanne about where the cabin is because she might twig on that I'm planning to run away and be angry that I thought of it first. She might set off before me, in her car, and beat me to it.

I hate her.

And I'm annoyed with myself for not taking notice of road signs along the way. I'm so stupid!!!

Wednesday 7th October 2009

'Dorable Dorian,

Last night Roxanne asked if I'd like a cream cake for after school today. She never does this usually, so I know she's trying to keep me sweet. Ha! Trying to make sure I don't grass her up to Dad. I told her I'd like a strawberry tart, even though sugar doughnuts and iced buns are way better and I hate strawberries. Strawberry tarts are more expensive though and she has to realise that my silence comes at a price. She gave me a funny look, like she knew. Good!

After a raven-filled day at school followed by a plateful of Roxanne's beef stew, I licked all the cream off my strawberry tart and then left the rest untouched. Roxanne looked really annoyed, but she didn't say or do anything about it.

I'm totally ~~enpow~~ empowered!

I excused myself from the table (Dad, the hapless idiot, is completely ignorant to what's going on around him) and stole Roxanne's phone from the sideboard. I wanted to find Uncle Dean's number so I could call him, but by the time I'd figured the stupid passcode to unlock the phone I heard Roxanne coming upstairs.

She was coming to see me so I summoned Uncle Dean's ravens to stop her from entering, but they didn't seem to work on her. She came straight into my room without knocking!!

I thought she was going to tell me off for wasting the strawberry tart, but she didn't. I think it's eating her up, not knowing if I'll tell Dad about Uncle Dean. She was being nice to me again, which is very unlike her. She asked how school is and then started asking about Pollyanna. Like how I'm coping with things. I told her I didn't want to talk about Pollyanna but she tried to push the issue. So I went in a sulk and wouldn't look away from the wall until she left.

I don't want to talk about Pollyanna ever again though, Dorian. She makes me angry. Too angry.

I know I have a darkness inside of me and I know some of it escaped a little bit at the cabin. But sometimes I can't control it. I can feel it crawling around inside my head all of the time. It's a spider and it tickles behind my eyes. Pollyanna used to annoy me so much that I'd want to scratch my eyes out.

Roxanne says I'm too angry for my own good. Sometimes she looks at me like she's scared of me. Like I'm a monster. She gives me this certain look sometimes too, where her eyes zone out and I don't know whether she might get angry or cry, and I get the feeling she's thinking she'd be better off if I didn't exist. I think if she could go back in time she wouldn't have had me. Then she wouldn't be with Dad, because neither of them would be scared about which one would have to keep me.

They made me see a doctor earlier this year, I think they wanted me to be taken away from them so that I was no longer their responsibility. But the doctor said there was nothing wrong with me. I didn't let the spider out of its box for a long while then. I knew we were playing a game, and I've always been better at playing games than anyone.

*Besides, **EVERYONE** has a spider inside of them. Sometimes it's so small like a money spider and it can't be felt most of the time. Mine is a black widow. Her name is Lucy.*

*I think Uncle Dean must have a tarantula or a Brazilian wandering spider living inside of him. I'm sure he's done many things that he knows he shouldn't have, but isn't sorry for all the same. And I'm not sorry for what I've done either. For hacking into Dad's Facebook account and 'friending' lots of dirty women and putting Roxanne's diamond bracelet down the drain outside and feeding Gran's dog chocolate. I'm not even sorry for tampering with the trampoline that broke Pollyanna's back. I was only sorry that it wasn't her neck. But that doesn't matter at all anymore because now she's **DEAD**.*

Ha ha ha!

27

'Pollyanna is dead?' Callie looked up to gauge whether anyone else looked as disturbed as she felt.

Thurston shifted his weight and licked his lips with a cool-eyed grimace. 'The girl isn't a full shilling, is she? She didn't mean Pollyanna's dead in a literal sense. Obviously.'

'Didn't she?' Callie wondered at that.

'Seriously?' Thurston's eyebrows peaked and he huffed with such a considerable amount of impatience it lent his face some colour. 'After everything you've read you actually question that last sentence like it's got some grounds for truth? Like everything she said before was actually plausible.' He smiled unkindly. 'I suppose you think there might be a spider living inside you? And that Sarah Jane Miller really did employ ravens to protect her from schoolyard bullies?'

'Fuck off, Thurston.' Callie angled her body away from him. 'Of course I don't.'

'So why would you consider that Pollyanna is dead?' he said, with his palms upturned. His hands were rust-red, the dried blood more burgundy in the creases of his wrists. 'You know she isn't. She's downstairs for God's sake.'

Needing to inject some harsh reality into the situation by reminding them all that this was very much happening and that Whispering Woods was still outside, Smiler strode boldly into the red and white room from his post by the door and tore the thick curtains open. A gauzy glow from heavily filtered daylight seeped in and painted the bedding cautionary-red. Somehow the room looked infinitely worse during the day. Fog had closed in further still, making it look as though nothing existed beyond the first row of trees. But of course this wasn't true. Whispering Woods was always there, even when you weren't looking. And sooner or later they would need to go outside and confront it, Smiler knew, because inside the cabin the level of paranoia was intensifying. They were becoming overly tetchy as their desperation stretched on. Theirs was a collective jumble of frayed nerves, like damaged threads that would never knit together again, not neatly in any case, because it felt like too much damage had been imposed already.

'Don't you guys see what's wrong?' Smiler said, turning to face Callie and Thurston. The fog was a phantasmal miasma at his back, which threatened to roll closer and seep through the glass to smother him and steal him away into the woods. Callie and Thurston looked at each other, both equally vague about what the answer to Smiler's question might be because by their reckoning there was an awful lot that was wrong. When they hazarded no guesses, Smiler told them, 'The diary was written in 2009. *Seven years ago.*'

No less clueless, Callie shrugged. 'So?'

'So Pollyanna can't have been here for seven years.'

'Who says she has? Maybe she came back with Sarah Jane more recently.'

'That would contradict Pollyanna's story. She said she came here the day they met Uncle Dean and never left again.'

'So what are you saying?' Callie lifted her legs onto the bed, bending them so her feet rested snugly against her backside. At the same time, she swivelled her body round to face Smiler. Behind him a row of spiky-limbed wraith-like giants reached up to the sky, perhaps in an effort to pull it down on top of their heads with skeletal fingers that were made of bark and knots and knuckles. 'That you think Pollyanna was left here in 2009 and that nobody ever bothered to come back for her?'

'I don't know.' Smiler seemed to be shrinking within the ghostly aura that looked as though it emanated from his upper body but was definitely outside. Callie wished he would come away from the window.

'I'm sure Roxanne Miller would have noticed she'd forgotten to take her niece home,' she said, casting her eyes at Thurston to see if he shared her scepticism.

'But it doesn't make sense,' Smiler complained, his voice becoming more forceful. 'Pollyanna is fourteen. That would mean seven years ago when this diary was written she was only seven.'

'Well, I'm pleased you worked that out for us,' Callie said with a dryness intended to ground his skittishness.

But Smiler simply clutched his head with both hands, as if the puzzle he'd presented was too much for his skull to contain and he hadn't heard her. 'Pollyanna and Sarah Jane are the same age. Sarah Jane Miller was *most definitely not* seven when she wrote those diary entries.'

'So what *are* you saying?' Callie said. 'That you think Pollyanna was fourteen seven years ago, which makes her what? *Dead?*'

Thurston exhaled irritably.

Smiler groaned with indecision. 'I don't know.' He seemed to shrink into the fog as it swelled around him with a phantom glow. That or the sun was burning a hole through it. 'I don't know what to think. I guess we need to clear a few things up. Maybe we should wake Pollyanna and show her the diary. Maybe we should just ask her to explain the bloody timeline.'

Thurston was quick to dispute the idea. 'No. The kid's weird. Maybe even more unhinged than her cousin. I think we should read some more of the diary between the three of us before we let her see it. I mean, do we really want her kicking off right now? Because I guarantee that's exactly what she'd do. And I bet *her* inner spider is a fucking Goliath birdeater called Beelzebub.'

Callie's lips parted with a groan. 'Slight exaggeration, don't you think?'

'Well would you like to find out?'

'Not really.'

'Besides, how do we know that Sarah Jane Miller isn't here as well?' Thurston looked up at the ceiling, as if indicating the tower. 'How do we know that she and Pollyanna, together, aren't messing with us?' He fell quiet for a moment, allowing Callie and Smiler to consider the possibilities of his suggestion, before saying, 'And aren't we being a little naïve anyway? Who says the diary was written in 2009? She might have written it last week for all we know!'

Callie nodded and she gnawed on her bottom lip. Subconsciously her fingers stroked red satin. Smiler was shaking his head adamantly though. 'Sarah Jane Miller isn't here,' he said. 'I'd know. I'd have noticed. I mean, where would she be?' He looked to the ceiling then. 'Because if you're thinking up there, you're dead wrong. The tower's empty except for a chest and a truckload of dust.'

'How the fuck should I know where she'd be?' Thurston said. 'I've haven't had the opportunity to take a look around, I've been a little incapacitated and preoccupied with other things.' He gestured to his chest with both hands, the effort a heated one.

Smiler squared his shoulders, finally stepping away from the window but not quite losing the fog. It clung to the memory of him standing there, his silhouette by the window burned onto Callie's and Thurston's retinas. Like a little bit of his soul had bled out perhaps. 'Yeah, well,' he said. 'I'm still wondering why Pollyanna's so convinced that *you're* Uncle Dean. That's a massive coincidence, don't you think?'

Thurston's face darkened, his mouth tight with as yet unsaid rebukes. Callie flashed Smiler a scowl of disapproval, but really she wondered the same thing. A wave of nausea surged from her hungry stomach and crested in her head, making her eyes busy with black and white fizz. She looked from Thurston to Smiler then back at Thurston, wondering which, if either, she could trust. She felt terribly hopeless and frighteningly alone.

It's him isn't it? Who?

Dean?

Before Thurston or Smiler could start tearing verbal strips out of each other, Callie did the only thing she could think to do: she opened Sarah Jane Miller's diary to the page where she'd left off and began to read again.

28

Wednesday 17th February 2010

Dear Deserted Dorian,

Sorry I haven't spoken to you in ages, but shit's been going down. Big style. And it's only now I feel capable of talking about any of it. All of my plans from before are ruined and I don't know what to do. It's like a dark veil has been pulled tight over my face, squashing my nose so I can't breathe properly and blurring my eyes so I can't see. I need to figure something out.

Ok, so basically it all started when Roxanne left home. Two days before Christmas. She'd packed a load of her stuff into two suitcases and told Dad when he got in from work that she wanted a divorce. She didn't even ask me to go to my room so they could talk, the horrible cow just went straight in for the kill. She may as well have thrown a pan of hot oil in his face. Seriously.

This is Roxanne Miller we're dealing with though, Dorian. I mean, why would you choose two days before Christmas to announce that you're retracting the sacred vows you once made in church unless you're a complete twat? And that you're deserting your only child on the penultimate eve of Christmas unless you're an even bigger twat? In fact, she's so much of a twatty twat, Dorian, it's unreal.

At first Dad was furious about her going. He shouted lots and they both fought over the suitcases: Roxanne trying to get them out the door and Dad pulling them back inside. It might have been funny if they had no association with me. But by proxy, until I'm 18, they sort of do. And so I hate them beyond any ~~reed~~ redeemable sense of family duty. They're both total freaks.

Dad was that angry he hurled one of the suitcases over the fence into next door's garden. He has such a blatant disregard for anyone else in the world though. I mean, why would you involve next door in your domestic disputes? Which is exactly what he did do because the suitcase broke the dial off Norman's sundial and Norman's very precious about his sundial and Dad had to pay for damages the next day because Norman threatened to call the police. Serves him right though. What he should have done was throw the suitcase through Roxanne's windscreen so she couldn't go anywhere. Not as easily as she'd intended anyway.

After she'd gone Dad's fury was pathetic. So pathetic I could have spat in his face. It only lasted for a day and then he got depressed. Like really mopey. I expected he might want to smash everything in the house, especially when I told him about Uncle Dean. But he didn't. On Christmas Eve he sat on the sofa and drank whiskey ALL DAY and listened to Coldplay and cried like a baby.

Personally, I wish Roxanne had left us years ago. But not like this!!! She'd run off to have the perfect Christmas with Uncle Dean (!), leaving me behind to live with Dad's wallowing and the shittyness of Peterlee's dirty slush. Which was actually rather symbolic of how my heart felt (and still feels): cold, grey and impure.

On Christmas day I didn't bother getting up till everyone

else in the world was probably loading their dinner plates into their dishwashers. It was a miserable day that couldn't be made any better. Dad spent it contemplating the sorrows of his failed marriage. I spent it contemplating whether to let Lucy loose. And also hoping that Roxanne would succumb to Whispering Woods and hang herself. Or that Uncle Dean would stab her in the head at least seventy times before feeding her to the animals that must dwell in the woods. Great big things I expect.

But none of those things happened. She phoned at 6pm. Dad answered and they had cross words. He tried to hand me the phone, but I shook my head. He gave me a don't-mess-the-fuck-about look and handed it to me anyway. She said 'Merry Christmas' then apologised for not being here. The level of fake sincerity was astounding (that's me being sarcastic by the way, Dorian). She obviously hadn't even tried to convince herself that she meant it.

She only called to keep up appearances. Other people (friends and family mostly, but also neighbours) will already know by now that she's a deserter. So if she hadn't called her only daughter to say 'Merry Christmas' on Christmas day she'd have been demoted to a 'black-hearted deserter' (which is what she is anyway).

*I can't remember what else she said to me because the sound of her voice made me **angry**. So, so **ANGRY!** And I could imagine that Uncle Dean was right there next to her, maybe even touching her. Or her touching him. Yes. Her touching him. She's **ALWAYS** touching him!!! Lucy started pacing then, scratching around behind my eyes till eventually they bled on the inside. Dad came and* *took the phone off me and said some stuff that I didn't really hear. I think Uncle Dean's ravens then carried me up to bed, and I stayed there for what felt like three weeks.*

When I eventually did resurface I checked the phone to find out what number The Deserter had called from. But the last number was Gran's. She must have called sometime in between. So I was left hanging for weeks.

I couldn't even talk to you about what was going on, Dorian. That's how bad it's been. I've felt so ill about it all, I had to let Lucy take over for a while. I've been resting and thinking and trying to heal. My heart hurts so much and my head is in bits. But it gets worse, Dorian. SO much worse...

The Deserter came back mid-January. I'd hoped Uncle Dean had kicked her out, but she'd come with paperwork for the divorce and to get the rest of her stuff packed together.

The atmosphere between her and Dad was tense. I wanted them to kill each other. I wanted Dad to knock her out with a fist to the face and for him to stamp on her unconscious body till it was dead and flattened on the carpet. Then for him to go and drown himself in the bath or something tragically depressing like that. None of that happened though. The Deserter slept in the spare room and Dad slammed doors a lot. That was all.

One day after school I came out and asked The Deserter straight up, because I NEEDED to know, if she'd been staying with Uncle Dean. She didn't deny it and I could feel Lucy freewheeling around the inside of my skull. Then I asked The Deserter if she and Uncle Dean were going to be a couple. She said 'probably' at first. Then nodded and said 'yes'.

I HATE HER!!!!

The Deserter announced that she'd be staying for a few weeks while she got things sorted with work (and I suspect while Uncle Dean got things sorted with his 'wife'. Claire. The bint). So Dad moved in with Gran. I only saw him on weekends when The Deserter dropped me off there. I presume she was meeting up with Uncle Dean and didn't have to take me, not now that everything was out in the open. Bitch.

I began to worry I'd never see Uncle Dean ever again and that my heart would remain a barely beating, mushy mess. But I saw him just three days ago! On Valentine's Day, of all days!! Which is bitter-sweet irony.

The Deserter tried to palm me off on Dad and Gran that day, but they refused to have me I think out of principle (because they knew they'd be ruining her slutty plans). And so I was used like some cheap-move chess piece.

Uncle Dean was forced to come and stay at our house instead though. So checkmate!

After school the Deserter made me a fish finger sandwich then sent me to my room. Uncle Dean arrived some time afterwards and I watched from the stairs as they cooked a meal together and drank wine. They never even saw me. I felt like a ghost, hovering outside of my body, looking down, unable to ~~interveen~~ intervene. Not even when Uncle Dean took a small box from his pocket and asked The Deserter to marry him. She said 'yes' and then they kissed. Next thing I remember I was in bed and it was morning and everything was red. And a couple of days later it still is a little bit.

So there you have it, Dorian, my heart is officially **DESTROYED**. *Uncle Dean and The Deserter are to be married.*

I asked Uncle Dean if I can live with him too, but before he got round to answering The Deserter butted in and said that I'd have to stay with Dad because of school and stuff. Uncle Dean winked at me with his blue eye and said I could visit whenever I liked. But that's not good enough, Dorian. I **NEED** *to be with him.*

So much it **HURTS**.

But I figure he'll have to let me live with him if I force the issue, because I have his ravens and I won't give them back if I have to stay here with Dad and Gran. Not ever.

29

'What are you all doing up there?' It was Pollyanna calling from downstairs.

Callie slammed the journal shut as though she'd been caught doing something she shouldn't.

'We'll be down in a tick,' Smiler yelled. Then to Callie and Thurston, because they were looking at him like he was Judas Iscariot, he said, '*What?* We have to show her what we found! She has a right to know.'

Callie sighed. She knew he was right, but involving Pollyanna with their find bothered her more than she could put into words. So she didn't try. She stood up and hugged the journal to her chest, feeling unreasonably possessive of it and not wanting it to leave her hands, not even for a moment. The answers she sought lay within the pages, she was sure of it, and even if those answers turned out to be sickening in whatever revelatory truth they unveiled, it was a truth that had to be known nonetheless. Everything Sarah Jane Miller, past or present, had planned, Callie needed to know. The teenager's spew of angry words and dangerous obsession was somehow key to why they were all there. Maybe even key to the death threats she'd received. The more diary entries she read the more she disliked the girl. And Pollyanna's direct familial association made her massively uneasy. 'Okay, let's go down,' she said, still hugging the journal. 'Smiler, could you give Thurston a hand?'

She expected Thurston would prove difficult and argue, but he didn't. He shuffled round and swung his legs over the edge of the bed, breathing hard with the effort like someone twice his age. He even looked like he'd aged about five years since the day before; his physical bearing less robust, though it had hardly been a thing of strength since he'd arrived, and his skin significantly paler as though the room had sapped something from him. Or as though the white walls had bled into his body.

Callie turned away and made the mistake of venturing too close to the window. Beyond it the fog was a soupy wall of thick grey, curling around indefinable edges and making everything in between blurred. The forefront of Whispering Woods was nothing but a suggestion; a row of what looked like weak day shadows standing upright. But the trees' voices were clear in her head, a cacophony of remembered hissed whispering. *Do you know any stories? Suppose that depends. Lived here as it happens. Something really awful. Take a guess. Suppose that depends. Why does anyone do anything? Suppose that depends. All except the small boy. But why? But why? But why? But why? That's just how it is, sweetheart.*

'We need to come up with some sound ideas,' Callie said, as much to the trees as to Smiler and Thurston, to let them know the trees and their words hadn't broken her. Yet. She resisted the urge to pull the curtains closed, because if she did they would have won. They were mocking her, subtly but all too perceptibly, and she knew she had to focus on zoning out from their insistent teasing else they'd worm further into her mind and wreak havoc with her subconscious. She whipped round and started pacing the room, and watched as Smiler stooped next to the bed to put Thurston's arm across his shoulders. 'I can't do this for much longer,' she admitted. 'We're floating about the place like dead people and it's driving me crazy. This cabin, that fog, those ravens, the trees – they're all driving me crazy! And *this diary?*' She held it out, making a point of uttering a small laugh that was hostile enough to express her abhorrence for all the book had revealed thus far. 'I need to get out. I have to go. I mean, look at me!' She pulled on the hem of the shirt she was wearing, aware of how hysterical she must sound, but not caring because what she said was true. Never had she been so close to the edge of what felt like categorical madness. 'And look at the pair of you. We're a right fucking state.'

'Calm down,' Thurston said, his voice gravelled yet calm. He was on his feet now and Smiler looked strained under the weight of him. 'We'll sort it. We've got this.' Still shirtless, he'd let the t-shirt he'd used to stem the blood flow fall to the floor. The left side of his chest was gaping open like a bloodied toothless mouth and Callie supposed that sooner or later one of them might well to have to stitch it up somehow. The thought made her queasy.

'Hey, why don't I bring Pollyanna upstairs,' Smiler suggested. His hands were planted firmly on Thurston's bare torso in an effort to keep him upright and his face was a blood-rush of red. 'That way you can stay right where you are, Thurston. I mean, you don't seem too good, man. You should probably lie down again.'

Thurston pushed away from Smiler a little, so he was standing more independently. 'I'm fine,' he said, though he was clearly lying. 'Let's just go.'

'Yes let's,' Callie agreed, glancing round the walls with no sense of diminished unease. The paint on the canvas above the bed looked as though it was wet like recent blood. She shuddered. 'I think it's best if he gets out of this room. If we all do.'

Daylight from the lounge lurked on the stairs with all the gloom of a wet October morning, but still it managed to make a faint shadow cage, as hazy as outside, around Callie's feet and lower legs from the wooden spindles of the bannister. At the bottom of the stairs Pollyanna was waiting. Annoyed impatience exaggerated the blackness of her eyes as though they were coals that had sparked the redness of her hair. 'What's going on?' she said. 'What took you so long? And what's that?' She lifted a hand and pointed, indicating the journal clutched to Callie's chest.

Callie held the book out and angled it about in the air, as if to allay any suspicion Pollyanna might have that she was trying to conceal it. 'It's your cousin's diary.'

'*Sarah Jane's?*' Pollyanna's anger was repressed by shock, making her eyes lessen in intensity and small mouth appear smaller still. 'But…where was it?'

'In the tower,' Smiler told her. He and Thurston had begun to climb down the stairs. His arm was tight around Thurston's waist and neither man looked comfortable with the arrangement. Their heavy, awkward footing caused a rowdy clobbering on the wooden steps, the sound of which the cabin seemed reluctant to absorb into any of its surfaces. But the echoing din wasn't enough of a distraction for Pollyanna. 'But you said you couldn't open the door,' she said, accusingly.

'Long story,' Smiler grunted, as he helped Thurston to negotiate the next step.

'We found a key to open it,' Callie explained more easily.

'Where?' Pollyanna scowled with what looked like mistrust but could easily be something else, including murder.

'Doesn't matter,' Callie said. The fact they had found the key to the tower buried in Thurston's chest was neither here nor there as far as Pollyanna was concerned. 'The main thing is, all four of us are going to sit down together till we've figured a way out of here.'

When Smiler and Thurston made it to the bottom of the stairs in a sweaty jumble that comprised arms and legs and blood-rusted skin, Callie offered her shoulder to support Thurston over to the couch, where slowly and carefully she helped him to lie down. She sat by his feet and Smiler collapsed in the armchair opposite. Pollyanna went to her usual spot by the window and looked out, even though there was nothing to see but fog clawing at the glass.

Callie thrummed her fingers on the journal's cover. She dreaded asking, but needed to know, 'Pollyanna, how old were you when you first came to the cabin?'

Apparently it was acceptable to ask the question, because Pollyanna replied civilly, 'Thirteen.'

'What about Sarah Jane?'

'Fourteen. She's two months older than me.'

'That was in 2009 right?'

'Yes.'

Callie shifted in her seat and felt Thurston's foot dig into the small of her back; a deliberate move, but one that showed support or deterrence for this line of conversation she wasn't sure. She avoided looking at him and asked Pollyanna, 'And do you know what year it is now?'

Pollyanna shrugged and shook her hair forward to conceal her face. 'I was never able to keep track of time. Late 2010?'

This time Thurston's foot in Callie's back was definitely a sign of dissuasion. She coughed into her hand and tried to think of something to say, anything that might derail them from the path of trauma they were currently headed down, but couldn't think of anything better than, 'Anyway, shall we continue?' while drawing attention to the journal that rested in her lap.

Pollyanna looked at everyone in turn then, her eyes unyieldingly scornful. 'You mean you already started reading it? Without me?'

Shit. 'So far we've flicked through as far as February 2010,' Callie said, feeling insensitive for the way she'd handled things, but not knowing how else she might have done it.

'Parts of the diary were written in *2010?* But that's not possible,' Pollyanna said, her mind stumbling with the knowledge and making her look vacant. 'Uncle Dean brought us here in October 2009.'

'Yes, the trip was mentioned.'

'But how did the diary end up in the tower? I'd have noticed if Sarah Jane had come back. I've been here all this time!'

For the first time since they'd met, Callie thought Pollyanna might cry. Her eyes glassed over and her mouth twisted with hurt frustration. To think that she'd been waiting all of this time for someone to come. But no one ever would. Not now. Not after seven years had passed. *Jesus.* 'That's what we need to find out,' Callie said, making her voice as soft as she could. She opened the book's cover and skimmed her finger over the words to find where she'd left off.

'I have to warn you,' Pollyanna said, with some prickle in her tone. 'You should take everything Sarah Jane says with a pinch of salt. She's a massive fantasist. A bloody big liar, in fact, and not a very nice person at all.' Callie was surprised by the admission and didn't quite know what to say before Pollyanna asked, 'Has she mentioned me at all?'

Callie looked at Smiler. He frowned. Then she flashed a sideways glance at Thurston who shrugged some despondency on the matter.

'Tell me,' Pollyanna urged. 'I want to know if she had anything to say about me.'

Callie took a deep breath. 'Okay. She said you made her angry.'

'Is that all?'

'For now,' Callie lied.

'What did she have to say about this place and what

happened and why they all left me?'

'We're not entirely sure what happened. It's not yet clear. Her folks split up and her mother got with Dean. Uncle Dean. Like you said, it's pretty obvious Sarah Jane was besotted with him.'

Pollyanna seemed to recede into herself, the stress of too much information. When it was clear she had nothing further to say, Callie started to read aloud from the diary.

No one interrupted. Everyone listened, including the cabin.

30

Wednesday 10th March 2010

Devoted Dorian,

Apologies yet again for the lateness of my thoughts. Almost another month has passed and everything is highly frustrating.

*First things first, I finally asked Uncle Dean where the cabin at Whispering Woods is, but I'm still no further forward! He started telling me stories about the holidays he's taken there since he was a boy, but didn't answer the actual question. Then The Deserter insisted I go to my room to do my homework, so I **STILL** don't know where it is. Argh! I've asked numerous times since, but it's almost as though they don't want me to know. The most I ever got out of Uncle Dean was that it's somewhere 'way up north' and The Deserter keeps telling me to mind my own business. Once she even shouted at me, saying 'I should never have bloody took you that day!'*

I still plan to go there. Some day. I'll find out where it is and take the ravens back and make it a place where The Deserter can't go. Hopefully she might be buried in the ground by then anyway, so when Uncle Dean goes to the cabin for holidays, there'll be just me and him. Him in his bedroom, with the stag's head and the burgundy throw, and me in the tower. I'll be right above him and he won't know. Eventually he will though. He'll sense me and call out for me. And that's when I'll go to him.

But till that day I'll bide my time. Like Rapunzel.

In other news the wedding has been set. June next year. A summer wedding. How awful. The print will ~~bearly~~ barely be dry on the divorce certificates or whatever it is you get when you get divorced.

Dad is sickeningly sad and The Deserter is infuriatingly happy. I hate her more than ever. But at least I get to see more of Uncle Dean.

To rub salt in the wound, The Deserter has asked me to be bridesmaid. It's the part of her that likes keeping up appearances that made her ask, otherwise she'd have run off into the sunset by now and never looked back. I've ruined her preferred colour scheme, so that's something at least! She wanted all bridesmaids in 'salmon pink' and Uncle Dean to have a matching silk tie. But then she realised it would clash with my hair, so she's decided to go with a sort of gold colour instead. I'm pleased I'm causing trouble for her. She doesn't deserve to be this happy.

Nothing good ever lasts though. I have to hold onto that thought.

Monday 22nd March 2010

Delightfully Deadly Dorian,

Had a massive argument with Dad today. I told him I'm going to take Uncle Dean's surname when him and The Deserter get married. Dad was really upset. I don't know why. It's not like he cares that much about what I do anyway. I only told him out of decency. I haven't discussed this with Uncle Dean yet. But I don't see why he wouldn't let me take his name. Not sure The Deserter will be happy, mind you. But I need a new start too, not just her. She's totally ruined my life with her selfishness, it's the least she can agree to.

In fact, Dorian, I've been doing some thinking and I've decided that as of next year I'm going to be someone else. Sarah Jane Miller is just too...ugh, I dunno, I just don't like being her anymore. Even if it can't be done legally, to have Uncle Dean's surname, like if Dad won't consent or whatever, I'll just do it anyway. Because Sarah Jane Miller's life isn't exciting and she needs a new name and image. A new persona.

Besides, Uncle Dean has come up with this cool new nickname for me. He calls The Deserter Roxie all the time, which makes her sound cool, even though she isn't. And he calls me Essie. The Deserter hates it, she says it's the height of laziness. But I love it! It's something shared between just me and him, and I think she hates it because it's mine and not hers and it's something he gave me that she can't have.

So next year I'm going to dye my hair blonde (a day or two before the wedding just to piss The Deserter off, because she could have had a 'salmon pink' colour scheme after all), and I'm going take Uncle Dean's surname and make the transition from Sarah Jane Miller to Essie Bennett.

31

Smiler made a strange noise. Everyone looked at him. The sound came from the back of his throat as though he'd swallowed something the wrong way. His eyes were wide.

'Are you okay?' Callie asked.

His eyes stayed unblinking and he shook his head, but he did so with such slowness and an uncharacteristic vacuity that seemed to suggest he wasn't answering her directly. Rather, he was engaged in some disturbing internal monologue.

'Seriously, Smiler, what's up?'

His jaw and lips began to move ever so slightly, as though he was chewing on the beginnings of a response, but it seemed his tongue was having problems turning his thoughts to actual words. Or maybe his thoughts failed to unjumble themselves into any sort of sense.

'Smiler!' Pollyanna tried to impose a look of impatience. It had been a while since anyone had seen her with a cigarette in her hand and it was this as well as her countenance that betrayed her concern. She was all stiff and angular, her small bony body fraught with apprehension. The reproving tone she managed to exude did the trick, however. Smiler snapped out of his trance, running a hand over his face. He looked at Callie and said, 'That's the girl I told you about.'

'What girl? When?'

'Essie Bennett. Yesterday.'

'Your ex-girlfriend?'

Smiler's complexion was waxen, too pale. He nodded.

'Shit!' The word hardly held enough weight to convey Callie's shock, but it was the first that came to her head.

A loud, sharp rap against the window made them all look. There was a raven on the wooden boards of the veranda outside. Watching them, intently. Its beak was poised, ready to hit the glass again, and its feathers were nightmare black against a backdrop of greedy fog, which had eaten the lake and the Bentley and anything else that had been out there.

Callie's heart began to thump.

Were the birds planning another attack? And was it because they were closing in on the truth?

'What happened with Essie Bennett?' Callie asked Smiler. 'Was it an amicable break up? Or did things get messy?'

'As I said, she got overly paranoid. Said I was sleeping with anyone and everyone I spoke to. She was the one who called it off when I said I wouldn't put my career on hold for her.' His face darkened then. 'But that's not to say it ended there. She went on to cause no end of trouble for me.'

Callie's eyes widened. 'Was that the trouble you mentioned before? Whatever it was you were acquitted of?' Her attention was split between Smiler and the raven. The raven's eyes gleamed with something: if not gloating then something perilously close to, like it knew more than she did on the matter.

'Yes. Essie orchestrated the whole thing.' Smiler rubbed at his chin with blood-rusted knuckles. His eyes were despondent as he began to process what all of this might mean, the fact the malicious teen who'd been so besotted with her mother's partner Dean, to the point of wild obsession, had been his own girlfriend at some point. Smiler was incredulous that he had been in a relationship with Pollyanna's cousin and was only realising now. Poor Pollyanna, the girl who should now be twenty-one, but looked and thought she was fourteen. 'I imagine after a whole lot of bribing and bullying tactics,' he said, 'Essie managed to persuade a group of schoolgirls to say that I'd exposed myself to them.'

Callie made a noise of disgust. 'That's sick.'

'Twisted,' Thurston agreed.

'Essie Bennett *is* twisted,' Smiler said. 'Thankfully the jury found me not guilty, but the media had already by that point damaged my reputation beyond what I could cope with. I mean, there's a certain stigma attached to stuff like that that never really disappears. No matter what. Even after an innocent verdict, there are people out there who still cast their eyes at you like you're some filthy fucking nonce. So yeah, Essie Bennett pretty much killed my career with her game of jealousy-induced revenge. *And* caused me to have a nervous breakdown at the same time.'

Cah-cah-cah. The raven laughed. It was an ugly sound, which the cabin readily welcomed into its wooden viscera. Callie refused to give the bird the attention it craved and kept her eyes on Smiler. 'How do you know for definite that it was Essie Bennett who set you up?'

'One of the girls cracked under the pressure of the case. Katie Pomfrey. She confessed to having lied about the whole thing. Then one by one most of the others did as well. They implied that someone older had coerced them into fabricating lewd stories about me, but none of them would give any names. About two months after the acquittal, I found a red rose taped to my apartment door. There was a note with it that said: Next time, Miles. It was quite obviously a threat. And it was quite obvious that it came from Essie. I could tell because of the way she put an '*x*' above the '*i*' in my name. She always did that.'

Callie was rendered speechless for a moment and it seemed nobody else had anything to say either. Not even the raven. 'I can't believe I didn't see any of this in the papers or on the news,' she said at last.

'Me neither.' Smiler shook his head. 'Where were you, on the moon?'

'Well I must have been up there with her,' Thurston said, 'because I don't remember hearing about any of that either.'

'Well, you have now.'

'Didn't it ever cross your mind that Essie might have been the one responsible for you being here?' Callie said.

'In the early days, maybe a little. Like maybe, I thought, she was trying to set me up. I mean, after everything, how bad does it look me being holed up with a minor?' He looked at Pollyanna apologetically for having referred to her as such. 'But I was never totally convinced. Essie's certainly dangerous and vengeful, but the longer this dragged on the more it didn't seem like her style. Essie is impatient. She wants everything done yesterday. She pretty much needs instant gratification otherwise she spits her dummy out. Whereas *this*, this is slow torture. Whoever set this up, I got to thinking, had to be in it for the long run. For the life of me I couldn't make any connection between me being here and Pollyanna being here.'

'Yet now,' Callie said, 'it's safe to say you're both here because of Sarah Jane Miller.'

Smiler's face fell into a troubled frown, as though the much-anticipated revelation was both mind-blowing and anti-climactic.

'What about me?' Thurston said. 'I don't know Sarah Jane Miller *or* Essie Bennett. So why am I here?' His head lolled against the couch's backrest and his heavy eyes suggested an increasing lethargy, but still he managed to inject a startling amount of aggression into his tone when he looked between Pollyanna and Smiler and warned, 'And the next person to accuse me of being

Uncle Dean gets a punch in the face, just so you know.'

The raven laughed again. Everyone looked at it.

An idea had formed in Callie's mind, one she'd rather not entertain, but one that seemed quite obvious. Too obvious to ignore. 'I think I know what's going on,' she said. 'Sarah Jane Miller became Essie Bennett, didn't she? Therefore, it wouldn't be unreasonable to assume that Essie Bennett might have got bored with herself and taken on another persona at a later date. And if that is indeed what happened, I'm going to suggest we *do* know Sarah Jane Miller.'

Thurston raised his eyebrows, but she could tell he wasn't about to oppose her idea because an unambiguous look of understanding was spreading over his face with as much presence as the fog outside; a murkiness that would become clear given time.

'Someone who links us together and fits into the correct age bracket,' Callie said, hoping she was wrong, 'makes me think that Sarah Jane Miller and Essie Bennett could be our Freya.'

Thurston closed his eyes to consider this within the confines of his own head. As he did, another raven flew at the window pane. It scrabbled about on the veranda, clawing, tapping and squawking.

'Sarah Jane's ravens,' Smiler said, his voice an eerie whisper. 'They know that we know her secrets. That Sarah Jane Miller is three different people.'

'We can't be sure,' Thurston said, his back straightening, his mouth pulled tight. Defensive. 'Not about Freya.'

'But I think it's highly bloody likely.' Callie reached across and touched his forearm, her fingers gentle but firm. 'Going off what you told me last night, you're about to break up with her. How long have you been thinking about it?'

'It's been in the back of my mind for a while now. I

just hadn't done anything about it.' His eyes were deep set in shadow. 'But this is the thing, I *haven't* broken up with her. As far as she's aware everything's fine. She has nothing to be angry or upset with me over.'

Smiler issued one snort of ironic laughter, like he knew differently, and Callie raised an eyebrow. 'If something wasn't right,' she said, 'chances are Freya knew. Woman's intuition.'

'Rubbish,' Thurston scoffed.

'I'm telling you, she'll have got vibes from you that something isn't right,' Callie reaffirmed. She pointed at the congealed bloodiness of his chest then thought to say, 'Don't you think that's highly symbolic?'

'Of what? A sadist!'

'Of Freya ripping your heart out and leaving the key to her secrets in its place.'

He breathed in deeply and massaged his temples. 'Sounds too messy and creative for Freya. She'd more likely key my car.' But Callie could tell he was already deliberating the implied motives of his girlfriend.

By now there were six ravens on the veranda brooding against a backdrop of intense dirty-white. They looked like sooty fallout from some infernal fire that was raging underground. A fire that was rising up and making enough smoke to seep through soil. Enough smoke to fill and suffocate the earthbound world.

'Let's suppose that Freya is Sarah Jane Miller,' Thurston said to Callie. 'Why are you here?'

'I don't know,' Callie admitted. 'But does Sarah Jane Miller need a reason to hate someone? Maybe she got bored. Or maybe she didn't like something I said last time we spoke on the phone. What I do know is that if Freya is Sarah Jane Miller, then I got off quite lightly compared to you guys.'

'I know why she wouldn't like you,' Pollyanna said, surprising everyone with her sudden input. She'd been quiet this whole time, her face hidden by her mass of red hair, but now she was looking from beneath her lashes at Callie. More ravens had gathered at the window, forming a line to her left like some implied extension of her. And the fog seemed to have darkened at its core, as though something evilly obscure within it drew closer. 'Because you're successful. She'd *hate* that.'

The ravens barked a ragged chorus that was much too enormous for how many were visible. Callie imagined there must be hundreds on the lawn, hidden within the swell of the fog. Even Thurston swivelled round to see if he could see.

Pollyanna smiled, managing to look even slier. 'Also, because Thurston likes you. That's more than enough reason for Sarah Jane to despise you.'

Soft thuds came from the roof. Callie jumped with a start and looked up. The birds were covering the cabin, looking for a way in. It wasn't long before she could hear wings flapping within the cabin. Upstairs. Behind Smiler's closed bedroom door. 'Don't be ridiculous,' she said, swallowing to keep her heart down. 'Me and Thurston are just friends.'

'Poll's right,' Smiler said. He had moved to the edge of the armchair and his eyes darted about with every scratch and bump exacted on the cabin. 'Because supposing Freya is Sarah Jane Miller, those are two very good reasons as to why she would hate you. The version of Sarah Jane that I knew was possessive and vindictive. Didn't apply logic or rational thought to the way she ran her life. Was devoid of empathy. And got off on ruining lives for fun.'

Callie felt sick. 'So you really do think I've been set up by a friend who begrudges my career and hates the fact I'm on speaking terms with her boyfriend?'

'Like you said, you got off lightly,' Smiler said.

'And we're speaking completely hypothetically,'

Thurston reminded them all. 'Read some more of that thing,' he said, indicating the diary with a troubled glance. 'Then we'll know for sure. But be quick, I think the ravens are about to go all Hitchcock on us.'

'Alright, alright.' Callie thumbed open the journal, feeling pressurised by the gathering black army outside. 'Should we skip straight ahead to the Essie Bennett stuff in that case?'

Thurston and Smiler nodded their agreement, but Pollyanna didn't say or do anything. Callie took her silence as an assent, not an objection. 'When were you seeing her, Smiler?'

Smiler shifted about in his seat. 'Er, actually, I'd be kind of uncomfortable if you were to read anything out that she might have written about me. I'd rather vet those parts myself. In private.'

'Of course.' Callie was already nodding. 'So what would be a safe date for us to resume?'

Smiler closed his eyes and thought. 'Say around November 2013. We broke up just before Halloween.'

'Okay, let's start December 2013, just in case.'

32

Sunday 1ˢᵗ December 2013

Dammit Dorian!

Stuff happened this weekend. Serious stuff! And now I'm in deep shit!!! But where to start? I can't think straight because Roxanne is going off on one downstairs. Again.

She went to her mate's hen weekend in York on Friday afternoon and as soon as she got home this evening Dean told on me! I can't believe it. I just don't know what to make of it or how to feel. But I'm jumping the gun, aren't I? I need to rewind...

Roxanne said she would drop me off at Dad's on her way to York, but I asked Dean if I could stay with him instead (since I had a load of college work to be getting on with). I promised I'd be no bother at all and he laughed and said, 'Shit, Essie, I can't believe you thought you had to ask, of course it's fine if you want to hang around here for the weekend!'

So I did.

On Friday evening me and Dean watched a few films together and shared a bottle of wine. It was the best night ever!

Yesterday he was out all day, so I just hung about the house. I took the opportunity to have a rummage through his and Roxanne's bedroom, to see what I could find.

*And I **FINALLY** found it, Dorian! The key and address for the cabin!!! (Though I'm no longer sure I want to go there now, not after what's happened. I don't know if it's appropriate. Or maybe it's perfect?? I dunno. I need time to think).*

Anyway, I'm going off on a tangent again. Dean didn't arrive home till quite late last night. He smelled of booze and seemed quite merry. I made him a coffee and he stayed up to chat for about an hour. I love it when he's drunk, he opens up and talks about his days in the army. About the gorier stuff that usually he would keep to himself. I wanted to ask him so many questions, but I could tell he'd had enough when his white eye stayed shut and his blue eye struggled to stay open. After he'd gone to bed, I watched more telly on my own for a while. Then during the night is when it all happened! When everything went wrong.

I mistimed. Misjudged. Got set up!

*I woke and it was raining really heavy against the windows and because of this the ravens were unsettled. They wouldn't let me go to sleep again, so I had to get up. They're so bloody stubborn! On the way past Dean's room, one of them pushed the door open. Then they **ALL** flew inside!*

The bedroom was dark and smelled pleasantly sour. A mixture of alcohol and Dean's aftershave. Dean was lying beneath the duvet, breathing heavily and murmuring about something. I crept inside, pleased that he was drunk, and waved furiously at the ravens, bidding them to come back to me. But they totally ignored me. Instead they perched themselves in a line along the headboard, their blinky black eyes full of mischief. Like one of them might crow at any minute, to wake Dean and get me in trouble. Then as if to wind me up further they started jumping down onto the bed, one by one, where they hopped about on Roxanne's pillow and started burrowing beneath the duvet!

The rain was still loud and by this time I could hear thunder in the distance. I rushed over to the bed and tried to shoo the ravens away. But all of them, every last one, seemed intent on disobeying me and disappeared beneath the duvet!

I thought about leaving. Splitting on them and running. And in hindsight I should have. But I couldn't. So I went to Roxanne's side of the bed and lifted the duvet and found them all lying on their backs, looking up at me. They're so defiant! And their black feathers were everywhere!

There was a massive crash of thunder then and Dean groaned and turned. Frightened the ravens might cause even more mischief, I quickly climbed into the bed to flatten them to the mattress, so they wouldn't be able to touch Dean. Then I lay there for ages, unable to move.

After a while, Dean put his arm across me and stroked my arm with his thumb. I turned on my side to face him and watched him for ages. His warm breath on my face. When it seemed likely he wouldn't wake, I dared myself to reach up and stroke his face and touch his mouth with my fingers. And I'm not altogether sorry that I did either. Not even when lightning flashed and thunder boomed and Dean opened his eyes.

He was confused at first. Then furious. He started shouting at me and told me to get out. I've never seen him like that before. When I jumped out of bed, the ravens scattered to the cream carpet like flakes of ash and I could hear them cackling. Sometimes they can be so cruel! It's not the first time they've set me up. Though this was their worst prank so far.

I haven't seen them at all today. They know I'm not happy with them. And Dean hasn't spoken to me. I stayed in my room with Lucy and didn't venture out. When Roxanne came home I heard her talking with Dean, then she stomped up the stairs and barged into my room. She looked like she wanted to kill me. Dean had come upstairs too and was standing right behind her. He looked awkward and I instantly wondered if he regretted telling her. But he had. The damage is done and can't be taken back.

Roxanne asked me what in the fuck I thought I was playing at. I said I was sorry (even though I wasn't) and said I must have sleep walked. I said I remembered nothing till Dean had woken me by shouting. I don't think either of them believed me, but Dean calmed her down (slightly) and took her back downstairs.

When everything had gone quiet, I eventually went down to see how bad things were. And as it happens, Dorian, it's pretty fucking bad! Roxanne says she wants me out. That I've gone too far this time and have to go and live with Dad or Gran.

Shit, why did this have to happen?!

I feel betrayed by the ravens and betrayed by Dean!

33

'DEAN!' A woman's cry cut through the cabin's wooden entrails, as well as the skin and bone of everyone in it.

Callie stopped reading and looked up. 'Did you all hear that?'

'Of course we fucking did,' Thurston said. He'd scrabbled round on the couch so his feet were on the floor, his ragged body ready for action. Ready for something.

Smiler, on the other hand, was pushing himself as far back as he could, as though he hoped to hide inside the armchair. 'You were right,' he said. 'There *is* someone else here.'

Callie placed the journal on the arm of the couch and stood up. The sound of the woman's fear was still ringing in her head. The way she'd cried out was as though someone was about to be murdered. But who? The woman herself? Dean? Someone else? Was the cabin some sort of murder house? Pollyanna had already said how Uncle Dean had hinted to her and Sarah Jane of it having a grisly past. Were spirits trapped here like bad karma, the cabin unable or unwilling to let go? And what did Whispering Woods have to do with it? The voices she'd heard outside. Were they current ponderings of the dead? Or a replay of words that had already been spoken, which the place possessively held onto and refused to let drift into the ether of the past. Nonsensical verses that were destined to hang around forever; able to break the soundest of minds in the here and now. *Do you know any stories? Suppose that depends. Lived here as it happens. Something really awful. Take a guess. Suppose that depends. Why does anyone do anything? Suppose that depends. All except the small boy. But why? But why? But why? But why? That's just how it is, sweetheart.*

Callie crept to the foot of the stairs and Thurston made to follow. Thinking he'd be more of a hindrance than a help, she urged him to stay where he was with a frantic hand gesture and fierce scowl. Quietly and light-footedly, she then made the ascent, listening all the while for anything else the woman might say. But there was just silence. A cabin filled with held breath and heightened pulses. And Callie's feet treading softly on the wooden stairs, a sound that was barely there. Once at the top, in the solemn gloom of the landing and the impending quiet, Callie forgot about the threat of the ravens and whipped the door to Smiler's room open. What she saw made her cry out in fright. The bed was a writhing black mass of feathered bodies and over by the window, disturbing in terrible contrast, there was a woman. A figure so blurry she might well have been fog that had seeped in through the broken pane. Except it definitely was a woman, or at least some spectral projection of what used to be, because Callie immediately recognised her as the woman she'd seen in the bathroom mirror.

Aside from the ethereal quality of her presence, the woman didn't look dead. More like a hazy, low quality playback. But this couldn't be the case, Callie thought, because when the ghostly woman turned, her eyes caught Callie's for the briefest of moments. The contact made Callie's skin prickle with gooseflesh. She shuddered. The woman then looked towards the raven-infested bed, as though someone might be on it, beneath the birds, and said, 'She's here, Dean. I saw her. I think she saw me.'

Then, as though Callie had witnessed as much as the

cabin had planned for her, the woman fizzled away to nothing. As easily as blinking away sleep. As quickly as shifting the brainstorm that comes with standing too fast. Callie was left unable to move.

I saw her. I think she saw me.

But why couldn't I see Dean? Why were the ravens gathered in his place?

As if goaded by her thoughts, the ravens broke their eerie stretch of silence with a headachy raucous of excitable chatter. They began to jump up and down, landing on each other's backs and jabbing each other with overly zealous beaks. Some of them scattered to the floor in the commotion, which prompted Callie to jump backwards and swing the door shut, to keep them locked within.

'There's a ghost,' she said, hurrying back down the stairs. Her hands were trembling and she was sorry she'd gone to look, sorry that her curiosity had been sated. 'It's a woman. I've seen her twice now.'

'What does she look like?' Pollyanna wanted to know. There was a quiet dread etched onto her face, making her small mouth slightly downturned. Callie could already guess what she was wondering.

'Mid-thirties, maybe. Long dark hair. Slim build. Pretty.'

'Aunt Roxanne,' Pollyanna confirmed, her forehead puckering with a building permission to grieve at last.

'Do you think it's possible Sarah Jane killed her?' Callie asked.

'I've been here all this time. How could she have?' Pollyanna said. 'I don't get it.'

'Me neither,' Smiler said.

'I do.' Everyone looked at Thurston. His shoulders were slumped and he rubbed at the dried blood that discoloured his fingers. His expression was so concentrated he looked almost stultified. 'We've got it wrong,' he said. 'That is, we're looking at it from the wrong angle.'

Callie almost didn't dare ask, but had to. 'What are you talking about?'

He stopped rubbing and showed her his hands, a gesture of openness and sincerity. 'Look at us. We can't get out. We're trapped here. Think about it. *Really think.* Pollyanna should be twenty-one, for chrissakes.' He shook his head at the absurdity of that idea. 'And look at Smiler. He looks like Death warmed up. Then there's me. I've got a dirty big hole in my chest and I think it might be worth mentioning, though I really didn't want to have to, that I can't feel my heart.'

'What the hell are you saying, Thurston?' Callie forced him to maintain eye contact, hoping to see a glimmer of humour, however sardonic, so she could know he wasn't being totally serious. But all she saw there was sombreness. 'That you think it's us who're dead? That you think we're the ones haunting this place?'

He held his arm out to her. 'Check for a pulse.'

'You're being silly. You're not well, that's all.'

'That's what I've been trying to convince myself. But I *know* that's not true. I first realised after we'd been outside, when those things were out there. I was scared witless and ran back to the cabin with you, yet when we got inside I couldn't feel my heartbeat.'

'Maybe it's something to do with the wound.' Callie shrugged, her eyes denoting a certain amount of rising fear. 'Maybe you have low blood pressure? I dunno, I'm not a doctor. There must be a logical explanation.'

'Yeah, that's what I wanted to believe. But since then, no matter how much I try, I just can't find a pulse.'

'I don't think it's as easy to find your own.'

'So find one for me, prove me wrong. I dare you.' Again he held out his arm. When she made no attempt to do any such thing, he said, 'You said you thought you'd got off lightly, Cal, but I don't think you did. I think we're dead. All of us who're sitting here in this room. That's why none of this has been making any sense.'

'Sense! And you think that what you're saying does make sense?' Callie responded, with a snort. 'I don't know what's going on with your heart, but that fever must really be getting to your brain, Thurston.'

He waved his arm at her, offering up his wrist. 'Go on then, *check!* Feel for a pulse. If you find one, then I'll admit I'm wrong.'

Callie was aware now that Smiler and Pollyanna were watching, their faces steeped with an interest that was perversely fortified with dread. They were waiting, she realised, for her to make the argument in favour of them not being dead. So she did the only thing she could do and took hold of Thurston's wrist. Her fingers searched for a pulse. For the tiniest, faintest rhythmic beat. But after much probing, she found nothing. She shook her head and said in a voice that was high with fear and thin with indecision, 'Like I said, I'm not a doctor.'

But Callie had more or less substantiated Thurston's claim; a frightening prospect, because it made his outlandish idea that little bit more real and he'd rather have been disproven. 'Put your hand inside my chest again if you like,' he urged, becoming visibly worked up. His eyes were wide and he'd begun to tremble. 'You don't need to be a doctor to feel for a heart. I'll bet you can't find one, because Freya tore it out, just like you said. Only a little more literally than you originally thought.'

'Stop it,' Callie snapped. 'We're *not* dead. The woman I saw upstairs is.'

'Says who?' Thurston was not calmed in the least by her adamant claim, his complexion becoming less peaky because of his agitation. 'Maybe Roxanne and Dean are here on some other plane of existence. Maybe they're alive and *we're* the ones scaring the shit out of *them!*'

Callie inhaled loudly, her fists winding tight. 'If I was a ghost why the fuck do you think I'd haunt this place?' she almost screamed. 'I'd never even been here before two days ago.'

'Who says we get a say?' Thurston shouted back. 'If Sarah Jane Miller killed us, then maybe our souls are like a stamp collection and we've wound up in her sordid fucking scrapbook.'

'In which case, there could be quite a few of us living here by the end of the year,' Pollyanna said, with no sense of irony. She'd lit a cigarette and appeared creepily unfazed by the discussion. She stared at Callie, unblinking. 'I think Thurston's right. We *are* dead. It's certainly not a new concept to me.'

'No!' Callie rubbed her forehead, as if to massage the thought away. 'I don't believe I am dead. I can't be. Just no. Smiler, *you* check for a pulse.'

At the request, Smiler made a whimpering noise and shook his head. 'I don't want to.' He regarded Thurston with eyes that were glassy with fear. He knew that to touch him would be to seal their doom-filled fate. 'What good would it do? I'm not a doctor either.'

'I don't know, maybe you could just…'

'Hey guys,' Pollyanna said with such profoundness it made the hairs on Callie's neck rise. 'Have you seen outside?'

Callie hardly dared look, but when she did she saw that the veranda was a moving black thing, every square inch of its wood buried beneath an army of feathered bodies. The ravens were mostly facing the cabin. Hundreds of eyes. Watching.

'Sarah Jane's ravens,' Callie said, echoing Smiler's earlier words and believing them wholeheartedly.

'To hell with the ravens.' Thurston pointed to the journal resting on the couch's arm. 'Let's find out if

Essie Bennett definitely did become Freya. Go right to the end, Cal. Read the last entry.' He cast a look to the window again, his right leg having adopted a tic fuelled by nervous energy. 'Because I get the feeling we're a little pressed for time. Something's about to happen. Something big.'

'End of level bad guy,' Pollyanna said.

No one thought to disagree.

34

Monday 22nd September 2014

Dasvidaniya Dorian,

This is my final note to you. You've been a good friend and I'll miss you. I must go, though, and I can't say for sure if I'll ever be back. I'm off to university – much to Roxanne's delight – to make a fresh start. I need to forget about Dean and be someone else. I need to forge a new life for myself, no matter how much it hurts to walk away.

I need to forget about the cabin at the lake too. And Whispering Woods. Sometimes I doubt they ever even existed. Dean never took us back there. Not me, in any case. I wonder if that weekend ever truly happened. It was so long ago.

*I remember the cabin's rooms vividly. Or at least I think I do. Mine and Pollyanna's room with the twin beds overlooking the woods. Dean's room with the stag's head and the velvet throw. The room next to his with the blue bedspread and swan. Only, I never quite picture it that way. In my head it's always red, because I associate it with **HER**. Inevitably she was there that weekend and I feel I have to box her in somewhere so that she doesn't taint the rest of the cabin. Or my memories. So every time I imagine that room, I see it filled with all of her smuttiness. All of her filthy whoredom. All of her blood. In my head it's always red.*

*I hate her for leading the life **I** want. For masquerading as a beautiful swan and making Dean her own.*

But now it's time for this ugly duckling to become a swan. Only, I'll be black with red eyes and a forked tongue, so the white swan better watch out!

Maybe one day I will go to the cabin. I can't pretend I'll forget about it completely. It's almost as much a part of me as Dean. Neither can be erased. My heart pumps them round my veins and my brain feeds me dreams in which all three of us are together. Always.

I know that if I go back to the cabin, I'll never leave again.

But for now, as much as I love him (and always will), I need to distance myself from Dean. I need to get on with my life. I need to be someone new. I can no longer have the names that he gave to me. They're too painful to bear.

I don't yet know who I'm to become, but I know I won't be Sarah Jane Miller again, and I can't ever be Essie Bennett. I'll be stronger next time. Better than either of them ever were. I'm older now. Fiercer. I'll have new friends too. Better ones. And I'll try to love again. Someone else besides Dean.

My new love won't have it easy, granted. He'll have a lot to compete with to make me love him. He'll have to be powerful and beautiful, with a name like thunder.

Maybe Tarrant or Tarren. Or Thor. Would that be too much? Yes, probably. Tyrell. Keme. Thorin. Torbin.

Yes! Torbin. I like that. I like that a lot. And he'll look just like Dean.

35

Callie looked up, her eyes wide with consternation, 'Can somebody please tell me what I just read?'

But nobody could, least of all Thurston. The fog pressed closer to the window and the ravens shuffled restlessly, their hoarse baying softened by the nothingness that closed in all around them. Eventually Smiler broke the conversational silence. 'How could she have known?'

'Known what?'

'That she'd end up with someone called Torbin who looked like Dean.'

Thurston ran his hands through his hair and laughed; an ill-humoured sound. 'I admire your spirit, Golden. But *really?* I mean, that last entry was pretty profound and my head is in bits, but surely you get it? Surely.'

'It's a massive coincidence, that's all,' Callie said, squeezing her eyes closed and trying to think of a way of making it so in her head. But a greater instinctive part of her knew it was beyond any such thing.

'It's worse than being dead, that's what it is!' Thurston stood up. He began pacing the floor, his chest as gruesome as ever but no longer seeming to cause him pain. Whether this was a case of mind over matter or pure shock, Callie couldn't decide.

'You're not thinking about it logically,' she said, hoping to convince him so that he in turn might convince her of something she hadn't yet thought of. She cast the journal onto the coffee table, no longer able to bear the feel of its leathery waxiness. The dead skin of its front and back cover held pages of depravity at its rawest, which petrified her. Did it even exist? Did *she?* 'It's a sick prank. That's all.'

Thurston shook his head, a maniacal grin curving his mouth. 'No. No it isn't. Watch.' He showed her his hand, as if to prove that whatever he was about to demonstrate wasn't a trick, then delved it into the bloody hole of his chest. Wrist deep. Then further still. Callie looked away, too disturbed. Smiler dry-heaved. Thurston made desperate grunting sounds as he poked his fingers through the spaces between his own ribcage, and his eyes soon exuded a profound misery of confirmation. 'See?' he said, pulling his hand free. It emerged slippery black. 'Empty. No heart. Just like I said.'

Callie bit her bottom lip and began to sob. Either he was telling the truth or had completely lost his mind. Smiler buried his face in his hands and Pollyanna gawped in shocked silence. None of them said anything; each of them trying to process the hideous thing that Thurston had just done to himself, as well as Sarah Jane Miller's last written words.

'We were dreamed up by a delusional, self-obsessed psychopath,' Thurston thought to say, when still none of the others had spoken. He laughed then; a demented sound which made Callie cower away from him. 'We're nothing but characters inside her head.'

'No.' Callie groaned, shaking her head at his theory. 'There has to be a rational explanation.'

'Yes, there *has* to be,' Smiler agreed. 'It's got to be some sick joke.'

Pollyanna said nothing.

'Seriously?' Thurston said, his voice rising to near hysteria. 'If you're all finding it hard to believe, then feel free to have a dig about.' He indicated the yawning slick hole in his chest, offering it to anyone who might like to. Nobody did. So he ran his hands over his head, which left his blonde hair bloodied, and moved about in a bid to expel some restless energy. He looked at Callie and

wagged a finger at her. 'That life of stardom you thought you were leading, well really you aren't.' Then he looked at Smiler. 'And don't bother losing any more sleep over that ruined reputation of yours, mate, because guess what? You never had one. And my film production company? Never was. Pollyanna's accident? Never happened.' He was becoming more and more frenetic, his arms gesticulating, his eyes wild. 'And the reason we can't get out of this *shithole* is because we're stuck within the confines of Sarah Jane Miller's fucking head.' He struck the side of his own head with the heel of his hand.

'No,' Smiler said. His own stance was shrunken, as though he was trying to retreat within himself, away from Thurston's frenzy. Despite his refusal to accept what Thurston said, his eyes were racked with all the dread of a condemned man. 'That can't be right. What about the village? How could it be inside Sarah Jane Miller's head when she couldn't even remember where the cabin was?'

Callie groaned; a sound that indicated a new level of trepidation. 'That's a valid point, Smiler, but it actually substantiates Thurston's theory. Sarah Jane Miller, subconsciously or not, would have recalled bits of the village as they drove through it to get to the cabin, her mind probably filling in the blanks. The village itself was never really important though, hence the empty interiors and lack of people. It was never anything more than a scenic buffer for the cabin, a vignette of proposed reality.'

'No!' Smiler was shaking his head in abject denial. 'I can't believe that.'

'Well I certainly don't *want* to,' Callie said, taking to pacing the floor space in front of the couch while gnawing on the skin around her fingernails. 'But scarily enough it's starting to make the most sense, because there's also the whispering to take into account.'

'What whispering?'

'I've been hearing voices. I thought it was the trees. But now I wonder if it was her all along. Like what if the voices are her memories? Snippets of conversations she'd remembered from here. In fact, it has to be. It was never the bloody trees! When Dean told her about the woods and the murders, he planted a voracious seed in her head that grew and grew into something huge. Especially as he reinforced a sense of mystery surrounding the cabin by never revealing where it was or bringing her on a return visit. This is *all* about Dean, don't you see? It always has been. She's dangerously, obsessively infatuated.'

'And *I* was meant to be his substitute,' Thurston said. A great deal of contempt cast a shadow over his face. 'But I didn't quite live up to the ex-army sergeant. Obviously.'

'You never would have,' Callie said. 'No matter what, it was always going to be Dean she'd come back to eventually.'

'Should that make me feel better?' His reply was a little too harsh.

'Hey, we've all had the same news,' Smiler reminded him.

'Yeah, but your name isn't written down in black and white,' Thurston said, pointing at the journal, which was sitting on the coffee table with as much of an air of guilt as a bloodied axe at a murder scene. 'You didn't have to sit and listen to the childish process of her choosing a name for you. One she liked best. One that rolled nicest off her tongue. Did you?'

'No. But if we really are cast members of her fucked up fantasy world, as you suggest, then that's how it must have happened all the same, because *here I am!*' Smiler retorted, holding his arms out. 'In fact, if you flip back a few years I'm pretty sure that same childish process *is* jotted down for Miles Golden. Only, it's even worse for me. I was like some practice run. A lesser model that led to you.'

'Anyone other than Dean was never going to be good enough,' Pollyanna reminded them. The ravens continued to bustle about on the other side of the glass from her; just as fake, yet no less real than she was.

There was a loud bang upstairs, a door crashing open, then a huge raven swooped down and perched on the stair post. It was easily twice as big as its counterparts outside and it regarded them all with shrewd black eyes. 'Oonin,' it cawed, the consonants rolling awkwardly from its powerful beak. 'Oonin.'

Callie and Thurston both stopped pacing. The bird was like some portent of imminent doom.

'Shit, that's it!' Thurston said, raking his fingers down his face. 'You were right, Cal. The tattoo on my back *is* relevant.'

'How?'

'I thought I liked ravens,' he said, 'but I guess maybe I never really did. It was Sarah Jane Miller's idea to put them there. Obviously. But they do have significance. They're Odin's ravens.'

'Who's Odin?'

Thurston breathed a weary sigh into his hand. 'A god from Norse mythology. Top dog. He's blind in one eye and Thor's dad, would you believe?'

'Easily,' Callie said. 'Dean couldn't be anything less, could he?'

'Odin's ravens are called Hugin and Munin. Their names mean 'thought' and 'desire'.'

'Oonin,' the raven on the stair post said as if in confirmation.

'Which is Munin?' Callie asked.

'Desire.'

Callie looked from Thurston to Smiler, then she glanced at Pollyanna near the window. 'I think Sarah Jane Miller's here at the cabin. Or at least close by. When I saw the woman upstairs, probably Roxanne, I heard her say 'She's here, Dean. I saw her. I think she saw me.' At first I thought she meant me, but she didn't. She meant Sarah Jane Miller. Freya.'

'*Freya!* Of course.' Thurston groaned, his eyes expressing recognition of his own idiocy on the matter. He'd been slow on the uptake, realising only now. 'In Norse mythology, Freya is Odin's wife.'

'And now she's come back to do whatever she has to do to get Odin,' Pollyanna said.

Callie nodded. 'She's going to kill Roxanne. We have to intervene. We have to stop her.'

The raven on the stair post laughed; a croaky sound that filled their heads with the threat of infinite death and uncertain purgatory. Then all of the ravens outside started to beat their wings, their own laughter a deafening furore like a prolonged tremor of thunder.

'How the hell are we supposed to intervene?' Thurston cried. 'We don't even exist!'

'Don't say that!' Callie said, furiously unwilling to accept this fact. 'We're here and I'm talking to you. I'm thinking. I'm feeling. Therefore, I do exist!'

'What if we make her think about us,' Smiler suggested. 'If we get to the forefront of her mind we can maybe talk her out of whatever it is she's going to do.'

'But why do we care?' Thurston wondered aloud.

'Because it'd prove we're human,' Callie said. 'It'd prove that we're more than what she wanted us to be. That we have freewill. That we have our own minds.'

'Do we though?' Thurston said, casting her a disparaging look. 'How do we know we're not just aspects of her subconscious? Conflicting morals that are probably too weak to stop her anyway.'

'No. I won't have that. I'm *not* her, I'm me.' Callie ground her jaw tight. 'Freya tried to talk me out of the part I played in *Ampato Curse*. She said she was worried about my mental health. I'd had a few breakdowns and she suggested that I should take a career break. That's what she *wanted* me to do, I can see that now. But I didn't, I went against her advice and did what *I* wanted to do. Just as Smiler did when he chose his career over Essie Bennett. That's why she wrote us off, confined us to this box in her head, because we wouldn't conform to her will. But here we all are, guys, plotting and thinking and living independently from her.'

'Similarly,' Smiler said, 'every time it looked like Pollyanna was going to make a name for herself, Sarah Jane Miller stuck a spanner in the works.'

'And no matter how much she wanted *you* to love her,' Callie said, to Thurston, 'no matter how hard she tried to make you, you never did.'

'No,' he agreed, 'not even a little bit.'

'Therefore don't you see? We *do* have freewill.'

Thurston didn't look wholly convinced, but she could tell that he was contemplating what she'd said.

'So now, for all of our sakes,' Callie urged, 'we need to challenge her.'

'Yes,' Pollyanna said, her voice filling the room like a memory. A sad memory of a girl who was once normal. 'It's time to confront her.'

36

She sat by the lake. Brazen as can be. Well, technically it was a loch. She was in Scottish Highlands territory. The Munros in the distance were almost how she remembered them, but darker, as if they'd brooded a lot during their wait for her to come home. She breathed in deeply and smiled. *Home.* Finally, she was home. All she had to do was officially announce her return.

The bathroom window to the rear of the cabin was open and she had thought about sneaking in that way, to take Dean and Roxanne by surprise, but decided against it. She was sick of skulking and hiding and not being seen. Besides, when they did see her, if they hadn't already, there was no risk of them phoning for the police, she'd already cut the phone line. Not that she imagined there was a police station within close proximity. The biggest town she remembered passing, before things got fairly remote, four days ago, was Fort William. There was no mobile signal at the cabin and although Dean's car was on the drive, it wasn't going anywhere. She'd removed the tyre valves and filled the exhaust with expanding foam. So the three of them would have to negotiate this surprise homecoming between themselves, with no outside interference. It was the only way.

Dean was ex-military, of course, she had to be careful not to underestimate him or overestimate herself. But she wasn't going to give them any reason, initially, to suspect they were in danger. Though she suspected that Roxanne *would* suspect. She always did. Mother's intuition. The restraining order Roxanne had taken out was still valid, but if a restraining order was the best she could do, it was quite laughable: even Hell's hound Garm from the underworld couldn't keep her away from Dean!

For the past two nights she'd slept rough in Whispering Woods. It had accepted her willingly, even though it scared her. But that was okay, she loved feeling scared. The adrenaline rush reminded her of when she was younger. With the thunder and the lightning, and the wind and rain battering the cabin, and Dean close by. Besides, whatever was in the woods, whatever might want to harm her, Dean had protectors. Odin's wolves, Geri and Freki. The ravenous ones. They'd protect her too, just as Dean's storytelling of ravens always had. Hugin and Munin, especially. Soon all of them would be together at last. There was just one problem to fix: Roxanne.

The idea of seeing Dean again gave her internal and external chills of excitement. She hadn't spoken to him in just over a year. For the special reunion she wore all black: skinny jeans, bodysuit, duster jacket and biker boots. She was the black swan and had come back for him, whether he consciously chose her or not. It felt as though her entire life had been leading up to this moment. This was her time to shine.

She grinned and hugged her knees to her chest, and watched as a lone female mallard glided across the loch. When she heard a gruff voice behind her, her heart fluttered and for a moment she couldn't breathe. 'Essie, what are you doing here?' It was him. Dean. He sounded stern, not exactly welcoming. But that was okay. She imagined he must be shocked about her turning up like this. It was only natural.

Then she heard Roxanne. 'How did you find us, Sarah Jane?'

'It's Freya. You know that.' Freya stood up and dusted the seat of her jeans. She turned round and smiled, her attention immediately fixed on Dean. Her heart felt as though it would rupture with long term affliction, and she thought when it did it might shatter her ribs and that she'd weep real tears of blood; such was her sense of loss for not having seen him in such a long time. His dirty blonde hair was still long and unkempt and he had facial hair that was too long to be stubble but too short to be a proper beard. His face was more slender now, sunken beneath his cheekbones. She couldn't decide whether this sign of ageing was what her memory measured against the first time they'd met, or whether he had indeed aged so much over the past year. Perhaps, if the latter was true, it was because he had mourned her loss. She liked that idea most. His live eye made her feel woozy and calm; the blue always managing to suppress the red behind her eyes, mostly triggered by encounters with Roxanne. His dead eye looked right through her. Since marrying Roxanne he'd stopped working out as much, lapsing into a more sedentary lifestyle. Therefore, his body had visibly softened, but still he looked good. So much so, Freya wondered at the inevitability of her heart bursting and wondered how long she had till it did.

'Why are you here?' Roxanne demanded to know.

'Pleased to see you too,' Freya said, with a sense of irony not bitter enough to cause an argument, but bitter enough to show resentment. Slowly she started across the lawn to the veranda where Roxanne and Dean were standing. Keeping her head bowed low, in what she hoped would be taken as submissive body language, she shrugged and offered them another smile. 'I just came to see you guys. I've been feeling bad about the way things turned out and I wanted to say I'm sorry for all the shit I've put you through over the years.'

Roxanne rolled her eyes and groaned. 'For God's sake.'

'Hey, I know I shouldn't be here.' Freya came to a

stop and held her hands up. 'I know where I stand. With you and the law. But I just had to say sorry. Face to face. I *had* to see you both again.'

'How did you get here?' Roxanne did a sweep of the garden, her hand gripping Dean's arm. 'I don't see a car.'

'I left it back at the village.'

'Why would you do that?' Roxanne's eyes narrowed some more.

'I didn't think it would cope with the potholes very well,' Freya said, maintaining a level of nonchalance, just as planned. She couldn't let them think she'd made the one-way trip by hitchhiking and walking, because then they might realise too soon that she had no intention of leaving. She pointed to the Land Rover on the drive, as if to shame them, and said, '*I* don't have a flashy car like you guys.'

Ever the diplomat, Dean scratched his chin and nodded. 'You'd better come in.'

All three of them stood awkwardly in the hallway, Dean towering above both women. He and Roxanne blocked the way to the lounge and Freya had made it no further than the doormat. Feeling the need to exert control, or be the one to do something at least, Dean put his hand on Roxanne's shoulder and squeezed. 'Why don't you put the kettle on, love?'

Roxanne flashed him a look of incredulity and opened her mouth to argue, but Dean insisted, 'Let her talk for a while, then she can go.'

Accepting her husband's judgement, rightly or wrongly, Roxanne turned and headed for the kitchen. Dean then led Freya through to the lounge. On the way Freya breathed in deeply, the smell of the cabin's wood as well as Dean making her feel in some way close to content. In the lounge Dean motioned for her to sit down on the couch, but she walked to the window instead and looked out at the loch.

'How did you find the cabin?' he said, taking a seat for himself. 'And how did you know we'd be here?'

Freya continued to stare out of the window at a sky lined with pewter that concealed a heartbeat. A storm was coming. 'Do you remember that story you started to tell me about Whispering Woods?' she said, purposefully ignoring his question. 'About Old Mally Murgatroyd and the family he killed. And how afterwards the trees told him to kill himself.'

Dean said nothing, but she could feel his discomfort like a palpable new fizz in the air. She smiled, pleased she could make him feel something unpleasant. It was payback, however miniscule, for the way he'd made her feel for all these years. All the agonised suffering she'd had to endure. Her poor heart.

'Do you want to know why I think Old Mally Murgatroyd and the trees spared that little boy?' she said, turning to him then.

Dean shook his head, his blue eye lessening in brilliance as vagueness befell him. He waited for her to tell him.

'Because he was you!' she said. 'He was you all along.'

Dean raised his eyebrows and began to speak, but she talked over the top of him, 'The trees want you here. They always have done. You can hear them, can't you? What do they say to you?'

'Whoa, Essie,' he said, holding up his hands. 'Of course I remember telling you that story, but it was just a bit of fun, that's all.'

'Fun?' Freya repeated the word as though it had no meaning. Then her eyes became awash with fearful bewilderment at the implied possibility of what he meant.

'It was just some local folklore. A daft tale that I

thought you'd like.' Dean shrugged. 'Kids like that kind of thing, don't they?'

Freya shook her head, unable to accept this. 'But it *is* true. The trees *do* talk. I've heard them myself.'

Dean regarded her with something like pity. 'It was just make-believe, Essie. A story created to stop local kids from wandering too far into the woods.'

'No.' Freya's face had paled. She imagined her blood had too. All of the red had left her and Lucy cowered in some cerebrum nook inside her head. 'It was real. It really happened. All of it.'

'Sorry, Essie, but no.'

Roxanne came in then, carrying a tray. She set it down on the coffee table and sat on the couch, close to Dean. Nobody moved to claim a cup of tea. The tray and its contents were simply there as a focus. A prop of civility in this surreal gathering. She may as well have brought three empty cups.

'Why did you come here, Sarah Jane?' Roxanne said, fidgeting with her hands in her lap.

'I already told you,' Freya said. Her voice sounded distant and she stared at the floor, trancelike, still pondering Dean's words. 'It's Freya.'

'Whatever.' Roxanne inhaled deeply. 'Why did you *really* come?'

'I wanted to see you guys. To apologise.'

Roxanne shook her head and snorted with derision. Her brown eyes sparked with something dangerous. Territorial anger, perhaps. 'I don't believe a word of that. You don't have a remorseful bone in your body. Is it money you want?'

Freya looked at her mother then and laughed. 'What the hell must you think of me? I don't want your money.'

'So what do you want?'

'You're the only family I have.'

'Hardly.'

'Gran's in the nuthouse and Dad's not far behind. He was never the same after you left him. Not that I came here to piss on your parade. Bit late for that anyway. Besides, you did what you had to. But it really did finish him off. So now you're the only family I have. You and Dean.'

'You've never been the sentimental type either, Sarah Jane.'

'Don't you think it's sad that we don't talk anymore? That you have a restraining order against me, your own daughter?' Freya frowned to convey her deep-rooted hurt. 'I mean, shit, what did you think I'd do to you?'

Roxanne hadn't relaxed in the slightest. She looked tightly wound. Ready to snap. The tendons in her neck were massively pronounced. 'Continue to harass us.'

'Harass you?'

'Yes, because you're bloody obsessed!'

Freya's expression clouded. 'With what?'

'You damn well know.'

Dean shifted in his seat and looked somewhat uncomfortable. Embarrassed even.

Freya fixed her attention on him and smiled, her eyes becoming darkly mischievous. 'I think she's trying to say that I'm obsessed with you, *Uncle Dean*. Do you agree?'

'Look, Essie,' he started to say, but she cut him off.

'It's okay, if you agree with her then just say so. We can only move forward as a family if we're open and honest with each other. Perhaps you'd even like to hear my take on it?'

His blue eye flashed angry and his white one remained all-seeing and not so blind to what was going on. To how she felt. He *knew* she was obsessed with him. She knew he always had done. It was never that he'd encouraged her attention per se, he'd just simply been

there. And there was never anything he could have done
to dissuade her about the way she felt. She loved the
very essence of him. 'Just say what you came to say,
Essie,' he said, hard-faced. 'Then I think it's best if you
leave.'

His firm demand was like a blow to the gut and part of
her wanted to die, but Freya managed to smile through
it. 'Me and Roxanne always did rub each other up the
wrong way, didn't we? But why can't we just be a
normal family?'

'Because there's nothing bloody normal about you,'
Roxanne told her.

Freya laughed again, although she didn't feel like it.
'You never were the motherly type were you?' She held
her hands up to show defeat. 'I get it, though. You wish I
wasn't here. I can tell I'm not welcome. I just thought, I
dunno, I thought things could be different now that I'm
grown up. But I can see that it's always going to be
difficult for you when you just don't have the feelings
for me that you should. But hey, don't feel bad. I get it.
There are anomalies in the wild sometimes too, you
know. Animals that eat their young. So you're by no
means a freak of nature. It happens. And for the record, I
think I'd be a lousy mother too.' She clapped her hands
together to signify a truce. 'So then. Now I've said what
I came to say and we all know where we stand, I guess
I'll be off. I'll leave you alone to live happy ever after.
You can't say I didn't try, though, you have to give me
that much.' She'd kept her voice calm and as she made
her way towards the hallway Dean and Roxanne both
looked uncertain. At the door she turned and spread her
arms wide. 'But don't I at least get a hug before I go?'

Roxanne looked to Dean, as if needing some moral
advice. He shrugged one shoulder and cocked an
eyebrow, in as much as to say *please yourself*, but made
no attempt to move, perhaps not wanting to encourage

his step-daughter's fixation by giving her physical contact. Under a strained sense of obligation, Roxanne rose from the couch, slowly and stiffly, and went to Freya. Her reluctance to do so made her grimace.

It was Freya who forced the embrace, bundling her mother into her arms. A little too keenly perhaps. Roxanne's body was bony and sinewy, and she didn't relax into the hug at all, which made Freya hate her more than ever. Holding her mother close, Freya breathed in the clean coconut scent of her hair. 'There once was an ugly duckling,' she began to sing. 'With feathers all stubby and brown.' She felt her mother stiffen and, as such, almost trembled with exhilaration as she slid the metal file she'd kept hidden up her coat sleeve into her hand.

This was it.

Time for the white swan to die.

Freya pulled way from the hug, enjoying the look of bemusement that had befallen her mother's face. With a quick swipe, she brought her hand up and drove the file into the side of Roxanne's neck. There was a wet choking sound. 'And her mother said in so many words.' Freya pulled the file free and pushed her mother to the floor. 'Get out of town.'

Roxanne dropped hard onto her knees and gripped her gushing throat with both hands. The white swan was fatally bloodied and there was a satisfying and distinct look of acceptance in her eyes, Freya saw, of the inescapable death that her daughter had dealt out to her. And there was so much blood. Red everywhere. Freya gaped in open-mouthed wonder. She'd dreamed of this moment for years and now that it was really happening it felt like just another dream.

It was Dean's shouting that broke through the surreal red. He was off the couch, lurching straight towards her.

'Get back!' she screamed. Snatching a handful of

Roxanne's hair, Freya then held the file just millimetres away from her mother's eyeball and told him, 'Or I'll put her eye out.'

37

To Callie, Thurston, Smiler and Pollyanna the cabin's rooms and contents transformed as soon as Freya entered. It was as though the memory of the place in her head had decayed over time, distorting into a place that was close to dilapidation. But upon Freya's return all of that changed. The furniture and décor, they saw, was actually clean and tidy. Dean and Roxanne Bennett were right there in the room too, not as ghostly figures but as real people. Yet still they were unable to communicate with them in any way.

Thurston couldn't stop staring at Dean. The likeness between the two men was unreal. Pollyanna stayed by the window, quietly seething. Freya had transformed into a woman while all this time she had been trapped in the body of a girl. Smiler fidgeted by the hearth, hardly daring to look at Freya. And Callie paced back and forth in front of the couch, feeling uneasy for Dean, but more so Roxanne. She cried out and told Roxanne to sit down when Freya requested a hug, then pleaded with Freya when she saw the silver flash of death graze her hand. But it was all in vain; Callie had no voice in their world.

It all happened quickly thereafter: an awkward hug turned into a deathly embrace. Roxanne Bennett crashed to her knees, blood pouring from her neck, and Callie found that she couldn't determine which were or weren't her own cries because Dean, Thurston and Smiler were also yelling at the same time.

When Freya threatened to stab Roxanne in the eye with the metal file, Callie couldn't stand it anymore. She screamed and screamed; her horror so intense everyone fell quiet and Freya flinched.

'Did you see that?' Thurston said. 'She heard you! *She heard you!*'

'Do it again,' Smiler urged.

But Callie didn't think she could. The most she could muster was a weary, 'Freya, stop it. Please.' This sombre appeal did nothing but emphasise the massive divide between their two worlds though, because she got no reaction. Nothing at all.

Roxanne coughed up blood and scrunched her eyes shut against the threat of the file's narrow tip; the file that was saturated with her own blood. She tried to move away, but Freya's fingers worked tighter in her hair. She yelped, a sound that gargled around in her throat, and looked wide-eyed at Dean.

Dean edged closer; unable to do nothing, yet not able to do anything to help his wife.

'There's nothing you could have done to stop this, Dean,' Freya said, her face devoid of remorse for the act of violence she'd just committed. 'You'll get over it eventually, though, because it was always meant to happen this way. It's the way it should be. Just me and you, here in the cabin.' She then applied enough pressure to scrape the surface of her mother's eyelid. Her expression had a demented guile that suggested she was ready to drive it home any second.

Callie's stomach roiled at the thought. *'STOP IT!'* she screamed.

Freya scrunched her eyes shut, as though pained with a sudden headache. 'No, not you!'

Callie's heart thumped. 'Yes, it's me. Me, me, *me!*'

'Go away!'

'You were supposed to be my friend, Freya. How could you do this to me?'

Freya's jaw clamped tight and she screamed through her teeth. 'Go. Away!'

'But why?' Callie insisted. 'Why did you do it? How

could you bring me here and leave me to rot?'

'I said *go away!*'

'Tell me.'

'No!'

'TELL ME.'

Freya looked Callie in the eye, her lips thin with hatred. 'Because you slept with Thurston behind my back, you fat cow.'

Dean closed the gap between him and Roxanne. 'Who's Thurston, Essie?' he said. His voice was calm as though he was talking to an upset child, but his blue eye was overwrought with terror.

'No, no, no!' Freya said, scowling and waving the metal file at him. 'I'm not talking to you. Stay back!'

'But it's not true,' Callie said, scared in case she lost contact with Freya. 'I've *never* slept with Thurston.'

'Liar! You've been trying to take him off me for ages.' Freya's fingers wound tighter in her mother's hair, but Roxanne Bennett barely seemed to notice, her consciousness was waning fast. 'And I know he has feelings for you.'

'Wow, you're so wrong it's almost funny,' Callie said. 'Even though you wanted me to, I never did sleep with him.'

'You *did!*'

'No, I didn't,' Callie insisted. 'And while we're on the subject I may as well tell you, he never loved you.'

'Liar!'

'It's true.'

'How would you know?'

'Because he told me.'

'When?'

'Last night. He's here with me right now.' Callie looked at Thurston, who was standing close to Dean like a nightmare version of him. 'So is Miles Golden. And Pollyanna. We're all getting along just great without

267

you.'

Freya's face contorted with rage, then as though summoned by her unspoken anger two massive ravens blustered down the stairs. Callie whipped round, turning her back to them, and covered her head with her arms. But the birds swooped hard and fast, mostly aiming for her face with their beaks and claws.

Dean leapt forward and shoved Freya away from Roxanne. Freya stumbled backwards but quickly righted herself. She screamed in anger and swung her arm in an upwards arc, aiming the file at Dean who was already scooping his wife into his arms. The whole cabin sucked in air then gasped loudly as the file popped the already scarred membrane of Dean's white eye. The metal shaft glided almost handle-deep inside his skull, puncturing soft tissue. His initial scream surpassed everything else that was going on. Even the ravens were startled and forgot about Callie for a moment.

'No! No! No! Look what you made me do!' Freya cried. Though to whom she was talking, nobody knew.

The ravens began a more frenzied attack on Callie, bloodying her arms and scalp within seconds. Thurston pitched himself forward and plucked one from the air. Its wings flapped furiously against his arms and it squawked its wrath till his ears hurt, but he managed to crank its neck to the side with one sharp jolt. It fell silent. Flinging its limp body to the ground, he reached for the second bird. This one fought harder. It gouged wedges of skin from his hands and almost severed one of his fingertips in its powerful beak, but Thurston wrestled it to the ground and repeatedly hit it with his fist till it was still.

Freya crumpled to the floor and clutched her head. 'NO!' She touched Dean's face with tentative fingers and stroked his hair, then shoved her mother's lifeless body away from him. 'This wasn't how it was meant to be,' she said, laying her head on his unmoving chest. 'This wasn't how it was meant to be!'

Everything seemed to stand still then, as though time and everything bound to it was irrelevant. And maybe it was, Callie supposed. What did time mean for her now anyway? What did anything mean? The injuries on her arms might be nothing at all or very real. They were hurting and bleeding what looked like real blood, so maybe they were real. She felt that they were. She looked down at Freya and felt an array of negative emotions. Then she heard Smiler's voice. *'Poll?'*

Callie turned to see.

Pollyanna was trying to stand, a look darker than rage plaguing her face.

'What are you doing, Poll?' Smiler asked.

'What I should have done years ago.' Pollyanna's arms trembled under the weight of hauling herself up. 'If I'm really not real, then I can do what I like. I can move my legs. I can walk.' But when she let go of the arms of the chair, her legs folded beneath her and she crashed to the floor. Smiler dashed over to help but she smacked his hands away and started dragging herself across the carpet towards Freya; her cousin who was lying with Dean's body and finally showing remorse for something she'd done.

Pollyanna's nails dug into the thick pile of the carpet and she moved quickly, perhaps fuelled by anger and hate and seven years' worth of retribution. The others just stood and watched. When Pollyanna reached Freya, she stretched up and grabbed a heavy looking snow globe off the coffee table and raised it high. Without a moment's hesitation, she then brought it down on the side of Freya's head. The subsequent crunching of skull bone, Callie thought, was a noise that would stay with her forever. Freya tried to move away, but Pollyanna brought the snow globe down on her head again and again and again, screaming wildly as she did, as if to give greater strength to every subsequent blow. Callie, Thurston and Smiler continued to watch on, dumbfounded. Sickened. Avenged. It was only when Freya's head was a bloodied mess and she was no longer breathing that Pollyanna let go of the snow globe. It rolled some way across the carpet then all of them watched, mesmerised, as snow fell down behind the blood-smeared glass dome onto a beautiful white swan.

38

Callie, Thurston, Smiler and Pollyanna weren't dead. Freya was, but they weren't.

'What happens now?' Smiler asked, his voice a dread-filled whisper. 'Why are we still here?'

None of them had dared to move in case they drew attention to the fact that they shouldn't be there, thus prompting the great fabric of existence to fold in on them.

'Because we're real,' Callie suggested. 'Not in Roxanne and Dean Bennett's world, but in our own. Though who's to say their world is any more real than ours?'

'But Sarah Jane Miller *imagined* us,' Smiler said. 'If she's dead then how can we be real? I don't get it.'

'We've all been living independently from her for a long while. We took control of our own destinies. She tried but failed to control us.'

'Did she though?' Thurston still appeared to be sceptical on that point.

'Yes,' Callie insisted. 'Remember that time we slept together?'

'No.' Thurston shot her a look of bemusement.

'Exactly!' She grinned. 'We evolved outside her head. We do what *we* want to do.'

'So what, are you saying you really don't want to sleep with me?' He flashed her a playful wink.

To which she laughed and said, 'You're a total dickhead, Torbin Thurston.'

'Hmmm.' He became quiet then, growing more serious because the situation demanded it.

The cabin felt full, the air around them swollen with

too much emotion and violent death. Smiler had wandered over to the window to escape the redness of it all.

'Maybe now we're among the dreams of the dead,' Smiler suggested. 'And maybe shit's gonna get a whole lot worse for us.'

'Yeah, Mr Pessimism,' Callie said, with a sigh. 'Maybe we are and maybe it is.' She and Thurston went to join him. Beyond the cabin they could see that the ravens had gone and the fog had shifted at last. The sky was burnt grey though; a scorch mark of uncertainty that blocked out the sun. The lake was blacker than it ever had been. Callie was awestricken by the desolation of it all.

Maybe now we are *among the dreams of the dead*, she thought. *And maybe shit* is *gonna get a whole lot worse.*

She felt a rush of despair, but this was replaced by some small comfort when Thurston took hold of her hand and gently squeezed. They held hands and continued to stare out of the window till, eventually, Callie said, 'I'm leaving. I refuse to stay here any longer.'

'Agreed,' Smiler said. 'But where should we go?'

'Let's see where our feet and imagination take us.'

'What if there's still nowhere out there?'

'There will be.'

'How do you know?'

'I just do.'

'But what if there isn't?'

'Then I know of another place besides the cabin.'

'You do?' Thurston looked down at her, a mix of surprise and concern widening his eyes, emphasising true blue.

She smiled. 'Were you ever a churchgoer, Thurston?'

He shook his head. 'Nah, can't say I ever was.'

'Me neither,' she said. 'But this one's different.'

'Sounds intriguing, but what about the wolfmen? Will we need to run for our lives to get through Whispering Woods?'

'Considering we survived Freya's death then there's every chance that those two vicious bastards could still be out there.'

'In that case,' Smiler said, 'should we take weapons with us?'

Callie shrugged. 'Can't hurt.'

'Weapons such as what though?' Thurston wanted to know.

'Whatever we can find.' Smiler looked about them. 'It's all about improvisation.'

At that moment Pollyanna snapped out of whatever trance she'd fallen into, her blood-spattered expression becoming fully cognisant, and said, 'Snow globe anyone?'

Callie couldn't help but laugh.

'Are you up for an adventure then, Poll?' Smiler asked, hopefully.

'I'd say I've been cooped up long enough,' she said, holding a bloodied hand out. 'Pass me some cigarettes and let's get the hell out of this lousy, stinking cabin.'

'Before it drives us mad,' Callie thought to add. 'If it hasn't already.'

Thurston squeezed her hand and threw her a wink, his eyes intense blue. 'That's just how it is, sweetheart.'

Outside the wind picked up and the remaining post-summer leaves on the trees in Whispering Woods began to chatter. To the side of the cabin, the branches of the ash tree were filled with large, black feathery bodies. Huddled, quietly. Waiting.

Acknowledgements

Firstly, thanks to all of my readers who enjoyed *Emergence* and chose to follow me on this new adventure. I appreciate each and every one of you! Thanks also to all of my new readers who are discovering me now with this latest book *Ravens* – I hope you'll stick around for the long haul.

Thanks to Hannah Thompson for going through the *Ravens* manuscript and whipping it into shape, for being politely stern about my bad habits (I suspect that had I been with you during the editing process I'd have got a (well deserved) slap on the wrist with a ruler) and for the helpful suggestions you made. Hopefully editing *Ravens* was nothing compared to a Force 11 storm at sea. If it was, I apologise. Wholeheartedly.

Thanks to my mam and dad for being my Horden representatives! You'll be pleased to know that I'm bringing the horror home again next time round.

Thanks to my good friend Benn Clarkson who was always on hand and happy to discuss Norse mythology and other random musings, and for being something of a beta reader and confidence coach in the early stages of *Ravens*.

Thanks to friends and family for appreciating the vast amount of time and effort that goes into writing a book and, subsequently, for understanding that sometimes I just need to be a hermit for a while.

And lastly, but absolutely by no means least, thanks to Derek who showed me an unending amount of support, belief and love throughout the quagmire that was 2016. I couldn't have done any of this without you, mister!

About The Author

R. H. Dixon is a horror enthusiast who, when not escaping into the fantastical realms of fiction, lives in the northeast of England with her husband and two whippets.

Visit her website for horror features, short stories, promotions and news of her upcoming books: **www.rhdixon.com**

IF YOU ENJOYED READING THIS BOOK, PLEASE LEAVE A REVIEW ON AMAZON. THANK YOU!

CPSIA information can be obtained
at www.ICGtesting.com
Printed in the USA
LVHW031723081218
599771LV00001B/53/P

9 781999 718022